P

All Spel

"Exceptional…Shearin has proven herself to be an expert storyteller with the enviable ability to provide both humor and jaw-dropping action."

—*RT Book Reviews*

"*All Spell Breaks Loose* not only lived up to my expectations but was even BETTER!"

—*Dangerous Romance*

Con & Conjure

"Tons of action and adventure but it also has a bit of romance and humor…All of the characters are excellent…The complexities of the world that Ms. Shearin has developed are fabulous."

—*Night Owl Reviews*

"Action packed and fast paced, this was a fabulous read."

—*Fresh Fiction*

"*Con & Conjure* is a great addition to a wonderful series, and I'm looking forward to *All Spell Breaks Loose* and whatever else [Shearin writes] with high anticipation."

—*Dear Author*

Bewitched & Betrayed

"Once again, Ms. Shearin has given her readers a book that you don't want to put down. With Raine, the adventures never end."

—*Night Owl Reviews*

"*Bewitched & Betrayed* might just be the best in the series so far!…an amazingly exciting fourth installment that really tugs at the heart strings."

—*Ink and Paper*

"If you're new to Shearin's work, and you enjoy fantasy interspersed with an enticing romance, a little bit of humor, and a whole lot of grade-A action, this is the series for you."

—*Lurv a la Mode*

The Trouble with Demons

"The book reads more like an urban fantasy with pirates and sharp wit and humor. I found the mix quite refreshing. Lisa Shearin's fun, action-packed writing style gives this world life and vibrancy."

—*Fresh Fiction*

"Lisa Shearin represents that much needed voice in fantasy that combines practiced craft and a wicked sense of humor."

—*Bitten by Books*

"The brisk pace and increasingly complex character development propel the story on a rollercoaster ride through demons, goblins, elves, and mages while maintaining a satisfying level of romantic attention…that will leave readers chomping at the bit for more."

—*Monsters and Critics*

"This book has the action starting as soon as you start the story and it keeps going right to the end…All of the characters are interesting, from the naked demon queen to the Guardians guarding Raine. All have a purpose and it comes across with clarity and detail."

—*Night Owl Reviews*

Armed & Magical

"Fresh, original, and fall-out-of-your-chair funny, Lisa Shearin's *Armed & Magical* combines deft characterization, snarky dialogue, and nonstop action—plus a yummy hint of romance—to create one of the best reads of the year. This book is a bona fide winner, the series a keeper, and Shearin a definite star on the rise."

—*Linnea Sinclair, RITA Award-winning author of* Rebels and Lovers

"An exciting, catch-me-if-you-can, lightning-fast-paced tale of magic and evil filled with goblins, elves, mages, and a hint of love interest that will leave fantasy readers anxiously awaiting Raine's next adventure."

—*Monsters and Critics*

"The kind of book you hope to find when you go to the bookstore. It takes you away to a world of danger, magic, and adventure, and it does so with dazzling wit and clever humor. It's gritty, funny, and sexy—a wonderful addition to the urban fantasy genre. I absolutely loved it. From now on Lisa Shearin is on my auto-buy list!"

—*Ilona Andrews, #1* New York Times *bestselling author of* Magic Shifts

"*Armed & Magical*, like its predecessor, is an enchanting read from the very first page. I absolutely loved it. Shearin weaves a web of magic with a dash of romance that thoroughly snares the reader. She's definitely an author to watch!"

—*Anya Bast,* New York Times *bestselling author of* Embrace of the Damned

Magic Lost, Trouble Found

"Take a witty, kick-ass heroine and put her in a vividly realized fantasy world where the stakes are high, and you've got a fun, page-turning read in Magic Lost, Trouble Found. I can't wait to read more of Raine Benares's adventures."

—*Shanna Swendson, author of* Don't Hex with Texas

"A wonderful fantasy tale full of different races and myths and legends [that] are drawn so perfectly readers will believe they actually exist. Raine is a strong female, a leader who wants to do the right thing even when she isn't sure what that is...Lisa Shearin has the magic touch."

—*Midwest Book Review*

"Shearin serves up an imaginative fantasy...The strong, well-executed story line and characters, along with a nice twist to the 'object of unspeakable power' theme, make for an enjoyable, fast-paced read."

—*Monsters and Critics*

"Lisa Shearin turns expectation on its ear and gives us a different kind of urban fantasy with *Magic Lost, Trouble Found.* For once, the urban is as fantastic as the fantasy, as Shearin presents an otherworld city peopled with beautiful goblins, piratical elves, and hardly a human to be found. Littered with entertaining characters and a protagonist whose self-serving lifestyle is compromised only by her loyalty to her friends, Magic Lost is an absolutely enjoyable read. I look forward to the next one!"

—*C. E. Murphy, author of* Raven Calls

"Nicely done. I actively enjoyed the characters and their banter."

—*Critical Mass*

"Fun, fascinating, and loaded with excitement! *Magic Lost, Trouble Found* is a top-notch read of magic, mayhem, and some of the most charming elves and goblins I've ever encountered. Enthralling characters and a thrilling plot…I now need to cast a spell on Ms. Shearin to ensure there's a sequel."

—*Linnea Sinclair, RITA Award–winning author of* Rebels and Lovers

TREASURE & TREASON

Also by Lisa Shearin

The Raine Benares Series

MAGIC LOST, TROUBLE FOUND
ARMED & MAGICAL
THE TROUBLE WITH DEMONS
BEWITCHED & BETRAYED
CON & CONJURE
ALL SPELL BREAKS LOOSE
WILD CARD (A RAINE BENARES NOVELLA)
WEDDING BELLS, MAGIC SPELLS

The SPI Files Series

THE GRENDEL AFFAIR
THE DRAGON CONSPIRACY
THE BRIMSTONE DECEPTION
THE GHOUL VENDETTA

NIGHT SHIFT (anthology)
containing LUCKY CHARMS,
a SPI Files novella

Treasure & Treason

A RAINE BENARES WORLD NOVEL

LISA SHEARIN

NLA Digital, LLC
1732 Wazee Street, Suite 207
Denver, CO 80202

This book is a work of fiction. The characters, incidents, and dialogue are drawn from the author's imagination and are not to be construed as real. Any resemblance to actual events or persons, living or dead, is entirely coincidental.

Production Manager: Lori Bennett
Cover art and design: Aleta Rafton
Interior design: Angie Hodapp

ISBN 978-1-62051-254-8

As always, for Derek.

Acknowledgments

They say it takes a village to raise a child. Well, it takes a team to make a book. I wouldn't be able to do this without the simply amazing ladies at Nelson Literary Agency and NLA Digital: Kristin Nelson (my agent), Lori Bennett (production manager), and Angie Hodapp (interior design). Then there's the legendary Betsy Mitchell (my editor), the incomparable Martha Trachtenberg (my copy editor), the supremely talented Aleta Rafton (my cover artist), and the marvelous Logan Hyatt (my assistant).

I also needed help naming three of the dragons in this book. I received so many great suggestions. The winning name for the little firedrake on the cover was "Indigo" sent in by Kirsten Parriott. For two of the much larger sentry dragons: Scott Balliet thought of the name "Amaranth" and David Gray came through with "Mithryn." I can always count on my fans to come through with character names or book titles. You guys are awesome!

For my fans who have always wanted to read a book about Tam and Phaelan…ask and you shall receive. This one's for you.

"There is nothing more difficult to carry out, nor more doubtful of success, nor more dangerous to handle, than to initiate a new order of things."

The Prince

Niccolò Machiavelli

1

I pinched the bridge of my nose and closed my eyes against an oncoming headache.

A headache named Phaelan Benares.

"I would ask if you're joking," I said, "but I know you're not."

Laughter came from inside the massive crystal ball on my desk. Laughter that didn't make me feel any better about the situation I was about to land in—or what was about to land on me.

Raine Benares's face and shoulders were all that was visible inside the ball, making her seem even smaller than she was in person. It'd only been two weeks since I'd attended her wedding to Mychael Eiliesor on the Isle of Mid. Considering what she'd been through over the past few months, it was good to hear her laugh.

Too bad this time it was at my expense.

I settled back in my chair. "Married life agrees with you."

"Don't change the subject."

"I didn't change it," I objected mildly. "I merely injected an observation."

"About me and not Phaelan."

"I have many observations about Phaelan," I assured her. "Unfortunately, the telepath on your end wouldn't be able to hold the connection long enough for me to get through the list."

Raine gave me a flat look. "It's Ben, the best telepath the Guardians have. He's up to it."

"I seriously doubt that."

"Tam, you and Phaelan simply don't know each other well enough."

"And you apparently want to remedy that—vengefully remedy that. Generally, when a woman is vindictive toward me, I at least know what I've done to deserve it."

"What I want is for your expedition to have the best protection available. Sandrina Ghalfari and her Khrynsani are the least of your problems. She's made friends with off-world invaders who killed every person on the planet of Timurus, and whose magic isn't like anything we've ever seen. Yeah, it's been seven hundred years since then, but that probably just gave them time to get better at it. And now they've got the Seven Kingdoms in their sights. Your ships need the best there is to have your backs. That would be Phaelan and his crew."

"*And* his crew?"

"Uncle Ryn is overseeing the outfitting of the fleet here," Raine said. "The *Fortune* needs some repairs, and Phaelan doesn't want his crew cooling their heels in port while it gets done."

"Ah, now we're getting to the real reason. Mychael doesn't want a bored pirate crew roaming his city."

Raine snorted. "No one wants that." She paused, her gray eyes serious. "Tam, Phaelan volunteered. He knows what's at stake here. He wants to help. Gwyn and Gavyn are more than capable of protecting your ships, but Phaelan thinks he can do it better. He's the older brother. He saw those two in diapers." Raine made a face. "Then again, so did I. But they turned out well. You almost wouldn't know their last name is Benares."

The last name of the most notorious family of pirates in the Seven Kingdoms—and now my expedition's seafaring bodyguards. Though in all honesty, considering where we were going, what we were looking for, and who we would likely encounter, the entire Benares fleet might not be enough to ensure we made it home again.

"Uncle Ryn has a new ship in Beag's End, the *Kraken,*" Raine continued. "Gwyn and Gavyn will man it with enough crew from their ships to get it to you in Regor."

I put a hand to my temple and started rubbing. That ship wouldn't be the next thing arriving under full sail—my headache was coming in right now. Three Benares siblings who were captains of three Benares ships. Pirate ships. Though in their favor, Benares crews were well known not only as fierce fighters, but disciplined soldiers.

While at sea.

Getting to Aquas was merely the first part of our journey, and the easiest. The continent was dry, barren, inhospitable, and uninhabited. Though the last quality was open for debate.

The Khrynsani had a long and unsuccessful history with Aquas. Over the centuries, they had launched many an expedition to the purported lost city of Nidaar, which was said to be populated by an ancient race of golden-skinned goblins. Between the eastern coast of Aquas and the mountain range where Nidaar was said to be were nearly a hundred miles of desert. I had assembled a team to cross that desert and find that city—and most critically, what was inside—before the Khrynsani could.

Legend said that the city of Nidaar was made of gold.

The Khrynsani had gold. While they always wanted more, riches were not the reason for their obsession.

They wanted power.

At the center of Nidaar was said to be a stone of such power that it had run the entire city. It was called the Heart of Nidaar, and it had provided light, powered the pumps to provide water, anything that was needed—in addition to powering and amplifying magical spells.

The Heart of Nidaar was unknown outside of the Khrynsani. I wasn't a member of the Khrynsani brotherhood. I never had been and I never would be. However, I was a dark mage, as were all Khrynsani. While I'd renounced the dark path I'd traveled, I still retained all of the knowledge. When you had an enemy as lethal as the Khrynsani, survival meant knowing what they knew. Over the years, I'd educated myself on every object of power the Khrynsani could possibly want to possess.

With the Saghred destroyed, Sandrina Ghalfari would kill every man, woman, and child in the Seven Kingdoms to possess the Heart of Nidaar. And now she had allied the

Khrynsani with an alien army, giving her the manpower to find the Heart of Nidaar and do just that.

I had told Raine and Mychael that the Khrynsani and their allies would in all likelihood use Nidaar as a staging point for their invasion of the Seven Kingdoms. I had not lied. While they staged, they would search for the Heart of Nidaar. If they found it before my team and I could, the alliances the kingdoms had forged wouldn't be enough to save any of us.

Two weeks ago, a peace treaty had been signed by six out of the seven kingdoms, and a promise had been made to form an alliance to fight together against the Khrynsani and the off-world invaders. I had vowed to the alliance that I would travel to Aquas and find where the Khrynsani and the invaders were staging, making my trip essentially a scouting mission.

I didn't intend to stop at scouting.

My goal was to find, secure, and if necessary destroy the Heart of Nidaar.

And prevent a repeat of what had happened with the Saghred.

When the Saghred had surfaced, every race had clamored to secure it for themselves. Goblin, elf, or human—all wanted to possess the stone and the power it contained. Some had wanted to keep the Saghred out of the wrong hands. Others wanted the Saghred in their hands.

As far as I was concerned, the power-hungry couldn't want that which they didn't know existed.

The lives lost because of the Saghred hadn't been limited to those who had been sacrificed to the stone. My goal was to prevent *any* lives being lost because of the Heart of Nidaar.

Right now that meant keeping its very existence a closely guarded secret.

"Tam, you can trust Phaelan," Raine was saying. "You may find it hard to believe, but I actually feel better about you going to Aquas knowing Phaelan will be there with you. I didn't insist that he offer to go, but let's just say I strongly indicated I'd be in favor of it. This is his world, too. His home. My cousin will fight to the death to protect his home and family from whatever invasion we're up against, and so will his friends. Believe it or not, you've become one of them. He doesn't like or trust your magic—or anyone else's for that matter—but not all that deep down, Phaelan likes and trusts you. He knows what's coming. Don't worry about Phaelan; he'll be all business, and you'll be glad he's there. He's hauled my butt out of the fire many times."

"And just how are Phaelan and his crew getting here?" I asked. "We sail the day after tomorrow. We can't wait any longer."

Raine grinned. "Here's the really unbelievable part—and the part that proves how serious Phaelan is about this."

I stopped rubbing my temple. It wasn't helping. Nothing would help. "I'm on pins and needles with anticipation."

"Mirrors."

I dropped my hand and leaned forward. "I don't believe I heard you correctly. Did you just say 'mirrors'?"

Raine added nodding to her grinning. "Yeah, mirrors. Phaelan's willing to go through a *mirror* to get to you. I was drinking coffee when he told me and I nearly choked to death. His crew will be getting there the same way."

"And they also volunteered?"

Another snort. "Are you kidding? Phaelan said he'll arrive first, then his crew *will* follow—with kicks from his first mate and quartermaster, if necessary. I assume you can set up a mirror near the docks?"

"Raine, I have mirrors all over this city."

"Of course you do."

"Having an exit nearby is always good."

"See, you and Phaelan have something in common."

"Well, that's one."

"There'll be more."

"I can't wait. Speaking of waiting, when can I expect Phaelan and his merry band of cutthroats?"

"Mychael thought it'd be a good idea if Phaelan arrived first, before Gwyn and Gavyn arrive. Would noon tomorrow work for you?"

"I have a mirror here in my study and a mirror mage on retainer to run it. I'll have it ready by noon tomorrow. What about Phaelan's crew?"

"I assume you don't want a pirate crew coming through your house."

"You assume correctly."

"I spoke with Gwyn an hour ago. They've had fair weather and good winds, so they're still on schedule to arrive on tomorrow's afternoon tide. She'll contact me once they've dropped anchor and met with you. Is there a place large enough near the waterfront to take in Phaelan's crew?"

"There's a warehouse I'm using to store supplies for our ship. It's half empty. I'll have a mirror set up there. It would be better to have heavily armed elf pirates arrive out of the public eye."

Raine chuckled. "Good thinking. Elves appearing out of thin air surrounded by goblins. That'd be a misunderstanding of epic proportions waiting to happen."

"I'd rather not have any bloodshed before we reach Aquas."

"Tam, you're going to locate Sandrina Ghalfari and her new allies, not start a war all by yourself."

I raised my hands defensively. "No direct contact unless necessary. But if there's a way we can delay or stop them, we're going to do it."

"Just don't get yourself killed in the process."

"Avoiding death is my main goal in life." I leaned back in my office chair. "Have you heard anything else from the Caesolians?"

Raine rolled her eyes. "More apologies from their amb-assador. Though I don't doubt he's sincere. It wouldn't be the first time an ambassador had to back out of a promise once he got home."

"At least they're still agreeable to joining their armies with the other kingdoms," I said. "Sending a ship with our expedition to Aquas was more than we could realistically expect them to go through with. They probably consider it a suicide mission. The Caesolian ambassador is a man of his word. He was genuinely apologetic when we spoke. I assured him that the king and the goblin people did not hold this against Caesolia. I wasn't sure if he believed me, but hopefully my assurances would help him sleep at night."

Truth be told, I was glad the Caesolians had backed out. On a mission such as this, I needed people I could trust, not a boatload of unknown quantities. In terms of what we might have to do if we encountered Sandrina or any of her Khrynsani… Let's just say the fewer people who saw the aftermath of that exchange, the better. As far as I was concerned, no course of action was off the table, including black magic. Our world was at stake, and I would do what needed to be done, and I'd rather not have any squeamish Caesolian witnesses when I did.

"So, what preparations are being made on Mid?" I asked, changing the subject.

"Any student in the Conclave college with a war-applicable major is being fast-tracked, and every other major is being focused on defense and offense. Even love potions could be useful if we could get some into a couple of the invaders' battle dragons. Anything we can do to distract those big brutes is worth doing. Mychael has accelerated Guardian cadet and squire training, too." Raine smiled with pride. "He made Piaras a squire last week."

I laughed. "Only because Mychael couldn't knight him directly from cadet."

"Actually he could've skipped right over it if he'd wanted to. Though there's only been a few instances before, and all of those were battlefield knightings. We're not at that point, at least not yet. How about Talon?"

"I'm keeping him with me."

That earned me two raised eyebrows.

I knew exactly what Raine was thinking. My mother had perfectly described Talon after taking one look at him. She had asked me whether he was impulsive, stubborn, arrogant, and believes himself irresistible to women and impervious to death. My mother's shots were always on target, whether from a crossbow, or simply speaking as an incredibly insightful grandmother being introduced for the first time to her previously unsuspected grandson.

"I'm well aware of what I'm setting myself up for," I told Raine. "I want my son with me, and I'm pleased to say I think that's where he wants to be. He's entirely too similar to the way I was at that age. I know the mistakes I made, and the prices I—and others—paid when I made them. Who better to keep him from making the same mistakes than me?"

"Kesyn Badru."

"He'll be going with us, too."

Raine laughed. "Poor guy can't get a break."

"He volunteered for the job of teaching Talon. He knew what he was getting into. He taught me, remember?"

"He can't get a break, *and* he's a glutton for punishment."

"He's also one of the most powerful mages I know," I said. "I trust him with my life, and beyond."

"Let's hope it doesn't come to that."

"I'll be doing all I can to ensure it doesn't. However, if anything does happen to me, I've asked Kesyn to be Talon's second fal'kasair."

Raine nodded in approval. "Good choice for a godfather." She gave me a quick grin. "And I'm sure Mychael won't mind sharing the burden."

"Since Talon is as much of a challenge as I was, I've asked A'Zahra Nuru to stand as mor'kasair. Between the three of them, Talon should turn out just fine."

"He'll turn out just fine because you'll be there."

"Contingencies, Raine. Merely preparing for any and all contingencies. I have no intention of dying. However, if I do, I intend to take those responsible with me."

Raine glanced off to the side. "Ben needs to end the connection."

I gave her a crooked grin. "I told you he couldn't hold on long enough for my list of Phaelan's faults."

Raine ignored my comment, her expression solemn. "Tam, be careful."

"It's my middle name."

"No, it isn't."

I shrugged. "Then I'll do what I can. I promise. As I said, I'm not dying anytime soon." I sighed. "I have way too much work to do right here."

"Watch your back."

"Always."

The crystal ball went dark.

Raine knew what I was referring to. The Mal'Salin dynasty had reigned over Rheskilia and the goblins for millennia. The late but not lamented Sathrik Mal'Salin had been in power for only a few years, but he'd done enough damage to last ten lifetimes. The goblin court had always been a vipers' nest of intrigue, scheming, betrayal, and bloodshed. Treason was a full-contact sport, treachery was an art, and murder merely a way to rearrange the game board in your favor. When you put goblin aristocrats in close proximity with each other, that simply was what happened.

Sathrik had been insane, the cruel and evil kind of insane that led him to imprison, torture, and murder his own people, people whose only crime had been to disagree with him. Yes, that disagreement led to more than a few attempts on his life, but that was what you earned when you turned on your subjects—your subjects turned on you. We goblins tolerated only so much murderous behavior from our monarchs, then we would take action. Decisive, permanent action. For goblins, a king or queen killing to protect and defend the safety and prosperity of their subjects was perfectly fine. But killing your subjects to preserve your own wretched life was cause for a coup.

Sathrik had called it treason. I called it an extermination that was long overdue.

Besides, it's not treason if you win.

I'm Tamnais Nathrach, chief mage for the House of Mal'Salin.

Again.

I had served Sathrik's mother, Gilcara Mal'Salin, for five years, an eternity when it came to survival in the goblin court. Sathrik had me framed for my wife's murder, then driven from my post and my country. Once I was gone, he killed his mother with his own hands. I risked my life to put his younger brother Chigaru on the throne, and there's no doubt in my mind that as his chief mage and chancellor, I'll have to put my life on the line to keep him there.

Sathrik is gone, but his allies still plot in dimly lit rooms and shadowed corridors. My enemies from the goblin court haven't forgotten me; they're just waiting for me to turn my back.

Just like old times.

I smiled. It was good to be home.

2

"You didn't tell her," said a voice from behind me.

I hadn't heard or sensed him until he spoke. Kesyn Badru had always been able to sneak up on me—now he could do it even through a locked and warded door. Good thing he didn't want to kill me. At least not most of the time. I glanced over his shoulder to the door. He'd even relocked and warded it without my hearing. Definitely a good thing he was on my side.

"You don't really think I should have?" I asked.

The old man barked a laugh. "Not unless you wanted to give the girl nightmares."

"Precisely. And I don't trust communications of any kind right now." I nodded toward the crystal ball. "I'm taking chances even using that."

"You suspected what Sandrina was really after, when you

were on the Isle of Mid for Raine and Mychael's wedding. You had ample opportunity to tell them then."

"I didn't know for certain."

"You knew enough."

"What good would it have done? Word would have leaked, we would have had a race to Aquas, and it would have been a bloodbath when we arrived."

Kesyn was grinning.

"What?"

"I never said I disagreed with you," he said. "I'm just playing devil's advocate and enjoying the sight of you not only thinking things through, but opting for caution and subtlety once you did. It's a new experience for me—and a good look on you."

"Do I detect a compliment?"

"Would I do that?"

"You never have. Why start now?"

"Why indeed. I was simply stating a fact. And savoring seeing caution and subtlety in the father, because I'm sure as hell not getting it from the son."

I winced. "Sorry about that."

Kesyn waved a hand and dropped into a nearby chair. "It's not your fault."

"I'm his father, and he's me made over."

My teacher shrugged. "Talon hasn't done anything that I haven't already seen from you. Power level, that is. Talent wise, he's an entirely different bird." Kesyn leaned back and regarded me. "The boy's half elf."

"Yes."

"The skills in his magic arsenal aren't the same as yours."

"I know."

"They're from his mother, I take it?"

I nodded once, tightly. I knew where this was going and it wasn't a place I wanted to go, even for a brief visit. I'd been slamming the doors in my head every time Talon did anything new. I couldn't keep doing that. The older Talon got, the more talents from his mother's family would emerge. It had to be faced and dealt with, and soon.

"Who was she?" Kesyn asked quietly. "You don't have to give me a name, son. Just tell me what she was packing—and her family. If I'm to continue teaching the boy, I need to know."

"She was a spellsinger," I said. "But she and her family were omnitalents."

Kesyn swore softly. "Couldn't you have fallen for a normal girl?"

I gave him a half smile. "I never have, and I doubt I ever will."

"Other than spellsinging, did she or her family have a particular talent?"

I hesitated. "Mirror magic."

Kesyn sat unmoving, unspeaking. An elven family of mirror mages. I didn't need to give him the name. He knew.

After a few moments, he slowly nodded once. "Duly noted."

"I appreciate you going with me—and Talon."

"I've made the commitment," Kesyn said. "You can't get rid of me now."

"And I don't want to."

"I noticed you didn't say '*we* don't want to.' Talon would probably like nothing better than for the ground to open and swallow me whole."

"He said that?"

"Not yet. He's actually showing up on time for his lessons." My teacher slouched down in his chair, crossing his feet at the ankles. "Though I'll admit I'm enjoying the time off while the boy's out of town with Cyran and Deidre."

My parents, Talon, and my brother Nath were presently visiting our country estate. My family had led the goblin Resistance, with victory coming at the taking of the Khrynsani temple, the death of Sarad Nukpana, and the destruction of the Saghred. They deserved some peace and quiet, and Talon deserved to get to know his grandparents and uncle. He'd met them only two months ago, and I wanted Talon to be able to spend time with them before we left for Aquas. I didn't know how long we would be gone.

Or, to be completely honest with myself, if we'd come back.

"Do you really think taking him with you is the best idea?" Kesyn was asking. Talon was due back later this evening.

"The only mages going with me are those I trust to have my back—and not use it as a target. You're at the top of that list. If you're going, Talon's going. Aside from myself, you're the only one qualified to handle him. Talon's a couple of years older than I was when I started down the wrong path. I'm determined that he will never set foot on it." I hesitated. "I want my son with me. He spent most of his life on his own, and I never want him to feel abandoned again. I know if I tried to make him stay here, he'd simply stow away like he did last time."

"The boy is fond of you," Kesyn said, "though he'd never admit it. I'll continue his lessons on board the *Wraith*. Though I'll hold off an anything involving fire until we're not on a floating tinderbox."

"That would be wise."

"I thought so." Kesyn shifted in his chair. "Speaking of wise choices, how many people have you told what Sandrina Ghalfari is really after?"

"You."

"You haven't asked Cort Magali to go as the expedition gem mage?"

"I had no intention of asking him until I'd had the chance to meet with him first. That turned into a moot point since he refused to open his door to speak with me, let alone allow me into his home."

"He wouldn't even talk to you?"

"Oh, he talked to me. That is if you consider 'No' and 'Go away' the beginnings of a productive conversation. I got the feeling he didn't want me to be seen on his doorstep."

"Who would?"

"Kesyn, I'm no longer the queen's enforcer."

"You're her son's chancellor. A more civilized title for basically the same work—at least for the time being. You and Imala have been cutting quite the swath through the Khrynsani's leave-behinds."

"Anyone who allies themselves with sadistic monsters should hardly be surprised to receive a visit when said monsters are tossed out of power. I believe you've called it 'cleaning house.'"

"Not many people do it with an executioner's axe."

"What would you suggest we do with traitors? Tap them lightly on the wrist and tell them to play nice from now on? If Chigaru and Mirabai are going to survive their first few months on the throne, let alone their first year, heads will need to roll. Literally."

Kesyn held up a hand. “Again, I’m not disagreeing with you. You and Imala have to clear out the vipers and cut off some heads. I’m just saying that’s probably why Cort Magali won’t come outside and play with you. Got anyone else in mind?”

“I’ve heard Agata Azul is back in the city.” My eyes narrowed. “You wouldn’t happen to know anything about that, would you?”

I saw my teacher do something I’d never seen him do before. He squirmed.

“Well?” I pressed.

“Yeah, I knew Aggie was back.”

“Aggie? I knew you were her teacher at one time, but—”

“And she outgrew me.”

“Actually outgrew or, like me, just thought she did?”

“Actually outgrew. There wasn’t anything else I could teach her. A smart girl that turned into a brilliant woman. I can talk to Cort, if you’d like. He’s a fine gem mage. Once he stopped feeling squirrely around you, he’d do nicely.”

“Yes, ‘he’d do,’ but he’s not the best. From everything I’ve heard, Agata Azul is. I want the best. I *need* the best.”

“Son, did it ever occur to you that the best might not want you, or want to be near anything you’re involved in? You’re notorious, and that’s putting it nicely.”

“Since when do you put anything nicely?”

“Since you dragged my ass back to the royal court. I’m looking forward to weeks on a stinking ship just to get away from wearing fancy robes.”

“I seem to recall saying that you didn’t have to wear anything you didn’t want to.”

“Imala outvoted you.”

"Since when?"

"Since she's scarier than you are."

I just looked at him. "The chief of goblin intelligence is scarier than I am."

"There, you said it; I didn't. That little lady makes people disappear."

"Imala wouldn't make you disappear. She adores you."

Kesyn didn't say anything.

I gave my teacher a slow smile as realization set in. "And *you* adore *her.* She asked you to clean yourself up and you did it. For her."

"That's not the reason."

"It's the only reason. She's a spymaster and a woman. She knows how to get what she wants."

He barked a hollow laugh. "Ain't that the truth. And those are some dangerous dimples. One smile and a 'please,' and before I knew it I was wearing brocade. Gods help us if the woman had more magic than she does."

I nodded sagely. "With greater power would come even greater responsibility." I paused. "So you're saying Agata Azul wouldn't work with a reformed dark mage."

"Dark ain't got a thing to do with it. Whenever there's been a political shitstorm—or even a shitstorm of any kind—you've been in the middle of it. It's a fact and everyone knows it. Anyone who signs on to help you do anything will be taking their life into their own hands. There's no amount of money worth that, and I know for a fact that Aggie doesn't care about money."

"Tell me what does she does care about."

"It's been several years since I spent much time with her, so

I don't have an answer for you, but I can tell you that survival would be near or at the top of her list."

"If she cares about survival, she'll understand why she should agree to help."

"I have to admit if any gem mage can sniff out this Heart of Nidaar, it'll be Aggie." Kesyn paused and his brow furrowed. "Though you'd think if there were goblins living over there we'd have heard something from them by now."

I gave him a look. "If you were living a peaceful and tranquil life, would you reach out to us?"

"Good point. If we're not at war with each other, we're at war with someone else. We do excel at screwing things up for us and everyone else, don't we?"

"Not to mention, if you had a self-sustaining city, peaceful, and full of gold, would you want to share? Since Chigaru and Mirabai have confiscated all of the Nukpana and Ghalfari lands and given most of them to my family, I'm certain Sandrina wouldn't mind filling up a few bags of whatever treasure is there after she gets the Heart."

"I'm still wrapping my head around the fact that you're going after another rock."

"I'm not appreciative of the irony, but the Khrynsani lost their chance at the Saghred. They and their new off-world allies need an energy source to power Gates to give them access to any place in the Seven Kingdoms at any time. The Heart of Nidaar would meet their needs."

"So you're sure that thing's still in Nidaar?"

"The Khrynsani are convinced. Right now, that's enough for me. Sarad Nukpana believed it since he was a child. I first heard about the Heart of Nidaar from him, when he was younger and hadn't yet mastered discretion. Sarad had a tendency to brag. I had a tendency to listen. Later, I did my own research."

"And you've since lost the tendency to listen. How sad."

"You sound like my parents."

"The highest compliment you've ever paid me. Tam, you're going to search for a city that no one has gone looking for and survived."

I raised a finger. "Some have."

"Due to realizing they were in over their thick-skulled heads and turning around before it was too late."

"I won't be 'searching' for Nidaar. I know where it is. I've seen a map."

"Where?"

"The Khrynsani library."

My teacher swore. Expressively. "When?"

"Don't worry, it was after the Khrynsani were overthrown. I wouldn't set foot in that mausoleum of a temple unless there was the direst of needs. Like now."

"Tam, it's not safe for you of all people to be in there. Leave the cataloguing and removal of those books to people qualified to handle them."

"And not be tempted."

"I didn't say that, but yes, and not be tempted."

"I've only read those books with information on Aquas and the Heart of Nidaar."

"That's another thing. In case you haven't noticed yet from your experience with the Saghred, only really evil rocks get names."

"Denita Enric, Dakarai's sister, is overseeing the inventory and moving of the library. She sent a messenger over saying she'd found another book for me."

"When are you going to look at it?"

"I need to stop at my office and see A'Zahra as soon as we're finished here. Then I'll go to the temple."

"I want to go with you."

It wasn't necessary. I knew it. Kesyn probably knew it. However, we both knew it'd be a good idea. I was a dark mage, and I always would be. My magic was a part of me, a part that was still susceptible to temptation.

"If that's what you want," I told my teacher.

"It is."

"I've asked Denita to pull out any journals or records from previous Khrynsani expeditions," I continued. "Sarad had to have gotten his information from somewhere. Sandrina probably read them to him as bedtime stories. I've also done some digging on most of the previous goblin expeditions to Aquas. All were funded—some openly, most covertly—by the Khrynsani. Some of the expeditions even predate the discovery of the Saghred. Once the Guardians took the Saghred for safekeeping, Khrynsani sponsorship of the expeditions continued."

"So you're saying that the Khrynsani lost their chance at one all-powerful rock, so they need to get their all-evil hands on another."

"Exactly. Sandrina isn't taking her new allies to Aquas for the vacation ambience. The Khrynsani—Sandrina included—never had an evil master plan without an ace up their collective sleeve. For the past thousand years, that preferred ace has been a stone of power. They came entirely too close to success with the

Saghred. Sandrina's dreams were dashed on the broken pieces of the Khrynsani temple. She has nothing left to lose. Now she has everything to regain. Without the Saghred to power their Gates, the Khrynsani's plan to invade and conquer the Seven Kingdoms fell apart. The Saghred is gone. The Heart of Nidaar is the only chance Sandrina has left."

"I can't believe after what happened with the Saghred—and what nearly happened—that you would even consider going within a thousand miles of another soul-eating stone."

I almost smiled. "The Heart of Nidaar doesn't eat souls. It's said to be completely self-sustaining."

"That's one thing in its favor."

"It will power her Gates, and she doesn't have to sacrifice people to it. A win-win for her."

My teacher leveled his dark eyes at me.

"What?"

"Power without sacrifice. I can see in your eyes that Sandrina Ghalfari isn't the only one that notion appeals to. Just what do you intend to do with this rock if you get it before Sandrina?"

"To be honest, I don't really know. Considering what it is reputed to do, it's in the Seven Kingdoms' best interests that we locate and secure it first, as the Guardians did with the Saghred. I am well aware that we need to keep it out of the hands of anyone who would abuse its power. Is there a good way to use its power? I don't know enough about it to answer that question. I'll cross that bridge when I come to it."

Kesyn voice was quiet and solemn. "I'll contact Aggie for you, if that's what you really want. And once you cross that bridge, just make sure you take the right path afterward."

3

In the goblin court, no level of paranoia was excessive. It was a way of life, and of staying alive.

Walking into the Mal'Salin palace put all my defenses on high alert. I automatically murmured my shields into place, and cleared quick access to my weapons. Most people would think that a royal palace would be the safest place to be. Goblins weren't most people.

Admittedly, I was a special case. Any who had been loyal to Sathrik wanted me dead. Any who were loyal to Chigaru didn't trust me. I had been away from court for nearly three years. I was no longer the man I had been when I'd served as Queen Gilcara's magical enforcer. Goblins' allegiances could change with the wind, but the complete change I'd undergone had been met with anything from skepticism to outright disbelief.

However, those who hadn't personally witnessed the battle between me and Sarad Nukpana had heard about it. Sarad had drawn on all the knowledge and power he contained by consuming the souls of six of history's most evil mages. He had created a towering skinform that held a multitude of demons, all struggling to tear free of the confines Sarad had used to imprison them and bend them to his will. It had been nothing short of every nightmare brought to life.

I had used all of my black magic skills to summon a bull-horned demon lord.

It had been close, but in the end—thanks to Sarad's concentration wavering when he saw Raine about to destroy the Saghred—his creation had crumbled, and the demon lord I'd made a deal with had carried Sarad screaming into the Lower Hells.

As a result, everyone in the palace now gave me an even wider berth than they had before.

That wasn't a bad thing.

But death didn't have to be dealt up close. A crossbow had killed me once and it could do it again. Though that time I had stood still in the middle of a street on the Isle of Mid and begged for death. Sarad Nukpana's soul had taken over my body, possessing me, bringing with him the souls of those six mages. The only way to freedom had been death. At the moment of my death, Sarad had fled, taking the souls he had consumed with him. Mychael Eiliesor had frantically worked to repair the damage while the nachtmagus Vidor Kalta had forcefully held my soul in my dead body until my heart could beat again on its own.

I had no intention of being killed by a crossbow bolt again.

Someone had once said that you couldn't come home again. You could, but if you were a goblin in the royal court, you'd better watch your back.

Those courtiers who didn't want to kill me, also didn't know what to call me.

Chigaru and Mirabai had wanted me to have the title of prince, indicating that I was their heir until they produced one.

I told them that I'd be their chancellor, but I'd drawn the line way before prince.

Also, there would be no robes and no ceremony. If I held the position, it would be on my terms. No discussion.

Chigaru had enough to deal with without arguing about my wardrobe choices.

While I was away, A'Zahra Nuru was the mage who would be taking over my job. I couldn't even begin to say how many favors I would owe her when I returned. She already had apartments here, and she probably wouldn't even set foot outside the palace walls for the duration. She had taken Chigaru under her wing when he'd been exiled by his brother, and that wing hadn't moved since. There was not a doubt in my mind that had she not done so, Chigaru would not have grown into the fine man that he was. She had steadied an otherwise impetuous temperament, one that would have gotten him and many others killed long before now. The goblin people didn't know it, but they owed their very lives to this tiny woman with a will forged of nothing less than tempered steel.

A'Zahra had taught Chigaru's grandmother, as well as his mother, the late queen. After I had been forced to leave Regor and was no longer there to protect her, Sathrik had killed his mother and had taken the throne. Sathrik had banished Chigaru and strongly encouraged A'Zahra to retire. He'd provided her with a modest house and annual income in Mermeia, which was where I eventually ended up. A'Zahra Nuru had become my mentor. Black magic was like an addictive drug, and she had brought me back from the brink.

A'Zahra's job was to work with her granddaughter Imala Kalis to keep Chigaru and Mirabai not only alive, but healthy. Their food tasters had tasters. Her secondary job was one Imala and I had begun in earnest the night Sarad Nukpana had been defeated—finding any Khrynsani sympathizers and getting rid of them.

There had been a lot of executions since that night. It had been unavoidable. To imprison them offered the possibility of escape, and these men and women ever seeing the outside of a cell was too great a risk.

The ones who we knew were inner-circle or upper-level Khrynsani had been executed immediately. When there was any doubt as to a courtier or court official's allegiance, the person was interviewed and their mind examined. Refusal of either put them on the executioners' list. Few were wholly innocent. However, there were a significant number who had faked their Khrynsani ties in order to survive. Many a noble family had had members imprisoned in the Khrynsani temple dungeons, held to ensure a magically powerful or politically influential relative's cooperation. These were the people we wanted to make certain did not pay for doing what most would have done to save themselves or their family.

A'Zahra had been heading up the mages in charge of the interviews. If A'Zahra told me a man or woman could be trusted, I believed it without question. And mages she had recruited to work with were likewise beyond reproach.

Those people whose Khrynsani ties had been against their will were housed in a guest palace. They were guarded, but were taken good care of, and treated with dignity and respect. They, too, knew the qualifications of the mages interviewing them, and if they were truly innocent, this would be determined and they would be released and could reassume their lives free of suspicion and Khrynsani blackmail or influence.

We had few enough people whom we trusted without potentially alienating—or making enemies of—anyone. Hence, their treatment as temporary guests, not prisoners.

Imala had assigned four of her best agents to protect her grandmother. If A'Zahra hadn't sensed me, she would have instantly picked up on the increased alertness of her guards when I'd entered the outer office.

They didn't trust me.

I didn't take it personally. Some days I didn't trust me, either.

My office door was open. I stopped, leaned my shoulder against the frame and waited.

A'Zahra knew I was there, though I had made no sound. She had probably known the moment I had set foot in the palace.

Silence meant survival. At least it gave you a better chance. My enemies couldn't kill what they didn't know was there. The reverse was also true—stealth meant success in eliminating your enemies.

I hoped those days were over, but I wasn't about to hold my breath.

My mentor normally wore simple gowns of fine fabric, but since returning to court, precautions were called for, such as gowns that left room for body armor beneath. A'Zahra's magical talents were at an archmage level, so she would know before an assassin got within stabbing or shooting distance; but all it would take was a momentary distraction. All too often, mages had been killed due to a split second of inattention. I was determined that A'Zahra Nuru would not become a statistic. Entirely too much was at stake.

The diminutive goblin's silvery white hair was elaborately styled and held in place with tiny, jeweled pins. More pale gems glittered on the lobes of her upswept ears. Her pale gray skin was still smooth over high cheekbones and fine features. I'd been told A'Zahra had been breathtakingly beautiful in her youth. In my opinion, she still was.

Having taught three generations of the Mal'Salin ruling family, A'Zahra was advanced in years, but not as far as one would think. Three generations of students would indicate old age anywhere in the Seven Kingdoms, except in the goblin court.

Life expectancy was significantly shorter for Mal'Salin monarchs.

That was another statistic I was determined to change.

"You're looking comfortable in your new home," I noted.

A'Zahra responded without pausing in her writing. "I do wish you would stop referring to your office as my home, dear. I have no intention of keeping this arrangement any longer than necessary. The very hour you return, this distasteful and distressing position is again all your own."

I pushed off from the doorframe. "You can't tell me you don't enjoy the power, just a little," I chided gently.

My mentor glanced up at me and leaned back, her small form dwarfed by my office chair. Admittedly, it was large for me as well. In the goblin court, you employed every defensive measure, including making yourself and your surroundings as imposing as possible. My desk chair functioned much like the hood on an annoyed cobra. It was cheap theatrics, but it worked.

"I enjoy the power about as much as the accompanying and incessant itch between my shoulder blades," she said.

I grinned. "I can assure you, ma'am, that the daggers are more likely to come at you from the front. My court enemies usually dispensed with subtlety."

"Only because you goaded them to the point of exasperated rage."

"What can I say? I hate to be kept waiting. If someone wants to kill me, I want them to get on with it." I took a seat in one of my two guest chairs—after angling it ever so slightly to give me a view of the door, even though I'd closed it. I didn't take chances lightly.

The adjustment wasn't lost on A'Zahra. "I can assure you that my guards' trustworthiness is beyond reproach. Imala selected them herself."

I chuckled. "And after she did, you linked with each one to confirm that any homicidal tendencies they possessed wouldn't be directed at you."

"That goes without saying."

"And Imala wasn't offended at you vetting her choices."

"That also goes without saying."

"Imala and I are finding more people we can trust, but there aren't nearly enough of them."

"We're goblins, dear. Intrigue and subterfuge are in our blood."

"I am more than aware of that, but for once I'd like to experience it not being aimed at me and mine."

"Imala is doing an admirable job rooting out the riffraff. At the rate she's going, she'll have the court tidied up within the month—quite possibly by the time you return."

"That would be a wonderful homecoming gift."

A'Zahra put her pen back in its holder. "Is your ship all packed for your little excursion?"

"It is." I smiled. Eighty percent of the expeditions that had gone to Aquas never returned. Those that did make it home came back with less than half their original complement. Aquas did not welcome visitors. I hoped our expedition would be the exception.

A'Zahra wasn't the first to refer to our expedition using a term with lesser gravitas. My parents had taken to calling it my "little trip." While I seriously doubted prefacing their descriptions with "little" would positively affect our chances for survival, I could hardly blame them for trying.

I leaned forward. "Have you given any more thought to my proposal?"

"Aside from that it's dangerous? Not much. Paranoia over who's going to make the first attempt on Chigaru and Mirabai's lives is a full-time job."

"But you agree it's needed?"

"*If* we're invaded."

"It will have to be in place before then."

"I know. If we must battle Khrynsani and alien invaders in our very streets, we will need battle mages from every shade of magic—light to dark. I do not disagree with you on that point." From her tone, she knew and she didn't like it, but it was past time for the people I'd spoken to A'Zahra about to be able to come out of the shadows.

Some were dark mages; others were mages of mixed blood, either goblin and human, or goblin and elf. The time had long come and gone for talented individuals to stop fearing for their lives and hiding behind glamours and veils.

Even among goblins, black magic was scorned and feared. However, I knew through my own experience that sometimes the only solution, the only way to survive, was by using dark or even black magic. I didn't consider myself evil. I was a man who did what was necessary to defeat evil. On occasion, that meant meeting black magic with black magic.

Then there was the issue of half-breeds—goblins who were half goblin and half elf, or half goblin and half human. In our not-too-distant history, such children would have been killed at birth, and never allowed to reach adulthood.

I had told A'Zahra that even black magic had its use, and those of mixed blood should not have to fear for their lives at being known for what they were.

Chigaru and Mirabai had agreed.

I knew that A'Zahra agreed, even if her granddaughter Imala hadn't been of mixed goblin and elven blood. I also knew her one reason for reluctance.

The dark mages.

She had accepted what I was because she knew me. She knew she could trust me.

"You're playing with fire, you know that, don't you?" A'Zahra said quietly.

"I'm willing to risk getting burned to keep from being annihilated," I told her.

"These dark mages could be Khrynsani spies."

"And some of them are trusted friends and allies. Friends who I have enlisted more than once over the past few years to help me when no one else could. Talon wouldn't be alive today if not for them. Neither would Raine and Piaras. In fact, if you take the series of events to their conclusion, without the help of my team of dark mages whom I personally can vouch for, we wouldn't be sitting here in this office having this difference of opinion. There are others out there just like them. I only ask that we give those men and women a chance."

"It's not that I don't trust your instincts in this..."

I finished the thought that she was reluctant to voice. "It's that you distrust anyone who has even delved into black magic. I would not be taking four of these men and women to Aquas with me unless I trusted them implicitly. Once we land, we must reach Nidaar quickly, do what must be done, and get out. That can't be done with an army, regardless of how small." I paused. "When I return, we can discuss this further, but I assure you that we will be thoroughly confirming the loyalty of each and every one of the dark mages on the list that I gave you. Those more skilled in battle magic need to be brought on board first. Khrynsani mages were embedded with our army units, and now that they're not, we have large defensive and offensive gaps in our ground forces. If we are to stand any chance at all against invaders capable of decimating an entire world, we need these men and women on our side and at our side."

"Yes, I am more than aware of our present weaknesses. I

have them staring me in the face before my feet even hit the floor when I get out of bed. That is, when I've been to bed."

"You're not sleeping?"

"As much as you are."

I raised an eyebrow.

A'Zahra smiled. "Barrett is my spy in your household."

"Of course he is."

"He worries about you—especially now that you've returned. He's determined that nothing is going to happen to you. And he knows I worry about you, too. It is still dangerous here. Perhaps even more so now than in the past."

"Predators are at their most deadly when frightened or cornered," I said. "Goblin courtiers only believe what they see and hear for themselves, and even then they will continue to doubt. We have had Chigaru lay out very carefully how he will conduct his reign. Which things will change, what will remain the same. The people see his actions and hear his words, but until they accept both, then yes, the capital will remain a very dangerous place."

"As will any place you go."

I laughed quietly. "Kesyn said much the same thing. For me, threats are expected."

"On a ship, quarters are close—and so are your enemies."

"What's one more target on my back?"

"At least on a ship you'll have all the people who want to kill you in one place."

"I've taken every precaution possible to ensure my safety and Talon's. I always have and always will, as you well know."

"I'm not concerned about someone on board being bribed or blackmailed as much as I'm worried about mind control.

The victim wouldn't even be aware of it—before, during, or after."

"It's a scenario I've considered."

"The Khrynsani have mages who can manipulate their chosen operative over any distance—"

"Mages who have not been captured," I finished for her. "Believe me, I am only too aware of what the Khrynsani are still capable of, Sandrina Ghalfari in particular. She escaped from us once; it won't happen again."

"Is that pride I hear?"

"That's mortification that she escaped the first time. Sandrina is a mess that we made. We should be the ones to clean it up. In the meantime, I'm surrounding myself with good people, people I trust."

"And whom do you trust?"

"Aside from yourself, Kesyn, my family, and a few select friends, the same people I always trust—no one. Those I will watch. If I only took people with me whom I know and trust, I would be going to Aquas in a rowboat. This is far from the first time that I've had to watch my back, front, and both sides, and I'm still here." I paused meaningfully. "Most of those who have made attempts on my life are not."

"Most, not all."

I arched an eyebrow. "Advocating violence now, are we?"

"Advocating survival. There are times when you cannot achieve one without the other. Unfortunately, we are living in one of those times."

I smiled. "But we are living."

"Exercising caution will ensure that we continue to do so. I know that you will be careful—most of the time."

"And since you won't be there to remind me when you perceive that I'm slipping, you're doing it now."

"With you, dear, I must do what I can when I can."

I leaned across my desk and put my hand over hers. "I've always been grateful for it, even when I haven't said so."

A'Zahra turned her tiny hand beneath mine, entwining our fingers. "I know, but it is nice to have you say it."

I raised her fingers to my lips and gently kissed them.

She gave me a tiny smile. "Insufferable charmer. Now run along so I can get some work done—and attempt to straighten out the mess you're leaving me with. Your organizational skills are abominable."

I stood, went behind the desk, and dropped a kiss on top of her head. "I can't be the best at everything."

4

The Khrynsani temple was guarded day and night. All entrances had been found and sealed except for one.

Curiosity was a powerful thing. The Khrynsani had occupied this building for over a thousand years. Now, for the first time, it stood empty, with most of the main temple having been destroyed the night the Saghred had been shattered. Sarad had summoned the pair of sea dragons that lived in the caverns beneath the temple's many sublevels to join the battle in the temple itself. The dragons had ripped their way up through those sublevels and through the temple's floors. The Khrynsani temple had never been safe for anyone, now it was even less so. However, goblins were inquisitive by nature. We liked to explore, to discover.

The Khrynsani treasury had also been here in the temple. We had found it soon after the order had fallen, and the gold was now back in the royal treasury where it belonged—and from where vast quantities of it had been stolen.

That would not dissuade the greedy. Where there was one cache of treasure, there could very well be more. There probably was. It would be found and the contents would be taken to the royal treasury. Chigaru's intention was to repair the damage—to property and people—that the Khrynsani had done. Money would be needed, a lot of it.

Just because there were no Khrynsani here did not mean there was no danger.

The Saghred was destroyed, but there were other, lesser objects of power in the temple. Those that were out in the open had been deactivated or contained and removed. I was sure there were others that were still to be found. And they would be found, but only by those trained to encounter such objects, not a thief or curious youngsters who would endanger themselves and others by attempting to steal or manipulate them.

The only remaining way into the temple was through the repaired front doors. They were locked by ways both magical and mundane. Four guards were posted with four werehounds. What the guards couldn't sense, the hounds could.

The goblin people were safe from the temple, and the temple was safe from the people.

Kesyn didn't believe that I was safe from what it still contained. He was right. I wasn't. Thanks to his teaching—and me learning from my mistakes—I was much better able to resist the calls of the artifacts and books inside. I had been inside many times since the temple and the Khrynsani who had controlled it had fallen. I had been tempted each and every time, but had not come close to succumbing.

Bad experiences were good teachers.

Kesyn Badru was also a good teacher. The best, if truth be told. He hadn't known that I'd been inside the Khrynsani library multiple times without, shall we say, a magical chaperone. Now that he knew, he was determined that I wouldn't be doing it again. Just because I didn't need him with me didn't mean I didn't want him with me.

Books contained knowledge. Knowledge was consumed. In inexperienced or careless hands, the books in the Khrynsani library could consume *you*.

I smiled grimly. And there were people who actually believed that words had no power.

The guards knew me. They were Imala's people, chosen by her and approved by me and A'Zahra Nuru. They were mage-level talents, but especially gifted in locking things up and keeping them that way. They were called prison mages or vault mages. There were no living prisoners here, but none of the objects or books inside would be leaving without a qualified escort, so in a sense, that made them prisoners.

I was here to examine one of those prisoners that, unless I was careful, would be every bit as dangerous as a living Khrynsani dark mage.

The vault mages opened an access point in the wards they had laboriously conjured and constructed over the temple's massive set of black iron doors. To get inside, we had only opened one of those physical doors, but the resounding boom of it closing behind us gave me an unwelcome flashback to fighting for my life in here only a few months ago.

Kesyn's voice was an eerie echo in the empty space. "When is this mausoleum going to be torn down?"

"Once we've taken everything out that needs to go, and destroyed the rest." I shivered, and it wasn't from the cold. "That day can't come soon enough for me."

Kesyn glanced down the hall at the blue lightglobes flickering in their sconces.

"The lights are on in here all the time?"

"Oh yes. I've ordered that they be activated and glowing at full power day and night."

"Good."

I knew what Kesyn was worried about. The temple didn't have any windows, so noon appeared as midnight here, but some of the artifacts kept down in the lower levels fed off of darkness. I'd had those rooms lit even brighter than the rest of the temple. I was fully aware of the kinds of things Sarad Nukpana had liked to collect. I wasn't taking any chances.

Those who had to venture inside the temple were not safe, and we knew it. The mages and academics working inside had been specifically chosen for their tasks. They had the talent to recognize what needed to be contained, and the strength to both resist and contain them. But to ensure that none of the books or objects had subverted that strength, anyone working in the temple had to submit to regular mind examinations. Every precaution and safety measure was being taken.

The Khrynsani temple was full of black magic temptation. Seductive didn't even begin to describe it. Knowing a thing was evil only did so much to help you resist it. Though for me, knowing that Sarad Nukpana had brought it inside himself or had approved it, went a long way toward turning seductive into sickening.

Objects like the Saghred wanted to be used. They desired power as much as they craved the souls necessary to create it.

Those with the greatest power became prizes to be lured in and taken. Most of these objects were primitive and couldn't tell the difference between a mage who could be tempted, and one whose task was to collect and contain them.

Most evil objects weren't what you could call strategic thinkers.

It had made our job much easier.

As a result, the blue-lit halls we walked through were quiet, both of mortal sounds and magical power.

Secondary hallways branched off, confusing to those unfamiliar with the temple. It had been designed that way on purpose. Those who belonged there knew. Those who didn't risked their lives and immortal souls by stepping across the temple's threshold. I knew where I was going, but I still counted the hallways as I passed. The risk had been lessened due to the collapse of some of the hallways' walls and ceilings from the sea dragon rampage, rendering portions of the temple inaccessible. Getting lost in here, even temporarily, was the last thing I wanted to do. I had taken a wrong turn before, last week most recently. It had been like walking a gauntlet. In the older sections of the temple, the mortar had been mixed with the blood of sacrifices. Normally, I wasn't sensitive to spirits or the echoes produced in the wake of violent death. I knew those who were, and counted myself fortunate not to share their dubious gift. Perhaps it was the sheer numbers of those who had been murdered to mortar the granite blocks. I actually heard their screams, felt their agony as the sacrificial blade was driven through their hearts.

We had just passed the hall that led down to that level.

I walked faster, and without a word, Kesyn more than kept pace.

The Khrynsani archives were too extensive to transfer all at once; and quite frankly ensuring that Chigaru's new reign lasted through its first week had taken priority over moving books and scrolls. So Imala and I had done as we'd had to do for many of the Khrynsani buildings—post guards and wards to keep the curious and greedy out and the dangerous valuables in.

There were plenty of objects of monetary value, but what I was looking for would only have value to a very limited few. Though I imagine there were those who would have gladly killed to get access to the section of the temple that I had just entered.

The library.

The repository of all Khrynsani history, records, and knowledge, as well as whatever else might have been hoarded by the Khrynsani and thus unknown to the rest of the world.

Denita Enric was the senior scholar in charge of cataloguing and moving the library. It wasn't vast, but it certainly wasn't insignificant, either in the number of books and scrolls or in their power. Denita was incorruptible on every level—magical, political, and monetary. A'Zahra Nuru was one of her best friends and she trusted Denita completely. So did I.

Denita had selected those working with her on the basis of their shielding skills.

They couldn't have any talent other than shields, and those had to be the best.

Books and the words within them could be more seductive than any lover, and could promise you more than any mortal could ever dream of giving.

There were two more vault mage guards on either side of the library doors. Denita and her assistants were experts at protecting themselves from injury, both physical and psychic, but if one of the books decided to fight back against being boxed and got through their shields, I wanted a vault mage nearby to lock that book down.

Kesyn noted their presence with approval.

"I'm getting cautious in my old age," I said.

"Or you've been bitten enough."

"That, too."

The instant I crossed the library's threshold, the whispers began. The more power you had, and the darker that power was, the more insistent the entreaties. To open a cover, to read aloud, to give the words voice.

And life.

I'd trained myself long ago to shut out the temptations, or at least hold them at bay. I wasn't saying that my magic didn't respond. It did. Like reacting to the sight and scent of a beautiful woman, a physical response wasn't something that could be stopped, merely resisted.

I'd had a lot of practice resisting.

The first time I'd come here, I'd been alone.

That had been a mistake.

The lightglobes hadn't been lit that day; however, their illumination hadn't been needed. The pages of the books stacked on the reading desks and even those in boxes and still on the shelves had glowed and pulsed, dazzling my senses, tempting them.

Tempting me.

There had been no one here to prevent me from opening and reading any book I desired, one by one until I'd consumed them all.

The books knew.

I blinked and shook my head, dispelling the memory, scattering those thoughts. Thoughts that had no place there.

Denita Enric glanced up, and I detected concern in her dark eyes. It was there for only a moment, then her academic reserve slipped back into place.

I wasn't the only one who was concerned.

Some of her students were watching me as well. Not openly, but they were being cautious and curious.

They knew who and what I used to be.

Kesyn's reputation wasn't exactly warm and cuddly, either.

One young goblin clutched the book he'd been about to pack against his chest, eyes wide.

"My footsteps aren't going to burst into flames," I assured him.

All that earned me were a few nervous smiles.

"And I don't bite," I added.

Kesyn grinned, showing his fangs, one of them chipped. "I do."

Reputations. They died hard. It looked like I would need to drive a couple of extra daggers into mine when I got back from Aquas. For now, that was all the reassurance I could give them.

I turned my attention to Denita. "You sent word that you had another book for me."

Denita tilted her head toward a nearby table. "A few hours ago, I found what appears to be a travel journal from one of the earliest expeditions. It's been cataloged, and I had it set aside for you."

The Khrynsani were avid collectors of magically-imbued objects, and would travel to wherever they had to in order to get their hands on what they wanted. They documented those journeys—where they went and what they found and brought home with them—or failed to bring home, as in the case of the Heart of Nidaar. I had asked Denita to set aside every travel journal that she found. Not only would it be helpful for finding and securing the Heart of Nidaar, it could give us the upper hand in locating objects in the future.

"Considering where I found it I knew you'd want to see it," she told me. "It was inside Sarad Nukpana's personal shelf."

That got my attention, and Kesyn's.

"Inside?" he asked.

Denita flashed a grin. "When a bookshelf is set against a wall, I always knock on the back of the shelf with a little push of magic. I've found all kinds of interesting things that way."

"I'll bet you have," I said. "Was it warded?"

"Unexpectedly, no. And I was grateful it wasn't. Most are. And considering that it would have been Sarad Nukpana who would have done the warding…"

"I don't blame you."

"Maybe he left it unwarded so his mommy could get at it," Kesyn muttered.

I walked over to the journal and extended my hands over it. No magic residue. Good. I could do without any more surprises today.

Still I hesitated before touching it.

I laid my hand on the spine.

No telltale tingle of malevolent magic.

Denita came to stand beside me, and lowered her voice. "I knew the book's author would especially interest you. Rudra Muralin."

Rudra Muralin had been the head of the Khrynsani order nine hundred years ago, and his lifespan had been extended by direct contact with the Saghred. I knew this because I'd met him in person a few months ago.

Kesyn whispered a word that I completely agreed with.

"You said it, sir."

"And if you even think about touching that book, I'll say it again—after I get you in a headlock."

"I have to examine it," I told him.

"No, you don't." Then he muttered a low string of profanities because he knew I was right and he didn't like it. "At least have proper backup when you do it."

"Who would that be?"

"Me and A'Zahra."

"May I take it with me?" I asked Denita.

"I'd hoped you'd want to take it out of here," she said. "Though I have a feeling that little book isn't going anywhere it doesn't want to go."

And I had a feeling—a sinking one—that Rudra Muralin would love nothing more than for me to take his book home with me. "I think the book will cooperate."

Rudra was dead. Sarad Nukpana had killed him. Or to be more precise, Sarad had drained the life out of him, sucked out his soul and knowledge, leaving behind a dried husk.

I'd seen his body.

Imala had decapitated him.

That didn't stop the feeling that somehow, somewhere, Rudra Muralin was laughing.

5

A'Zahra Nuru wouldn't be available until tomorrow morning, and I'd have been lying if I said I wasn't relieved.

I also had another excuse to put off dealing with Rudra's book.

I had an appointment with Agata Azul.

I'd sent a messenger to her before I left to see A'Zahra. Kesyn had included a private message along with my request. Her reply had been waiting when we'd returned with the book.

I read the note again. "She said yes. And she wants to meet at her home."

Kesyn chuckled. "Don't get your hopes up. The lady said yes to a meeting, not to go sailing off to the other side of the world with you."

"What was in that note of yours?"

"That you have more sense than you used to, you're a relatively decent sort, and that I'd appreciate it if she listened to what you had to say."

"Charming."

Kesyn spread his arms. "If you got it, use it."

"What do you think are the chances she'll agree to go with us?"

"Well, she doesn't scare easily, so you'll probably be fine there."

"So you're saying that going to an uninhabited continent to find a legendary city and the all-powerful stone that powered it, before the Khrynsani and an army of alien invaders can get to it first, won't scare her."

"I don't think she'll bat an eye," Kesyn said. "Aggie always was the adventuresome sort. Just be honest with her, and you'll be fine." My teacher's eyes had an evil glint. "Probably."

I wasn't about to simply drop in on a gem mage of Azul's power, especially when her idea of landscaping was to cover every square inch of ground with crystals cut to a razor's sharpness and glowing with power held under check—or released—at her whim.

Guests prudently remained on the brick path to the front door.

Suicidal maniacs arrived uninvited.

Thus, I'd made an appointment to ensure that Agata Azul considered me a guest and not a threat. Whether I was a maniac was up to her to decide.

Kesyn had remained at my house to secure the book. My

home was wrapped in wards, but one simply didn't leave a book hidden by Sarad Nukpana and written by Rudra Muralin lying around as casual reading material.

Considering who I was now and who I had been—and those who didn't like either one—I'd half expected Agata Azul to insist that we meet in secret. I wanted to get and stay on the lady's good side, so when she agreed to meet at her home, I knew a little judicious shielding would help my case. Not shielding from her crystal sentries, but from anyone watching me. Chigaru may have been on the throne, but I still had a target on my back. Several actually. Though who was I kidding? I had so many they overlapped.

Kesyn was right. No one in their right mind would want to be anywhere near me. He'd said Agata was brilliant, yet she'd accepted my request for a meeting. Maybe her sanity was questionable. Considering what I was about to ask her to help me do, I wasn't too certain about my own.

I wasn't wearing a cloak and my clothes were plain. Doing the cloak-and-dagger thing just made anyone who saw you wonder what you were up to. So no cloak, no hood, but plenty of daggers and magic at the ready. I started my trip to meet with Agata Azul from the south side of Regor near the waterfront. No one had seen me leave my house. Since I'd returned home, I had been mending fences with my neighbors, so to speak, and while I wasn't in their good graces and didn't anticipate being so anytime soon, at least a few of them would speak to me, surreptitiously, of course.

To further prevent being recognized, I magically altered my face and decreased my height, but I didn't try to hide. To attempt to hide was to attract attention. To a goblin, a person skulking about was a person begging to be followed, simply to discover what they were up to, if nothing else. I had used this disguise before and it had never attracted either suspicion or curiosity. As Kesyn would no doubt say: If it ain't broke, don't fix it.

I had seen Agata Azul at a distance, but we had never met. As chief mage, I spent most of my time at court. As one of the Seven Kingdoms' top gem mages, Agata Azul only accepted clients from a few, highly select friends and colleagues, and to my knowledge had never set foot inside the Mal'Salin palace. Smart lady. Staying away from court meant that not only was she talented and selective, but highly intelligent and not in possession of a death wish.

Kesyn knew her well enough to call her Aggie. Whether this familiarity was due to affection on his part—or tolerance on hers—I didn't know and would not find out by behaving in any way other than the very height of propriety and good manners. My mother had taught me better—and being a professional assassin, my mother had also taught me how not to be stupid and get myself killed. I would be availing myself of all of her teachings this evening.

What Kesyn called an introduction consisted of sending word to Azul vouching for my sanity and good intentions, and that I warranted an audience. He said that the rest was up to me. I would need more than words to convince Agata Azul to help, so I'd brought irrefutable proof—the spy gem with the recording of the Rak'kari, the monster spiders the Khrynsani had sent to infest the Void between the kingdoms' travel mirrors. I'd edited out the part where the Guardians had pulled me out of a Rak'kari's clutches and had to cut away my armor and clothes beneath to keep its acidic venom from melting the skin off my bones. I didn't think full-frontal nudity would be appropriate for a first-time meeting. I'd also brought the recording of what we had seen when we opened a rift to Timurus—an invading army with their banner and the Khrynsani flag flying from a fortress's walls.

As I approached Agata Azul's house, I kept my eyes straight ahead, but furtively glanced at the crystals glittering in the moonlight.

They were beautiful.

And deadly.

I told myself that the flickers of light from the crystals on the edge of my vision were just my imagination.

I didn't believe me, either.

I reached the front door and knocked using the fist-sized quartz mounted in a brass knocker. It tingled against my palm, meaning the quartz was embedded with a questing spell. Ingenious. Determine your guests' state of mind and level of power before opening your door to them.

The rock probably announced "nervous" loud and clear.

I was nervous, but not for the reason Azul might think. Yes, I was a little apprehensive about meeting her, but the majority of my nervousness stemmed from fear of her saying no.

I needed Agata Azul on this expedition. I needed her desperately. I had others going with us who could get us to Aquas, find Nidaar, and keep us alive while we did both. What I did not have was anyone who came even close to Agata Azul's level of skill in locating gems of power. Money was no object. I could afford to pay whatever she demanded, but I suspected that money would not be the deciding factor.

I took a deep breath and waited.

Minutes passed.

There was no sound on the other side of the door.

I knew she was home.

One, I had an appointment. Two, she'd see me, from curiosity alone if nothing else. Three, this was some kind of a test. One that I couldn't afford to fail.

Mages of Agata Azul's power were living divining rods for crystals of power.

I needed her help.

I waited. Perfectly still. Imperfectly patient. I glanced down.

Beneath my feet was a slab of crystal, now faintly glowing.

I sighed. Then again, why even bother opening the door when she could know everything without having to?

Nearly a minute later, the door did open, and I was looking directly into the eyes of a woman as tall as my mother, who was tall even for a goblin. Her height wasn't surprising; her age was. I would guess she was in her mid-twenties. I had assumed that with her level of power, she'd be older. Her features were strong, but feminine, attractive rather than beautiful. Her cheekbones were high, her lips full, and her hair an ebony sheet that fell nearly to her waist. But it was her eyes that drew my attention and kept it there. Not through any level of craft, but from a vitality that shone from within with a keen intelligence and sharp wit. A humor that seemed to be enjoying my confusion.

I dropped the glamour from my face.

I inclined my head in a bow. "Magus Azul, I presume?"

"You were expecting someone else?"

"No. But I thought—"

"I answer my own door. Good help is hard enough to find these days. I'm not about to risk losing one to an incendiary spell intended for me."

"I'm not armed with an incendiary spell."

Agata Azul looked me up and down with clinical detachment. "No, you aren't."

"Fire magic isn't my specialty."

"I should hope not. An uncivilized way to kill someone, besides completely lacking in creativity."

I didn't know what to say to that.

"Don't just stand there," she told me, "come in so I can close the door."

I did, and once inside and the door closed behind me, I dropped the glamour from my height.

Mages of Agata Azul's level usually wore ornate robes. She was wearing a tunic, trousers, and boots. While the leather and fabric were the finest quality, it was a form-fitting cut that allowed for maximum speed and movement. My mother would have called what Agata Azul was wearing formal working clothes. My mother was a semi-retired mortekal, a title goblins reserved for assassins of the highest caliber. Agata Azul was dressed for confronting any situation, but looking good while doing it. Mother would have approved. And since I couldn't help but notice how the soft leather accentuated every curve, I approved as well.

"Am I not what you expected, Chancellor Nathrach?"

Honesty was all I had. "No, you're not."

"Is that good or bad?"

"I'm not sure."

She gestured me toward the front parlor. "You may as well make yourself comfortable while you decide. I've given my servants the night off, so if you require refreshment—"

"No, thank you. That won't be necessary."

The sentry crystals weren't the only source of heat. The simmer I'd felt since being allowed past her wards came from Magus Agata Azul herself. The gem mage was a banked fire, her power burning brightly under a perfectly controlled exterior.

I didn't sense that she felt threatened by me. If she had, her gate wards had been sufficient to fry me as I passed the threshold. Just because she wasn't afraid of me didn't mean her defenses were down. On the contrary, the lady looked ready for anything I could have brought to her doorstep.

Her dark eyes gleamed with unspoken challenge.

This was a test, a test I no longer needed to pass. I *wanted* to pass it.

6

There were no lights in the house. The only illumination came from crystals. Crystals in wall sconces, on tables, and piled in braziers standing in corners.

Considering Agata Azul's skill level, it was the same as being in a house full of trained attack werehounds. No soft, flickering glows came from these rocks. All around us, crystals of all shapes, sizes, and colors flared and faded, only to flare again, giving me the intensely unsettling impression of agitated serpents, weaving hypnotically forward and back, ready to strike at the first wrong move. All at Agata Azul's command.

She may have been home, but she didn't feel secure. And here I was about to ask her to sail right into the teeth of the beast.

For most people, turning your home into a guarded fortress meant that you were afraid of something. My initial impression of Agata Azul told me there was little that she feared. Thus arming her home to this extent indicated that she merely wanted to kill anything that came at her and get it right the first time. This was a woman who did not play games, at least not of the life-and-death kind.

I was no expert on magic- and power-infused gems and stones, but I'd had a crash course over the past few months, courtesy of the Saghred. While Agata Azul's collection didn't give off Saghred-level vibes, I'd be foolish to discount the energy that filled the room—or the lady who had painstakingly collected them.

She noted my interest. "I specialize in sentry crystals. Goblins have what I like to call a healthy paranoia. That's a good environment for a business like mine. At the same time, I work by referral only. During Sathrik's reign there was an increase in the demand for weaponized crystals."

"You make weapons?"

"Only for clients who wouldn't abuse them, and for defensive use only. Needless to say, that considerably narrowed the pool of potential clients. There are other gem mages who aren't so selective. For them it's all about the money and power. I have lines I will not cross for any price."

"I assure you, that isn't why I'm here."

"Please be seated, Chancellor Nathrach."

There weren't many chairs in the sitting room, and every one of them would put crystals at a guest's back. This may or may not have been another test, but I was going to treat it like one—or at least show Agata Azul that I trusted her.

I sat in the chair with three of the most lethal-looking crystals in the room directly behind me.

So there. I trust you not to kill me horribly.

The gem mage raised a bemused brow.

I shrugged. "At the very least you won't have your pet rocks reduce me to a puddle, because it would be impossible to extract my remains from the upholstery." I glanced down. "It's a lovely fabric. Caesolian silk?"

"Woven with rose gold thread." One side of her mouth slowly curled upward. "Though if I decided you needed killing, I would sacrifice the chair as a cost of doing business."

She sat in the chair directly opposite mine. I couldn't help but notice that the crystals behind her chair glowed a warm and welcoming pink.

I think mine were hissing.

A flicker of light drew my attention to a walking cane leaning against the side of Agata Azul's chair. The gem on top was the size of a child's fist and appeared to be a sapphire. I seriously doubted it was merely a cane. Agata had shown no trace of a limp, and the cane's shaft was just large enough to contain a slender sword. The lady was armed and stylishly so. Again, I approved.

Agata Azul leaned back in her chair. "And what business does the chancellor to the new, young king wish to discuss with me this evening?"

"Time-sensitive business, so I'll get right to the point."

"What delightfully unexpected behavior from a king's adviser."

"A great many things have changed at court, Magus Azul. With much more to come. We don't have time for anything else."

"Refreshing." All signs of amusement vanished. "I wish you luck—and a lifespan longer than a bottle fly."

"That is but one of my goals."

I not only needed Agata Azul on the expedition, I needed her as an unswerving ally. Mages such as she didn't grant their support and allegiance lightly. Being goblins within a hundred square miles of a court ruled by any Mal'Salin, regardless of his or her attested sanity, any loyalty was given in private or not at all.

What I would be asking was about as public as it could possibly be.

I decided to tell her everything.

I began with the peace talks that had been held on the Isle of Mid last month, and the Khrynsani's attempts to sabotage those talks and cripple all mirror travel, essentially isolating all seven kingdoms from each other.

"I'd heard all mirror travel had been suspended," Agata Azul said.

"Rak'kari infestation."

"Those things actually exist?"

"I can personally vouch for it, and I brought spy gems to prove it." I pulled the two spy gems out of the pouch at my waist. "One of the first attacks was on Markus Sevelien, the director of elven intelligence, when he came through a mirror from Silvanlar to Mid. The elven ambassador and his staff had been attacked on their ship before they could even reach Mid. The ambassador was killed and his staff taken captive. The gold used to pay the pirates was goblin imperial, the bags marked as having originated from the royal treasury. And the Rak'kari are a goblin black magic creation."

"Someone was trying to frame you."

"Not only me, but the new goblin government. Mal'Salin monarchs aren't known for honesty as far as their intentions toward other kingdoms are concerned."

"It is still as it has always been," Agata Azul mused. "The other kingdoms will believe we aren't going to invade them when they wake up without goblins on their collective doorstep."

"Precisely. And who would it benefit the most to have the other six kingdoms unwilling to trust, let alone sign a peace treaty with the goblins?"

"The Khrynsani, for one."

"Right again." I rolled the spy gem in my fingers. "To help Mychael Eiliesor determine whether the Rak'kari attack on Markus Sevelien was an isolated incident, or if the entire Void—and therefore all travel mirrors—had been infected, I volunteered to step through the Guardians' mirror that led to the palace here. The same one Imala Kalis and I would have used to get to Mid. After Mychael alerted us to the attack on Markus, we used the Passages instead."

Agata Azul blinked. "You traveled the Passages? By choice?"

"Considering the alternative of becoming food for a nest of giant spiders…yes, I found the Passages the more appealing option."

"And Imala?"

"You know Imala?"

"Relatively well. Enough to know that taking the Passages would not be her first, second, or any choice."

"It was more of a sprint, actually."

"I see."

"I shielded both of us the entire time."

"I'm sure that was a great comfort to her."

"Not really."

"I can imagine."

And from the gleam in her dark eyes, she was imagining that right now, and was enjoying what she had no doubt had transpired between the two of us.

"We arrived safely."

"I don't believe that would have absolved you in her opinion."

I recalled Imala's reaction. "No, it didn't."

"And then you stepped through the mirror as spider bait?"

"I trusted Mychael and his Guardians to pull me out if anything happened, and they didn't let me down. The other delegates were placing the blame for the Rak'kari squarely on my shoulders, insisting that Chigaru was a Mal'Salin and that the Mal'Salins had always been allied to the Khrynsani, and this was just the latest attempt to cripple the kingdoms' defenses to launch an attack." I shrugged. "So I thought the best way to prove that I had nothing to do with the Rak'kari would be to go into the Void myself with a spy gem attached to my harness."

"So getting yourself killed would prove them wrong."

"Imala said much the same thing."

"I'm not surprised."

"She described it as dragging a baited hook through shark-infested waters. I told her who better than a dark mage to survive against creatures spawned by black magic."

"You're here and in one piece, so it must have worked."

"It did." I held up the gem. "Do you have a crystal ball available?"

Agata Azul gave me a bemused look as she stood, retrieved a head-sized orb from a shelf, and put it on the table between us. I activated the spy gem to play its recording in the crystal ball.

The gem mage watched the recording, and I watched her.

"I take it you played this for the delegates?"

"We did."

"Their reaction?"

"They were convinced this marked the beginning of a joint and imminent Khrynsani/goblin attack on the Seven Kingdoms."

"And how did they account for the fact that you nearly died making the recording?"

"Insanity, or so I assume."

"A logical enough assumption. Since I haven't heard that we're at war, I take it you convinced them otherwise?"

"Dakarai Enric did. Thankfully most of the other ambassadors were intelligent and levelheaded."

"Most?"

"The Nebian ambassador, Aeron Corantine, arrived with his mind made up—or his pockets lined—and refused to budge in the face of either proof or logic."

"I haven't heard of him."

"Be grateful. Imala and I had to sit across a negotiating table from him for nearly a week. She had many interesting ideas as to how to make him disappear and have it look like an accident. By the end of the week, she had dispensed with the desire to make it look accidental. She merely wanted to lunge across the table and throttle him to death."

Agata Azul laughed. "I would've liked to have been

there." She held up a hand. "As an observer, not a participant. My patience can only be tried so far. What's on the other spy gem?"

I passed it to her. "This is what Sandrina Ghalfari and the remaining Khrynsani plan to do next. If they had succeeded in using the Rak'kari to cut the Seven Kingdoms off from each other it would have simplified their plans, but the Conclave college has some creative and ingenious faculty. They came up with a way to destroy the Rak'kari and clean out the Void."

I briefly told her about the invasion of Timurus seven hundred years ago by an off-world army that completely wiped out all life on the planet. No one knew who they were, where they'd come from, what they had wanted, why they had invaded then, and why they'd returned now.

"None of this would have been an issue for us had the Khrynsani not chosen Timurus as their fallback refuge if they were ever defeated," I continued, "and as the place to store the Rak'kari eggs until they were needed. The Khrynsani traveled to Timurus by way of the Passages, both to regroup and to release the Rak'kari into the Void. We believe they encountered the invaders when they arrived and had to bargain for their lives—or simply made them a deal."

"To serve us up on a silver platter to save their own miserable lives."

I indicated the spy gem she held. "Mychael had the portal mages in the Conclave college's dimensional studies department open a small rift—no more than a window really—on a mountainside overlooking the city of Astava on Timurus. That gem will show you the army we saw massing. The same army that wiped out the population seven hundred years ago is there again. Their banners as well as the Khrynsani flag are flying over the city. The people of Timurus had mages and magic, and while they weren't to our level of ability, they weren't exactly helpless. The invaders were said to control magic different from anything that has ever been recorded, so based on Timurus's fate, no single kingdom can hope to defeat them. The only way we stand a chance of avoiding Timurus's fate of total annihilation is to form alliances and combine our armies. All of the kingdoms agreed, with the exception of the Nebians."

"Hardly a surprise."

Then I told her my theory of Sandrina using Aquas as a staging area for the invaders—and wanting the Heart of Nidaar to power the portals and Gates to take the invaders and Khrynsani anywhere in the Seven Kingdoms they desired—and what we intended to do about it.

"To stop the Khrynsani and save the Seven Kingdoms," I told her, "we need your help."

7

When I finished, I sat silently and waited. Agata Azul had listened to the last part without interrupting to question, condemn, or contradict, her expression utterly devoid of emotion.

"The Khrynsani have never been overly fond of me," she said. "Should the Khrynsani and their allies gain power, my participation in this expedition of yours would be signing my own death warrant."

"If Sandrina secures the Heart of Nidaar we're all dead or worse," I said. "By all, I'm referring to the population of the Seven Kingdoms. Those of us on the expedition will merely be at the front of the line, and as such will be counted fortunate by many."

"I didn't say I had a problem wearing a target." She gave

the slightest hint of a smile. "Any outfit worth wearing isn't complete without one. Did you know that Sarad Nukpana tried for years to secure my assistance in finding the Saghred for him?"

I went utterly still. "I was not aware."

"You could hardly be expected to know. His attentions increased after you left the court. Attentions that he abandoned after discovering Raine Benares's link to the Saghred. He needed my willing cooperation, which I would never give. I owe Raine Benares my most heartfelt and sincere gratitude. I seriously doubt my gratitude would lessen the suffering she endured for those three months, but should I meet her, I would offer it nonetheless." Agata Azul regarded me in silence for a few moments. "So you want me to drop everything to leave the day after tomorrow on a months-long voyage to an uninhabited continent, to locate a possibly nonexistent city of legend, with an even more legendary stone of power."

"It doesn't sound very appealing when you put it like that."

"Is there any way it could be put to increase its appeal?"

"Not that I've been able to find."

"This isn't an endeavor I will accede to lightly—or possibly at all." Her dark eyes held mine. "Before I give you my answer, I will know something, Tamnais Nathrach, chief mage and king's chancellor."

"I've told you all that I know, but if there's anything else I can tell you, I will."

"I don't care about the details of the mission. I want to know what is in your heart, why you're doing this. Your motivation." She slowly leaned forward in her chair, unnervingly like one of the serpents I had imagined. "Your *true* motivation."

I realized what she was asking. No, she wasn't asking. She was demanding this as the price for her help.

"You want a mind link," I said quietly.

"Want and must have. I have not denied my services to others merely for the satisfaction of refusing them what they want, with them knowing full well that there was nothing they could do to force me, satisfying though that was. I will not use my gift to enable evil—even if that evil began its life as an intention to do good. What is good and noble now can twist into evil later. It does not take much, as you well know. I have seen it happen, and will not be a part of it happening again. You say you want the Heart of Nidaar to keep it out of Sandrina Ghalfari's hands. That seems like a noble enough reason, but is it really? Kesyn Badru told me that you are an honorable man. However, under enough pressure I have seen a man's honor fail him—and me. What is in your heart, Tamnais Nathrach? What is in that subtle and darkly brilliant mind of yours? What do you *truly* desire?"

I moved to the edge of the chair, my hands resting on my knees. "I welcome you finding out."

"You're quick to agree."

"I have no time to waste."

"Even to discover the truth about yourself?"

"I know the truth."

Agata Azul stood and closed the distance between us. I remained seated, my face tilted up toward hers. The gem mage placed her palms on my temples, her fingers a gentle pressure on the sides of my head. Neither of us closed our eyes.

I knew what she would see. I let it happen. I had no choice, not if I wanted her help. I had to have it. Without Agata Azul, the expedition would fail before it even started.

It stung to be compared in any way to Sarad Nukpana, though it was the truth. He had sought her cooperation in finding the Saghred. I needed her help now finding the Heart of Nidaar. Both were stones of power. That was where the similarities ended. Sarad was the embodiment of evil, and his intentions for the Saghred would have spread that evil over the Seven Kingdoms. He had never tried to hide what he was, and it was obvious to all who encountered him.

I had spent years running from what Sarad had openly embraced. Some thought I was just like Sarad and that I was either hiding it from everyone or denying it to myself.

I was neither.

Yes, I had once trod the same path that Sarad had eagerly run down. I had turned from that path. Yes, it still called to me, and I had used black magic since then, but only when there had been no other option. However, I had used the darkest of black magic to defeat Sarad. I had summoned a major demon against the creature, the abomination that Sarad had created. Many would say that it had been evil battling evil that night in the Khrynsani temple, and they would have been right.

It also had been the only way to defeat Sarad Nukpana. If I had had a choice, I would not have done it, but I didn't have a choice, not if I wanted to save my family, my friends, and my people. I had chosen, and it had taken all of my black magic power to succeed.

I did not regret what I had done.

I wanted the same with the Heart of Nidaar as I had with the Saghred. I wanted to keep it from Sarad's mother the same as I had with her son, and if I had to use black magic to accomplish that, so be it. If that made me evil and unworthy of help in Agata Azul's eyes, then so be it. I would not cancel the expedition. I had to stop Sandrina Ghalfari, even if I had to go it alone.

"Confident, aren't you?" Agata Azul murmured.

"I see it as determined."

She had read my thoughts, and I had let her. This was not the link. Not yet.

Her eyes darkened and her fingers tightened their hold.

I took a deep breath and slowly let it out.

Agata Azul went into my mind.

8

A link isn't about sensation—at least not initially. It's about knowledge.

I couldn't feel what Agata Azul was doing, but I saw and I knew.

She had clearly done a link before and knew how to find what she wanted. The closest approximation would be searching through a stack of documents, scanning each, and then moving on to the next until you found what you were looking for. Agata Azul searched my memories, her touch in my mind a methodical and careful review that was actually gentle.

I knew exactly where she would stop and take the link to the next, deeper level.

When the Saghred had forged an umi'atsu bond between me and Raine Benares.

The Saghred had used Raine as bait, knowing that I would be unable to resist the combination of her and the Saghred's dark power. Ultimately I had resisted, and Raine had broken the bond when she killed me to force Sarad Nukpana's soul out of my body. While Sarad's soul had held my body hostage, I had seen inside his mind, knew what his plans were once he had the Saghred, and precisely how he planned to execute those plans.

That knowledge had extinguished any desire I might have had for the power the Saghred had been pushing me to take. Raine lacked the magical knowledge and training to use the stone to its full potential. Sarad and I had that training, and if Sarad hadn't succeeded in obtaining the Saghred for himself, I had been the rock's second choice. Either one of us would have been exactly what that poisonous rock had been waiting millennia for. We were prizes to be taken and used.

In seeing inside Sarad's mind, I had seen the Saghred's other half. The stone had wanted to be fed and used, to perpetuate a cycle of death and destruction played out on a massive scale. Sarad had devoted his life to finding the Saghred so that he could feed and use it to remake the Seven Kingdoms into his vision of paradise—full to overflowing with suffering, enslavement, torture, and death. His paradise, our hell.

Agata Azul was seeing all of this through my eyes and thoughts as I had lived—and died—through it. She saw my dark and primal desire for the power that the Saghred offered through Raine. My struggle to stay away from Raine and the overwhelming temptation the Saghred had flaunted before me. And the time I had come closest to giving in to that temptation. Me and Raine, our bodies entwined, our magic even closer, my thoughts utterly consumed with only one goal, my breathing reduced to ragged panting. I know now that had it gone further, the Saghred would have eaten my soul. At that moment, I would have gladly given my soul to have possessed the woman in my arms. What had stopped me was knowing that I would have taken her down with me. The Saghred would have possessed and damned us both. To stop had been agony, but I had done it. We had done it.

I let Agata Azul see, hear, and feel all of it.

It might have been from the glow of her crystals, but her face appeared to be flushed when she released me.

Regardless, I couldn't resist. I had to say it. "Is it just me, or is it hot in here?"

"The Saghred knew what would break you—your desire for Raine Benares and the feeling of black magic coursing through your veins."

"You're not making this any better."

"I'm not trying to. I need to determine whether you can be trusted when the Heart of Nidaar is beneath your hands and you're tempted with its power."

"Power doesn't tempt me."

"Apparently pleasure can."

I shrugged. "I'm a man."

"So I saw. You didn't have to let me see that much."

"As I said, we don't have time for anything else." I half grinned. "Though at this point, you can call me 'Tam' if you'd like."

"I believe 'Chancellor Nathrach' continues to be appropriate." She returned to her chair and sat, her features inscrutable.

"The legend surrounding the Heart of Nidaar doesn't mention any manipulative qualities. However, until we find it, we won't know of any other defensive measures it can employ. We will proceed with caution."

"Are you saying you'll help?"

"I am. I told Kesyn if you passed my test, I would agree."

"He didn't mention that."

"Of course he didn't. You expected him to? That was one of his more annoying qualities during the time he was my teacher. He preferred to let his students discover the consequences of their mistakes on their own."

I scowled. "Like having an ill-prepared spell blow up in your face."

She smiled. "But it made you prepare properly next time, didn't it?"

"How long were you his student?"

"Until it became obvious that my abilities were out of his specialty. However, we've stayed in touch."

"This wouldn't be the first time he kept things from me," I said. "I've gotten used to it."

"Do you have the shard for me to examine?"

"I beg your pardon?"

"The shard, the piece of the Heart of Nidaar."

"How could I have a piece of the Heart of Nidaar?"

Agata Azul stared at me in disbelief, obviously wondering if I was a few arrows short of a full quiver. "I assumed you were organizing and leading the expedition not only to deny the Khrynsani of the stone, but to continue your ancestor's work."

I waited for my brain to convert words into meaning. It

didn't happen. "I'm afraid I don't know what you're talking about."

"The Heart of Nidaar. An ancestor of yours by the name of Kansbar Nathrach was on an expedition that went looking for it. The name is not familiar to you?"

"No, we have the same surname, but other than that, I've never heard of him. How long ago was this?"

"Approximately nine hundred years. In your defense, he may not have been a direct ancestor, perhaps a distant cousin. It's a hobby of mine to know about powerful gem mages and stones of power. The Heart of Nidaar is said to be as flames captured in stone."

"You're saying that this Kansbar Nathrach was a gem mage?"

"Not that I was aware, or that gem historians know of. Just that he had been on a voyage to explore Aquas. But as with any group who went there, they also looking for the lost city of Nidaar. Gold is a great motivator. By necessity and curiosity, I'm a keen student of history, especially goblin history and gem lore. It's said that those who ignore their history are doomed to repeat it. We goblins have proven to be exceptional at that. We pick and choose what parts of our history to remember, and it is rarely the parts where we made monumentally bad errors of judgment. According to the histories, Kansbar Nathrach was quite the adventurer."

"Many of my family have been."

"This one was captured and tortured by the Khrynsani."

I scowled. "That also has happened more than once, most recently to my parents and brother."

"I had heard. I am sorry."

"We made them pay with interest. Finding the Heart of Nidaar before the Khrynsani do can help us ensure that it does not happen to anyone's family ever again." I thought for a moment. "I wonder why I've never heard about him—or why he wasn't mentioned in the books I've read."

"It wasn't exactly what one could call a successful trip. In fact, if something could go wrong, it did. It was said that the expedition was cursed, especially the return voyage, when they carried with them objects taken from Aquas. It was determined that more than one of the objects was responsible for their bad luck. All of the objects were thrown overboard. Once they were disposed of, the sickness and storms vanished."

"So Kansbar Nathrach threw the shard overboard?"

"The shard wasn't mentioned in any account," Agata said. "The stories emerged after his death. When the expedition's survivors returned to Regor, Kansbar Nathrach was taken prisoner and tortured by the Khrynsani. He was released, but was closely watched for the rest of his life, short though it was."

"How did he die?"

"Impaled on his own sword."

I raised a brow.

"An investigation deemed it to be suicide."

"Uh-huh."

"The king at the time, Omari Mal'Salin, ordered the investigation himself."

"A known Khrynsani puppet, a known and insane Khrynsani puppet."

"After the investigation, Omari confiscated Kansbar Nathrach's house and property."

"That sounds familiar, as well." Sathrik had taken all of my property, too.

The pale stone Agata Azul wore around her neck flared as glass shattered in the front and back of the house, immediately followed by the thumps of something hitting the floor. A second later, two more hit the roof.

I knew those sounds. Gas or incendiary canisters.

9

Agata Azul's house was protected by crystals of every kind, but somehow the canisters had broken through.

I jumped to my feet and reached for Agata to shield us both, and was met with a sharp pop as my arm went numb.

"What the—"

The oval stone around her neck glowed fiercely. "I can shield myself. Do the same."

An instant later, twin detonations threw us to the floor, blasting apart the wall separating us from the front hall and showering us with plaster and splintered wood. I shielded as more explosions tore through the house, my shield buckling with each impact. Agata's crackled with the same energy that had permeated the crystals in her sitting room.

Flames and smoke rapidly filled the house. I didn't sense a firemage on the scene or any other kind of magic, just a well-orchestrated and executed operation. If I hadn't been the target, I could almost admire their work.

I swore silently. "Other doors out. Where are they?"

Agata Azul took in the destruction of her home, the rage in her eyes burning hotter than the flames closing in on us. "The two they just bombed," she snapped. "Under the table is a trapdoor to the tunnels."

Most houses in the old, central city had access to the tunnel system that ran through the bedrock Regor had been built on. The assassins probably had covered that, too, but I'd rather fight than fry.

Agata kicked over the table and pushed the rug aside.

I stopped her as she reached for the ring set into the wood. "They'll be waiting."

She smiled in a vicious baring of fangs. "Not alive, they won't."

I didn't know what surprise Agata had waiting below for uninvited guests, but she seemed confident that it'd done its job. That was good enough for me until I saw otherwise.

She opened the trapdoor, and my nose told me that whoever had been waiting below to ambush us would never ambush anyone ever again.

Burnt flesh. Not just burnt. Charred to the bones.

Before I could step around her to go first, Agata nimbly dropped down the hole and scrambled down the ladder.

I followed and landed in a crystal-powered crematorium.

Four assassins had been waiting for us to flee the burning house. They had been the ones incinerated.

Most people thought rocks were harmless. They'd never met the Saghred or Agata Azul's crystal sentries.

I maintained my shield and Agata was doing the same.

Just because four were dead didn't mean there weren't more waiting in either direction down the darkened tunnel. Above us, the house was an inferno. This was our only hope of escape, regardless of who or what was waiting down here. Goblins can see in the dark as well as an elf can see at high noon. We had just come from a brightly lit and now even more brightly burning house. If any remaining assassins had been lurking in the dark down here, their eyes were already perfectly adjusted. It would take the better part of a minute for our eyes to do the same.

"This way." Without looking to see if I was following, Agata Azul ran down the dark tunnel, one hand held out in front of her, keeping a shield in front of us, extending from wall to wall and floor to ceiling. I adjusted my shield to cover our rear.

I closed in behind her, keeping my voice just loud enough to be heard. "Where does this go?"

"Where we go depends on who just ordered me burned out of my home. Any guesses on who followed you?"

"I wasn't followed."

"You must have been. Kesyn knew you were coming, and I know he didn't tell anyone."

"Are you implying that I—"

"I imply nothing. You came to my door asking for my help. Within half an hour, my house is on fire." She hissed out a breath. "Kesyn warned me. Did I listen to him? No."

"I assure you that I took every precaution not to be seen before I passed your front gates."

"Yet assassins burn my home to the ground." She stopped and spun on me, putting us nearly nose to nose. *"My home!"*

"I'm sorry for your loss." I tried to sound sincere because I was. This was the last thing I wanted to happen, and I didn't think now would be the best time to ask if she was still willing to go to Nidaar. I had a feeling she'd answer such a question with her fist. Not knowing what else to say, I went back to my original question. "Where does this lead?"

"There's a fork about two hundred yards ahead. We can either go toward the palace, or to the waterfront."

"I would suggest the palace. There's a way out near my home."

Agata's response was a terse nod. I took that as an agreement, albeit not an enthusiastic one. At this point, I thought it'd be wise for me to take what I could get.

She continued to lead, and I racked my brains for who could have possibly known I was meeting with Agata and how they'd come by that information. The Khrynsani had been disbanded and outlawed, and those who hadn't been captured in the hours following Sarad Nukpana's death and the destruction of the Khrynsani temple had fled or gone into deep hiding. Perhaps some had crawled out from beneath their collective rock, but this didn't feel like a Khrynsani hit. For one, they would have used magic. They had the talent, and they would have used it. To rely on mundane incendiary grenades wasn't how they operated. As to how they got the grenades past Agata's house defenses, a negating spell of sufficient strength would have done the trick.

If enough Khrynsani remained in the city to pose a threat and wanted to come after me, they would have done so themselves. They refused to work through or hire outsiders. That didn't mean it wasn't them. Desperate times called for desperate measures.

If they knew I was inside, and had surrounded Agata's home on the surface and had an ambush waiting beneath, there would be assassins waiting near my home as well. By now they knew we had escaped. Or that we'd avoided their first and second traps. There had to be a third waiting either ahead in the tunnel, or in the streets near my home.

I reached out and touched Agata's shoulder. "Take a left up ahead. We'll surface and approach my house from the back."

She frowned as she considered it, unconvinced.

"If they think they have us on the run, they'll expect us to take the shortest route," I added. "We need to get topside. If it looks suspicious, I have other places we can go."

Agata gave me a trace of a smile. "The Mal'Salin's chief mage and chancellor needs multiple safe houses in his own capital. And people asked me why I never wanted to serve at court."

10

The attack came while we were still in the tunnels less than two blocks from home.

I heard it before I saw it.

A ball of blue flame three times the size of my head sped toward us out of the dark, trailing a blazing tail like a comet.

Agata and I acted in unison. We each spat a well-chosen word, then combined our shields to deflect that flaming death back the way it'd come.

Someone didn't want us going that way, and we certainly couldn't go back.

I chose a third option—get up on the street. Now.

I launched a fireball of my own as cover. "Ladder."

We'd just passed a ladder that led up to an iron grate and the street, so one word was enough.

Agata moved. Fast. So fast that she was halfway up the ladder before I'd even reached it. That was a problem. Street grates were heavy. Without magic, I'd be hard pressed to lift one of the things. Agata was at the top of the ladder, and in my way. I had that kind of magic; she didn't.

Turned out I was impressively wrong. I was wrong, and Agata Azul was impressive.

She balanced her feet in the center of the ladder rung with her arms raised over her head. Her hands were glowing with a silvery sheen as she raised the iron grate enough to displace it from its frame. Then with a heave that belied her size, she shoved it aside.

Damn.

The instant it was clear, she scurried up the ladder and pulled herself out, shooting me a look that asked what was taking me so long.

I shielded and quickly climbed the ladder.

We were one street over from my house. It was lined with trees, tall iron fences, and stone walls. We goblins weren't big on being friendly with our neighbors. We didn't mind our homes being seen, but we didn't want anyone dropping by uninvited. It didn't have anything to do with etiquette and everything to do with paranoia. There was a booming business in the capital for security mages. Depending on the level of protection you wanted or needed, a security mage would ward your gates, doors, and windows. Some of my neighbors even had nets of wards that arched over their houses. I took care of my own security, and I wasn't bragging when I said I put my neighbors' efforts to shame. I wasn't competitive; I simply attracted more trouble than all of them put together.

Needless to say, we wouldn't be knocking on any gates. In Regor, if you had trouble chasing you, you dealt with it yourself.

That was my plan. I just hoped we didn't have more than we could handle.

I spotted a hooded man two houses down. I was sure there were others around us and more on the way.

I pulled Agata into an inverted section of a house wall. "What are you packing?"

"Everything Kesyn taught me."

"Which is…"

In response, she picked up a smooth, apple-sized rock from a flower bed border and threw it at the hooded man. It was a decent throw, but it'd never reach him. The man was two houses—two mansion-sized houses—down the street.

The rock not only reached him, but accelerated before it hit him in the forehead. He grunted and fell face-down on the sidewalk.

Agata turned to me and smiled sweetly.

"How did you—"

She indicated herself. "Gem mage. It covers more than sparkly things. I can hit pretty much anything with a rock. All I have to do is get it started; the rock goes where I tell it."

"Impressiv—"

I heard a whistle of displaced air from behind me and grabbed Agata, taking us both to the ground. A crossbow bolt punched a hole in the exact spot where her head had been an instant before.

Agata saw and blanched. "You're not so bad yourself."

"Not really. Just too much practice. I've gotten shot at a lot."

The bolt had to have come from a tree or roof. Either way, we had entirely too much distance to cover and next to nowhere to hide.

Agata reached out and snagged another stone.

"I'm not trying to be pessimistic," I told her, "but you'll need more than one."

She glanced to where the felled assassin was still sprawled on the sidewalk. The next whistle I heard was the rock she'd hit him with coming back to her upraised hand. She caught it without a wince.

That did it. I grinned. "And you can call them back."

"I can't outrun anything weighted down with rocks. All I need is one per hand. If I'm not ready to catch it, it'll stop and hover."

The next bolt impaled itself in the tree by my head, and the tree burst into flame—an unnatural dark blue flame.

Magic. Black magic.

I swore under my breath. "They're not playing anymore. How strong are those shields of yours?"

The lady didn't seem to have nearly the confidence that she had a few minutes ago. "Blue fire on a bolt might be pushing it."

I reached out and took her hand. "Then we'll use mine," I said as my shields enveloped us both.

"Can I still throw rocks?"

I quickly scanned the street for more shooters. "I wouldn't dream of denying you the fun and me the help. Your rocks can get out through my shields, but they'll have to knock before coming back in."

"Good enough." Agata reached down and grabbed another stone. "Insurance."

I didn't have rocks at my beck and call, but I had a lot of nasty surprises in store for whoever was trying to stop us from getting behind the safety of my home wards. Just because those bolts were tipped with black magic didn't mean a dark mage was pulling the trigger. They could have been prepped ahead of time and held the charge for hours. Whoever wanted me dead knew what they'd have to throw at me to make death stick. I had a sinking suspicion that what I hoped would be a sprint was going to be a fight for every step, but that didn't mean I wasn't going to try running. My goal was to get home alive, not make a statement. Running was perfectly acceptable. I wasn't running away from assassins; I was running toward home and the wards I trusted to vaporize anything that made the mistake of attempting to follow.

"How fast can you run?" I asked Agata.

"Can you shield us both without us holding hands?"

"Not as well as I can with."

"Then I can keep up with you. My legs are just as long as yours."

Yes, they were. I hadn't intended to glance down at her shapely suede-wrapped legs, but my eyes had other ideas.

Cutting loose and meeting fire with fire would be easy. The problem was finding a target before becoming one ourselves.

We managed to cover half a block before all hell broke loose.

Literally.

They were demons.

We were screwed.

They were bipedal, and the resemblance to the mortal

assassins ended there. They appeared to be unarmed. I wasn't fooled. They didn't have weapons because they *were* weapons.

Agata and I instinctively went back to back.

"I don't think rocks are going to work with these," she said.

"You'd just piss them off," I agreed.

Since our backs were touching—even though it was through cloth and leather—I could release her hand and still keep the shields around us both.

I lobbed my best incendiary spell at the closest targets to see what would happen. They were standing close together; I was going after a two-for-one. In a flash of red, the demons were vaporized. I turned my attention to the next one—just as the demons I'd vaporized reappeared.

No, not reappeared. They had moved before my spell had arrived, and had been so preternaturally quick that my eyes hadn't registered it.

That was not good.

11

A dark figure stepped forward. Not just dark in that I couldn't see his face; dark in that I wasn't even sure that he, she, or it had one. The bottom suddenly dropped out of the temperature and I could see the frosty puffs of my breath. The things surrounding us didn't make puffs, frosty or otherwise.

That was bad.

Demons breathed. These didn't. Undead demons? Demon zombies? Regardless of what they were, they had been strong when they had been alive, and it was all too obvious they had retained that power in death. Regardless of how they had been brought back and by whom, they had been chosen because of strength and impermeability. Their skin glowed from within. And they were fast. If I so much as twitched, the demons darted in a blur to cover the opening. Nothing alive or mortal was that quick. I'd found through unpleasant experience that things that weren't alive to begin with were next to impossible to kill.

The demon zombies parted and the hooded and cloaked figure glided through as if it didn't need feet to walk. The demonic minions closed ranks behind their leader.

"Give me the gem mage, Chancellor Nathrach, and I will make your death quick."

Agata's voice rang with indignant anger. *"Give?"*

A decidedly female voice. Our adversary was a woman. A woman with mortal assassins and undead demons at her command. It wasn't Sandrina Ghalfari, but I didn't recognize the voice.

"You have me at a disadvantage in more ways than one, madam," I said. "You know my name; I do not know yours."

"And you do not need to."

"You'll let me die not knowing the name of my killer? There has to be a rule against that somewhere in the Khrynsani handbook."

"I am not Khrynsani."

She didn't sound happy about that or insulted that I even suggested it; she was simply stating a fact. That was more than a little concerning. If there was a club of evil worse than the Khrynsani, I didn't want to run into them in a dark alley, or residential street, especially not when they had their undead minions in tow.

Just because she wasn't Khrynsani didn't mean she wasn't a goblin, but I couldn't see her face or any skin at all.

As we talked, the demons began tightening their circle around us. Normally, I'd obliterate a few of them, make my own exit, and take my chances, but I saw more waiting motionless in the shadows. As soon as we made a run for it, they would be on us. If it had been just me, I would take the chance if all other options failed. Agata Azul was with me. I wouldn't risk her being injured.

"If you will not release her to me, then I will be forced to take her." Again, not a threat, just a promise, a statement of what the mage was about to do.

The street darkened.

It was already night, but that didn't stop the dark from coming at us from all sides, like a black mold sliding over everything in its path. The dark smoothly flowed up the lampposts around us, seeping inside the glass and consuming the flames that flickered there. I wondered if it even covered the stars overhead, but I wasn't about to take my eyes off the dark and the mage who had conjured it for one instant.

I was a goblin, by nature nocturnal. Darkness was comfortable. The darkness creeping toward us was neither natural nor comfortable.

Ominous power whispered from the shadows just beyond my sight. Normally, I could see all the way to the street corner. Not now.

The assassin Agata had hit with a rock began to stir. He pushed himself up with his hands, saw the darkness coming at him, and cried out. That cry rose to a scream as the dark flowed up his arms, and abruptly silenced when it reached and covered his face and body.

The same light- and life-consuming darkness was coming toward us.

There was only one thing left for me to do.

The spell qualified as black magic and it would take all of my strength to employ. If it failed, I'd be all but helpless, unable to stop the mage from taking Agata Azul. Her shields were good, and she had a few defensive tricks up her sleeves, but the mage standing before us wasn't using merely black magic, she was using demonic black magic. Agata would be defenseless. The mage wanted Agata. She wouldn't kill her. Me? I had a feeling I was expendable. If I didn't stop the dark tide before it got too close, I wouldn't get another chance.

I quickly focused, and a dark shimmer formed around my extended hands. My shoulders bowed under the weight of the spell's power. A shadow quickly spread like oil from my hands to coat the cobblestones all around us. My body was racked with chills from the cold as the darkness I created suffocated not only the light, but what little warmth the air held. Emptiness spread from my fingers, radiating from my body. In the sphere of my spell, in the spreading shadows, was a void, an emptiness where magic was not, where life did not exist. Death was the absence of life; what flowed from my hands was the absence of everything.

The demon zombies shifted uneasily, and a few stepped back. None fled.

My shadow magic met the mage's darkness and stopped.

I pushed, testing the barrier.

The mage's darkness held.

Dammit.

I could only hold my shadow barrier in place for a few minutes. I could gain a little more time—if I dropped the protective shield I held in place around us.

The mage stood easily as if she had all the time in the world.

"I had been told you were strong," she said, and her voice didn't sound strained at all. "I didn't believe it. I was wrong." The mage actually sounded happy about that.

I couldn't spare the strength to speak, so I let my shadow magic continue to do the talking for me.

The mage extended her hands and pushed against my shadows with her darkness.

It held.

Yes.

"Very impressive indeed," she murmured. Then she gestured to the demon nearest her, indicating that he come closer. When he was within reach, the mage reached out with one hand and simply touched him on the arm.

The demon disintegrated without even trying to escape.

He had sacrificed himself, his power flowing into her.

And my shadow barrier was kicked back five feet.

I pushed with everything I had to regain the lost ground.

Nothing.

The mage lowered her arms, no longer needing a physical gesture to focus her power. "I can endlessly replenish my strength. Can you say the same?"

I couldn't say anything. Everything I had was holding what little protection we had left.

The mage knew it.

And I suddenly knew fear.

The darkness pushed my shadows back, flowed to the edge of my shields, and stopped mere inches from my boots. Our captor—she could no longer be called anything else—would hardly destroy that which she wanted.

Agata Azul.

"Actually, Primaru Nathrach, you could prove quite valuable to me as well, too valuable to destroy."

She was skimming the surface of my thoughts. I slammed the door. It didn't even earn as much as a wince from her.

Primaru meant archmage of the royal blood. I seldom heard it anymore. It was a title from another time, another life. A time when I had battled and lost—my wife, my position, and nearly my life. A time when all I lived for was revenge. The time of Sarad Nukpana and his Khrynsani.

The mage smiled slowly. "Sarad speaks very highly of you. It was he who warned me of your strength."

Agata gasped from behind me. I would have done the same if I'd had enough air.

Sarad was dead. He had to be. I'd seen the demon lord I'd summoned carry him screaming into the Lower Hells. The demon may have played with him first, but he would have killed him. I'd chosen that particular demon for that reason.

Sarad Nukpana made a deal.

The words appeared in my mind, but I knew them to be true. Knew it down in my bones.

His mother had made a deal with an off-world invader, and her son had likewise bargained for his life with a demon lord.

Sarad Nukpana was alive.

12

"Magus Azul, if you will come with me, no harm need come to you," the mage was saying. "I am fully capable of taking you or having you taken by force, but I would rather have your willing cooperation."

Willing cooperation.

I'd heard those two words earlier this evening in reference to Sarad Nukpana. He'd wanted Agata's help finding the Saghred. The Saghred was gone, or at least beyond anyone's reach.

Until a moment ago, I'd thought the same of Sarad Nukpana.

"I am highly selective of whom I accept as clients," Agata said, her voice and expression cool and composed. We were surrounded by a darkness that could consume us with a touch.

By necessity, she stood with her body pressed against mine. I felt the faintest tremor; then again, that might have been me. "And any acceptance is contingent upon the work in question not conflicting with one I have already accepted."

"You have accepted work with Primaru Nathrach?" the mage asked.

"I have."

"May I inquire as to the nature of that work?"

"You may, but professional ethics prohibit me from answering."

The dark crept closer, touching the tips of my boots and Agata's.

Agata never looked down, but her fingers tightened on the back of my arm.

The mage's voice was quiet and almost gentle. "Are your ethics worth your life?"

"Do you expect me to willingly cooperate with my life under threat?"

"I expect you to be reasonable."

"Reasonable. An interesting word choice from a woman who sacrifices her own people to get what she wants."

Confusion passed over the mage's face. "The undead one that gave his power?"

"The human assassin across the street."

"He was none of mine, nor are any of his companions. They flushed you out into the open, earning my gratitude, so if they come no closer, they may leave here with their lives."

"You're popular this evening," I murmured to Agata.

"So it would seem," the mage said. "I can assure you, Magus Azul, that allying yourself with Tamnais Nathrach will only bring you suffering and result in your death. I, on the other hand, can guarantee your survival."

"I'd like to say I could match that offer," I said, "but she's got me there."

"And she's got us *here*."

I didn't need reminding. The mage's dark magic had absorbed not only light but the remaining heat. A cold beyond anything I had ever felt was seeping up through the cobblestones and through the soles of my boots, permeating my skin and numbing the muscles of my legs. Running was something I very much wanted to do, but even if I hadn't been surrounded by death-bringing dark, I didn't think I could move, let alone run. The mage had to know this, but she remained where she had first shown herself to us, making no move to come closer.

Perhaps she couldn't.

Even if maintaining her dark magic kept her from approaching, that didn't make our situation any less dire. No one was going anywhere until the darkness retreated, or was called off.

A flash lit the street like high noon, and agonized shrieks came from all around us.

When I could see again, the demon zombies surrounding us writhed in the street, clutching what passed for ears, dark blood pouring through their fingers. The zombies were down, but their boss lady wasn't. What she was was pissed. The darkness wasn't gone, but it had weakened. Her attention was on whoever had put down her demons, not on the couple she had trapped.

I had one shot, and I took it.

I lifted my hand, spread my fingers, and with a roar, sent five needles of red fire at the mage, bending them to hit head, torso and legs. She was shielded, but I was determined—and desperate.

Our rescuer launched a furious attack that hit everywhere on her that I didn't.

Green.

His magic was green.

Kesyn.

With a vicious grin, I redoubled my efforts, slashing with my hand as if I were using claws—stabbing, slicing, darting and attacking again from another angle.

The mage wrapped the darkness around her like a protective shroud, and our fire merely impacted on the surface—a surface that was sinking like molten tar into the cobblestones until only a black greasy circle remained.

When she vanished, so did the undead demons.

The air reeked with the overpowering stench of burnt flesh and brimstone.

So much for my neighbors ever speaking to me again.

13

Kesyn Badru was bent over, hands braced on his knees, sucking in air as if he'd run the length of the city.

He scowled at the two of us. "I was right."

"I don't know what you're right about, but congratulate yourself once we're behind my wards." I hooked an arm around my teacher's shoulders and pulled him upright to hurry him along—and to help me stay on my own feet. Just because the mage was gone and her minions along with her didn't mean she couldn't come back, this time with more demon zombies.

Or someone else entirely.

I dragged in a breath. "She said Sarad—"

"I heard," Kesyn snapped. "Send him to Hell and he still—"

I pulled Kesyn and Agata back into the shadows.

I'd seen movement up ahead. Not enough that my eyes could see, but my magic senses were on high alert. Nearly being eaten by black magic sludge would do that to you.

My house was being watched.

By goblins. Eight well-hidden and well-trained goblins.

Human assassins, demon zombies, and now goblin hitmen. At least I assumed they wanted me dead; everyone else tonight had.

I reached out with my mind, the barest brush of magic to determine their intentions.

They were armed, and all were ready to kill. I didn't push hard enough to get a name and possibly alert them; that they had my house surrounded was enough information for me.

Kesyn and Agata remained motionless. I didn't know if Agata could sense them, but Kesyn could; plus, he trusted my survival instincts. During my previous tenure in the goblin court I experienced at least one attempt on my life per day, and that was on a slow day. I was good at staying alive.

I indicated a detour and they followed. Rather than risk another fight when Kesyn was exhausted and I wasn't much better, I opted for an alternate way home.

The last time I'd used the tunnel beneath my house had been when Sathrik Mal'Salin still reigned with Sarad Nukpana by his side, and I had been forced to sneak back into my own home. That time, there had been eight of us. Now there were only three. I knew for a fact that we were alone. I had set the strongest wards and repelling spells possible to guard the approaches to my home from every direction. Since I had returned home from Mermeia and the Isle of Mid, and once again had my family around me, I was determined to keep them safe.

The wards were intact on the hidden wine cellar entrance. No one had tried to breach them tonight.

That was both good and bad, or at least suspicious.

I disabled the wards in one section of tunnel and replaced them once we'd passed through. The door to my wine cellar was well hidden by vines, but I had warded it as well. Paranoia had always kept me healthy, or at least alive to be paranoid again.

Once inside the cellar, I replaced the wards on the door.

When I finished, I turned to find Agata surveying the damage to the room. Kesyn had already seen it.

After I had been forced out of Regor, Sathrik had ordered all of my possessions confiscated for the crown, though I knew where most of them had gone—into Sarad Nukpana and Sandrina Ghalfari's homes and coffers. My wine cellar had once been the envy of the court. Now it was a room empty of wine and full of overturned and broken racks. Or at least it had been. Since I'd returned home, we'd swept the floor and piled the debris in one corner. The racks made excellent firewood. What wine I had now, I kept upstairs. Replacing my wine collection hadn't made my list of priorities since getting Chigaru on the throne.

"You're home early, Your Grace," said a voice from the stairs leading up into the house.

"And I've brought two guests." I stepped aside so Barrett could see them, especially Agata.

My majordomo had aged entirely too much during the

time I had been away. Most people wouldn't have noticed it, but I did. I had caused it. Not myself directly, but my actions had brought the wrath of Sathrik Mal'Salin and Sarad Nukpana down on my family, and I included Barrett as one of them. He'd played a large part in raising me, but as I had done with all who had tried to guide me, I had ignored his guidance, discarded his advice, and nearly destroyed my life, and by association his as well. Barrett and my parents and brother had welcomed me back with open arms. I hadn't deserved it, but I was beyond grateful for it, and was determined never to put any of them through that again.

"I take it your meeting went well only to a point," Barrett noted with his usual reserve. "And judging from your collective smokiness, I assume Magus Azul gracing us with her presence wasn't her choice."

"Unfortunately correct on both counts, Barrett," I said.

Agata sighed. "After Chancellor Nathrach's visit, my home is now a pile of smoldering cinders surrounded by assassins. I was left with little choice."

Barrett graciously inclined his head. "Regardless of the reason for your visit, be welcome in this house, Magus Azul. Since his return, His Grace has developed an annoying tendency of bringing guests in through the sewers. I'm beginning to fear he's lost any trace of the manners that I assure you he was taught."

Kesyn barked a laugh. "*Beginning* to fear?"

Barrett stood aside on the landing. "Hospitality and chivalry demand that we immediately see to Magus Azul's comfort and needs."

As always, Barrett saw to all of our comfort and needs.

Needs were met in the form of a guest room for Agata so she could clean up, and then food for all of us.

Our comfort came when Barrett informed us that the goblins lurking outside were lurking under Imala Kalis's orders. They were guards to protect me, not assassins sent to kill me.

That was an unexpected and pleasant surprise.

Though right now, I thought that Imala, who had just arrived, might be reconsidering their orders.

"They're armed and were lurking outside my house," I said. "What was I supposed to think?"

"If you had accepted my offer of guards the first five times I offered, you would have known about them and we wouldn't be having this pointless conversation." Imala's voice was a silk-covered stiletto. Most goblin women were tall and coldly beautiful. Imala Kalis was petite and—though I'd never say it to her face—adorable. Adorable and deadly, with dimples. She wasn't showing me her dimples now. In fact, I didn't think I'd be seeing them anytime soon. I towered over her by a good foot, but that had never stopped her from getting in my face, figuratively speaking.

"My wards are sufficient," I told her.

"Are they now? And what if this mage had decided to come here rather than capture you and Agata in the street? From what Kesyn told me, she would be more than able to get through your pride and joys."

I didn't say anything. Just because a statement might be true didn't mean I had to acknowledge it.

"You were lucky I happened along when I did," Kesyn

said, enjoying himself far too much at my expense. "I came by here earlier, thinking you'd be back, but Barrett told me you hadn't come home yet. I knew you couldn't still be talking to Aggie. She's got more sense than to fall for your tall, dark, and charming act. So I figured you—or the two of you—had gotten yourselves into trouble."

"We didn't get into trouble," Agata told him. "Trouble set fire to my house."

Kesyn's eyes flicked between the two of us. "Which one were they after?"

"The ones you met wanted Agata," I said. "And seemingly for the same reason I did. I don't know what the pyromaniacs wanted, other than to flush us out of the house."

"You think they were working together?" Imala asked.

My mind flashed back to the assassin being consumed by the black magic-spawned darkness. "I have a feeling they weren't."

Imala pushed back a curl of dark hair that'd escaped from her long battle braid. "I received intelligence that some out-of-town talent would be paying Regor a visit. Considering the level of the talent, I assumed they were here for Chigaru and Mirabai. When I determined that wasn't the case, you were second on my list of people most likely to have a price on their heads."

"Unfortunately, you were right."

"Yes, I was."

"You don't have to sound pleased about it."

"It's so rare to have you acknowledge when I'm right. How else am I supposed to act? When I found out that Agata's house had been firebombed, and knowing that you were going to ask her to go on the expedition—"

"Wait, how did you find out that—"

Imala just looked at me. "I'm the chief of goblin intelligence. It's my job to know everything." She flashed a dimpled grin, but it wasn't friendly. "When I got here, I asked Barrett where you were. I extrapolated the reason for your visit based on your not having asked Cort Magali yet."

Agata was glancing between us, sipping a cup of tea Barrett had prepared and enjoying the show. "Ah, so I *wasn't* your first choice. Cort Magali would have done a fine job."

I shot Kesyn a look. He had described Magali the same way.

"I didn't tell her about Cort," Kesyn said.

"He didn't have to," Agata said. "Cort was anticipating your visit, even though he did not know the reason for it. The thought of going to Aquas would have terrified him—and the thought of going to Aquas with you would have terrified him even more."

"Even he realized you were trouble with feet," Imala muttered.

"That wasn't what I meant, Imala," Agata said. "Well, at least not entirely. Cort Magali is deathly afraid of being out of sight of land. Then there's the seasickness. Cort would have been quite worthless to Chancellor Nathrach."

I realized something. "You ladies are on a first-name basis. Magus Azul said she knew you—"

"Imala is one of my best clients," Agata said. "I've kept the palace in sentry gems for the past year."

That gave me pause. "Impressive work. They're the best I've ever seen."

The gem mage inclined her head. "Thank you. My clients expect the best, and that is precisely what I give them."

"Agata is not only one of the best gem mages in the Seven Kingdoms," Imala said, "but better still, she is eminently sensible for one so young." Imala quirked a smile. "Which would be a highly desirable—and needed—addition to your expedition."

I ignored her last comment. "Did the Khrynsani ever seek you out to provide crystals for the temple?" I asked Agata.

"With annoying regularity."

"I take it they were on the list of clients you refused to work for."

"They were—and they are."

"Have you been contacted since the fall of the temple?"

"Oh yes."

"If I may be so bold as to ask, who wanted to hire you?"

"Unknown. They communicated with me via courier. Their letters were lengthy. My replies were quite short. There aren't all that many ways to say no."

"Why did they want to hire you?"

"They hadn't reached the point of revealing exactly what they wanted. But considering that I'm a gem mage, I suspect it's the same reason that it always has been—to locate and use a stone of power for them."

"Speaking of stones of power," I said, "this mage knows Sarad Nukpana."

Imala went still. "You mean knew."

"I wish I did. She said to me, and I quote: 'Sarad *speaks* very highly of you. It was he who warned me of your strength.'"

"Do you think she may have been merely toying with you?"

"I hope she was, but…"

"I saw that bull demon carry him away."

"Carried away doesn't equal killed," I reminded her. "That type of demon may play with its food, but it always kills and eats it, and not necessarily in that order."

Imala's silvery skin was a little paler than usual. "You're saying that—"

"I'm saying it's possible. When I eliminate an enemy, I prefer to see the dead body myself to ensure that it's absolutely positively deceased. I didn't have that option with Sarad."

Imala looked to Kesyn. "You believe it, too."

"I heard her," my teacher said. He tossed his now empty pipe in one of the trays I kept here for him. "I don't think she was lying. She planned on killing Tam and taking Aggie. She wanted to see the look on Tam's face before she finished him off. I didn't detect anything but the truth coming from her."

"So he could be here," Imala said.

"I don't think so," I told her. "If he warned her of my strength, that tells me he's not here. He may not still be in the Lower Hells, but if he were here, he wouldn't be able to resist showing himself."

Imala gave me a level look. "Unless he's on the Isle of Mid, showing himself to Raine."

14

I contacted the Isle of Mid and asked to speak with Mychael Eiliesor, not Raine.

Definitely not Raine.

I hadn't told her about the Heart of Nidaar when I had spoken to her earlier, so I sure as hell wasn't going to tell her that in all likelihood Sarad Nukpana wasn't only alive, he might be on the same plane of existence as the rest of us, possibly on the same island as her.

Considering what had happened this evening, I no longer had an option of keeping the search for the Heart of Nidaar a secret. Tonight had revealed that we had even more bad guys than we'd anticipated, and their interest in Agata Azul said that they knew not only about the expedition, but what we'd be searching for once we got there.

I needed every good guy I could get on my side, and good guys didn't get any better than Mychael Eiliesor. As the paladin and commander of the Conclave Guardians, Mychael needed to know not only about the Heart of Nidaar, but also that the Khrynsani and their invader allies were after it, and that I would be going after them. He also needed to know about Sarad Nukpana.

I told him everything.

If keeping him in the dark had annoyed him—and I knew it had—Mychael showed no sign. I was a goblin, and goblins kept secrets. We hoarded secrets like a miser hoarded gold. I hadn't done it without a good reason, and Mychael realized that.

Though there was one thing I didn't share.

The book written by Rudra Muralin and found behind Sarad Nukpana's Khrynsani temple bookshelf. I wasn't really keeping anything from Mychael, because other than where it was found and who wrote it, that was all I knew. Once I had a chance to examine it, and if it contained anything Mychael needed to know, then I'd tell him.

Though if Mychael valued his life—and the continued affections of his new bride—he'd tell her about Sarad Nukpana. I gave him permission to put the blame for not telling her about the Heart of Nidaar squarely on my shoulders. I was far enough away not to worry about the wrath of Raine. Hopefully, by the time I saw her in person again, she would have calmed down. If not, I'd take my medicine.

The Guardians had had the dubious honor of being the keepers and protectors of the Saghred for the past thousand years, give or take a couple of decades. Until about five months ago, they'd done a fine job. That was when the Saghred had selected Raine Benares to be its next keeper, and Sarad Nukpana caught up with her and the stone, sending the possible fate of the Seven Kingdoms into a death spiral.

We'd thought that was all over. Two weeks ago, right before her marriage to Mychael, Raine discovered that not only had she retained much of the power the Saghred had given her, but whatever had given the Saghred its power was now inside of her. That night in the Khrynsani temple, Raine had released the souls the Saghred had held prisoner, then she had shattered the empty orb.

Or what she and the rest of us had assumed was empty.

Even after the souls were gone, her hand had still been fused to the Saghred, meaning that it had merely appeared to be empty. It still had power. The orb had been the Saghred's body, and when Raine had been about to shatter it, the entity that was the Saghred saved itself in the only way it knew how.

The last soul the Saghred took through Raine Benares had been its own.

Only a few people knew the truth.

The entity, the power which we had called the Saghred, now resided inside of Raine. All that new power was going to take a lot of getting used to—and a lot of support from her family and friends.

That was the real reason I hadn't wanted to tell Raine anything I didn't have to. She had enough to deal with.

But with the possibility of Sarad Nukpana's return, that choice was no longer mine.

Raine needed to know, and Mychael would do the best job of telling her.

When I came back in my study, Imala and Agata had their heads together like a pair of conspirators. Believe me, I've seen enough of it to know it on sight. That I was the topic of their discussion was a given, but it was confirmed when they sat back with an identical glint in their eyes, which also confirmed that they didn't care if I knew it.

"We were discussing what Agata should call you," Imala said. "I assured her that being stuck on a ship with you for over a month will give her ample time and opportunity for name-calling. It's merely a matter of how long it will take for her to reach the breaking point. By the time the ships reach Aquas, she'll have all sorts of names she wants to call you."

I ignored everything that said or implied, and turned to Kesyn. "Speaking of epithets you want to call someone, that spell you blasted those demons with could've killed us."

"Not a chance. Well, not unless your shields were crap."

"They weren't."

"Of course, they weren't. I taught them to you. All I needed to do was put a little light on the subject." My teacher tossed a marble-sized ball of intense light in his hand. "Blow a little sun where the sun doesn't shine."

"With that?"

"How many times do I have to tell you, size isn't important." He grinned wickedly. "It's all in what you do with it."

I nodded in understanding. "You multiplied it."

"By a lot." Kesyn leaned toward Agata and lowered his voice. "He tends to overthink things."

"I've noticed. Though in his defense, I didn't see a way

out of our situation either." Agata addressed me. "As little as I like it—and for the record, I don't believe I have ever liked anything less—we need each other, as unfortunate as that arrangement is. You don't stand much of a chance of finding the Heart of Nidaar without my help, and I'm not going to be able to rid myself of Khrynsani attentions until that stone is either destroyed or permanently out of their reach. And to do that, I need you. I'm afraid we're rather stuck with each other for the duration."

I blinked. "Afraid we're *stuck*?"

"I take it you'd rather I worded it differently?"

Imala cleared her throat. "Tam's used to better reactions from women to the idea of spending time with him."

"I'm going to a continent few have journeyed to and survived," Agata continued, "to find a stone with the power a cult of psychopaths need to open passages to our world to conquer and enslave us all." She glanced back at me. "Can you honestly say that you're looking forward to this?"

"I have things that I would rather do," I admitted. "As if the Khrynsani and the possibility of Sarad Nukpana being back isn't enough, now we have someone who, if she isn't actually from the Lower Hells, has enough black magic to have her own mini army of demon zombies at her beck and call."

"We were lucky she put all of her effort into containing the two of you," Kesyn said. "She wasn't expecting an attack from the rear and didn't prepare for it. She won't make that mistake again. Arrogance will bite you in the ass every time. Remember that, boy."

"I've never forgotten."

My teacher snorted. "If I didn't know you'd forgotten,

I wouldn't need to remind you. You didn't expect someone bigger and badder than yourself. Granted, there aren't many of them around, but one of them found you, and you've got a lady and a hunk of rock that she wants. She'll be back, and she'll have an even uglier surprise for you next time."

Agata spoke. "We should be safe—at least from her—while traveling to Aquas. We'll be on a ship."

Imala and I traded an "oh crap, not again" glance.

"What?" Agata asked.

I told her. "The pirates who killed the elven ambassador and took his staff prisoner were killed by Khrynsani death curses."

No one said anything.

Agata looked confused. "And this affects our shipboard safety how?"

"A Khrynsani dark mage tore open a Gate on board the pirates' ship while it was in the middle of the Sea of Stillness."

Agata dark eyes widened. "A Gate can be opened on a ship under sail?"

"Unfortunately, yes. Any higher-level Khrynsani mage can open a Gate if they know a ship's exact location. All it would take would be to plant a tracking crystal on the ship when the Khrynsani agent initially hired them."

"What's to keep them from doing the same thing to our ship?"

"Extreme paranoia on our part. Anything being loaded on our ship is being checked before going onboard. And before we set sail, Kesyn and I will be going over the ship again."

Kesyn grunted. "Work in the palace long enough and you raise paranoia to an art form. If you don't, you're dead, and it won't be pretty."

The mention of palace intrigue made me remember what

Agata had said about my ancestor, Kansbar Nathrach, and the piece of the Heart of Nidaar that he'd supposedly brought back to Regor with him. The Khrynsani had searched his home nine hundred years ago—the same home we were in now. It had passed down through the Nathrach family through the centuries. The Khrynsani had searched my home two years ago, and I had a feeling they hadn't found what they were looking for. Were they still looking for the shard? And if so, was it still here? Or did it no longer exist—if it ever had?

I asked Agata to tell Kesyn, Imala, and Barrett about Kansbar Nathrach and the shard.

Afterward, I didn't feel nearly as bad about never having heard of him, as Barrett had no recollection of any ancestor by that name. Barrett's family had served my family for nearly two hundred years, and Barrett knew as much about the Nathrach family history as my parents. If they knew it, Barrett would know it. He didn't.

I frowned. "So Sarad and Sandrina destroyed our home out of spite."

Then Barrett and Kesyn shared a suspicious-looking glance.

"That's not entirely accurate, Your Grace," Barrett admitted.

My eyes narrowed. "What is it?"

"This may have had nothing to do with what happened here," Kesyn said, "but it could explain a few things."

Barrett spoke. "After Sathrik Mal'Salin had you declared a traitor to the crown, he confiscated this house and its contents. We managed to get some of the family valuables out; the rest we had to leave in the armory vault in your rooms and hope they weren't discovered. There simply wasn't time."

I clenched my teeth as the anger built. My family had been

forced to flee our home, grabbing what they could, risking capture, torture, and death by remaining one moment longer than necessary. I had repaid Sarad Nukpana—or so I thought. Like rats, they had taken over my home; and like rats, they had escaped.

Not for long.

I took a calming breath. "I wouldn't have wanted you to risk yourselves. Possessions can be replaced; my family cannot. And yes, Barrett, you are family."

"Thank you, Your Grace. What you saw when you returned from the Isle of Mid was much improved over what we found when we first got back into the house."

"It was worse?"

That earned a whistle from Kesyn. "Oh yeah. It was all too obvious that the house had been searched from top to bottom. And when they didn't find what they were looking for, they went deeper—as in holes in the walls, floors, and ceilings."

Since my return, my mother had told me that even after Kesyn was no longer my teacher, he had still maintained close ties with my family. I had abandoned them. Kesyn Badru had not. "Why didn't anyone tell me?"

Barrett stepped up next to Kesyn. "With all due respect, Your Grace, what purpose would it have served?"

"Most of it was done by Sandrina," Kesyn added. "Sarad was busy with his plans for kingdom domination, so Sandrina appointed herself demolisher in chief. She oversaw the search for whatever they were looking for. And they were looking for something. Hard. However, I got the impression that they didn't find it."

"Do you think it was the shard?" Agata asked him.

"It was right after Sarad had been outmaneuvered once again to get his hands on the Saghred. Though if they were looking for something like that, it wouldn't have been something they could have achieved with a simple burglary. They would have needed you out of your house permanently."

I knew exactly what he was saying, and so did Barrett and Imala. I didn't know if Agata Azul knew the story of my wife's death, but I wasn't up to telling her.

Sandrina Ghalfari had poisoned my wife Calida. It had been the first step in forcing me out of court and then out of the kingdom. I knew they'd wanted me out to open the way for Sathrik to kill the queen, his mother. What if it was more? What if it they simply needed me out of my house so they could ransack it for a piece of the Heart of Nidaar? Did my Calida die in agony for a sliver of rock?

I didn't say any of this out loud.

I met Imala's eyes. She knew.

"According to the histories, Kansbar Nathrach brought it back from Aquas with him," Agata said. She then told them about one or more of the objects brought from Aquas being cursed and causing storms and sickness on the return voyage, and that all objects were thrown overboard. That may or may not have included the shard. "However, once Kansbar returned to Regor, the Khrynsani captured and tortured him, and when he wasn't forthcoming about the shard's location, they watched him for the rest of his life, short though that was."

"No shard?" Imala asked.

"Not that anyone knew of."

"The house has always been in the Nathrach family," Barrett said.

"And if Sarad and Sandrina still didn't find it here," I noted, "chances are good that he hid it somewhere else, or it doesn't exist anymore."

"You forget a third option," Agata pointed out. "A rather obvious one."

"Which is?"

"Barrett, you said that you removed some of the family valuables before the house was confiscated and ransacked. I assume that included the family jewels?"

"It did."

"I take it they're back here now?"

"They are."

"Would you mind if I examined them? Being a gem mage, if a shard from a stone of power is among them, I should be able to find it."

15

Who knew my family had so much jewelry?

There were chests of it. They weren't particularly large chests, but they were still chests. I couldn't help but think that Phaelan Benares would love to come across these on a ship he'd just taken.

Thanks to my family's quick thinking, the Nathrach family jewels were all here rather than adorning Sandrina Ghalfari. My armory had survived as well, with the addition of the jewels and art my parents couldn't take with them. It had remained undiscovered during Sarad's sacking of my family home.

We goblins are most proficient at hiding things, be it money, jewels, alliances, dead enemies, or inconvenient emotions.

Imala had returned to the palace, leaving my house security in the capable hands of her team. Kesyn had adjourned to the nearest couch to take a nap.

I looked closely at the jewels spread on the table before me. They were easily worth a fortune.

My mother would possibly know if one of the pieces had a stone that flickered like flame. But my parents and Nath weren't due back from the country until tomorrow. Since Talon was going on the expedition with me, he would be coming back home via mirror in a few hours.

Mother had only had me and Nath; there'd been no daughter to pass the family jewels down to. Considering how Nath and I had turned out, that absence had to be a source of disappointment to her.

We were both doing everything we could to make our pasts up to her—especially me. She had given many pieces to Calida, but none of them had resembled "flames captured in stone."

I didn't remember my mother wearing such a stone, but then she had worn only a few pieces, not being much for socializing with the previous regime.

Barrett leaned over the table next to me. "Sir, may I recommend you examine one drawer at a time. The entire collection would be a bit overwhelming all at once."

"There's more?"

"Of course. The Nathrach ladies have always enjoyed their finery."

He didn't mention Calida, but I knew he was thinking about her, as was I. She had been exceedingly fond of jewels, but only the smaller, more understated pieces, which meant

I'd never seen some of these pieces in my life. Not all of the jewelry had been maintained. If it was attractive and wearable, it had been kept clean and polished. Garish pieces had been left to gather dust and tarnish. I shifted through a tray of bejeweled castoffs.

"Some of these are quite…large," Agata noted.

"And gaudy," I muttered.

"I didn't say that."

"You didn't have to."

"They do speak for themselves, don't they?" Agata said.

"Loudly," I agreed. "I assure you we have good taste, at least the last two generations do." I picked up a pendant with a ruby the size of a goose egg. "How would a woman even wear something like this?"

"The better question is why she would want to," Agata said. "Though it could be nice on a sword pommel."

We went through drawer after drawer in the jewelry cabinet, and chest after chest. Nothing looked like it was or ever had been flickering with flames. There was much that was bright, shiny, or sparkling, but there wasn't a flickerer in the lot.

I was getting discouraged.

I glanced at Agata. "Well?"

"Well, what?"

"Do you sense anything from any of this?"

"Other than the Nathrachs at several times in their history had questionable taste in jewelry—no, I don't sense anything. That being said, many gems of power are activated only by touch."

I took in all the pieces of jewelry, most set with more than one stone, the chests stacked with multiple trays, and sighed. "We're going to need coffee."

Agata nodded in agreement. "A lot of coffee."

Legend said the Heart of Nidaar was like flame contained inside of a stone. It didn't say what color the stone was, which wouldn't really have mattered in regards to what we were doing. I wasn't about to leave any stone unturned—no pun intended. Or untouched.

"Do you think the shard would react to me?" I asked, shuffling through a small pile of loose stones, turning them this way and that, looking for the telltale flame.

Agata was doing much the same. "Unless you have gem talent, it shouldn't. Do you have any gem mages in your family?"

"Before tonight, I would have said no. But tonight I discovered one of my ancestors had not only sailed to Aquas and returned, but also may have brought home a shard of the very rock we'll be searching for."

Agata turned an opal the size of a hen's egg in her fingers, gazing at the light playing in its sparkling depths. "Ignorance can be enlightening."

"I'm not enlightened yet."

"Patience is a virtue."

"Can you speak in anything except idioms?"

She gave me a hint of a smile with her eyes still on the opal. "Only time will tell."

I nodded toward the pile of jewelry and gems she had already examined. "Is there magic in any of those?"

"These? No." She pointed tentatively at a small chest that she'd set off to the side. "Those in there, on the other hand, you might want to consider getting rid of. Cursed. Nothing big, but in the right environment and wrong hands, they could be nasty. At the very least, securely lock them away from the, shall we say, inexperienced and dangerously talented."

Like Talon.

"Duly noted and done."

I looked in the last chest.

Empty.

What we had spread on the table before us was all there was, and none of it flickered like trapped flame.

"That's it," I said.

"What's it? You found it?"

"No. I meant that's all the jewelry." I waved my hand to encompass what was on the table. "This is all there is. No shard."

Agata didn't hear me, at least not entirely, but her head tilted to the side as if she were listening.

"What is it?" I whispered.

Agata held up one hand for quiet. After a few seconds, a slow smile spread across her face. She got up from her chair, walked around behind me, and peered down into the last chest.

"It's not empty," she murmured. "Not quite." She reached inside.

I stood and looked in.

The chest's interior was black, and so was the thin box Agata pried out of a hidden compartment in the bottom. She carefully placed it on the table and opened it.

There it was. Actually, there they were.

Cushioned on a bed of black velvet were a pendant and a ring—both set with stones in which firelight flickered from the depths. Both appeared to be made of gold and featured a dragon as part of the design.

Agata lifted the pendant out of the box by its golden chain.

The pendant was a small disk about an inch in diameter, and a quarter of an inch thick. A serpentine golden dragon completely encircled the gem, gripping it with its four claws. The disk appeared to be a slice from the Heart of Nidaar.

I picked up the ring.

The band consisted of the golden body of a dragon. Its four claws gripped the gem and its mouth was open as if breathing fire into it. Though the detail was exquisite, the gold—if it was gold—was dull, and the rough-cut stone cloudy. I reached for the polishing cloth and went to work on both.

I was soon rewarded with a warm glow, as if a tiny flame had been trapped inside, caught in mid-flicker.

I carefully picked it up and held it to the light.

Flames danced inside.

I didn't even need to move the ring. The flames inside the gem flickered with tongues of fire as I held it perfectly still. Agata had said that there hadn't been any description of the size of the gem, or even if there was more than one, but these had to be it. Two pieces of the Heart of Nidaar.

Neither looked like shards to me, but Shard of Nidaar sounded more impressive than Lump or Slice of Nidaar.

"I've never seen the Heart of Nidaar," Agata was saying, "but these certainly fit the description." She examined the pendant in her hand, holding it by the chain, being careful not to touch the stone, at least not yet.

"How do we determine if it is?" I asked.

"The legend said that one of the things the Heart of Nidaar powered was the city's lights."

Our eyes went to the lamp on the table. A small, but strong, lightglobe provided the light, which was then reflected around the room by small clear crystals. I waved my hand over the lamp, extinguishing it. I tossed an expectant glance at Agata.

"There's no time like the present," I told her.

"Especially with us leaving the day after tomorrow."

I felt Agata's shields go up on everywhere except where her fingers now held the disk's golden frame. If the rock decided to get nasty, she could quickly cut contact. I knew that hadn't worked with the Saghred, but that had been the entire stone. This was a very small piece of the Heart of Nidaar, or might be. Agata Azul was one of the best gem mages there was. She knew the risks and how to protect herself against them.

I felt Agata gathering and focusing her power. Not much, just enough to activate whatever power lay dormant in the disk. The flames flared where Agata's fingertip touched the surface. She showed no sign that it hurt. She touched the pendant's stone to the lightglobe.

Nothing.

That was disappointing.

The lightglobe suddenly blazed with light.

And exploded.

As did every other lightglobe in the house, judging from the loud pops and crashes.

We shared a wide-eyed look.

"That answers that question," I said.

Kesyn's testy voice came from behind us. "I can't leave you two alone for one minute."

16

Now that it wasn't in contact with the lightglobe—because it'd blown it up—the stone disk reverted to its neutral state.

I still held the ring, though now by its gold band. I wasn't in any hurry to touch the stone again. Or I should probably say the Shard of Nidaar, because there wasn't any doubt in my mind that was what we had.

Kesyn indicated the ring. "Does the legend say how dangerous it is to have that little nugget of boom anywhere near you?"

Agata shook her head. "The legend only refers to the Heart of Nidaar. Other than its existence, and that it was taken out of Aquas by Kansbar Nathrach, there's no mention of the shard's capabilities."

I probed it with my magic.

No reaction.

"You were holding your breath," Kesyn noted.

"Can you blame me?"

"Not really. I would advise not putting it on."

"I have no desire or urge to do so."

"Prudent." Kesyn glanced at Agata. "I told you there's hope that he has more sense than he used to." He indicated the ring. "May I?"

I gave it to him. "By all means."

Kesyn examined it, turning it this way and that, frowning the entire time. Even from where I was sitting I could see the flames inside.

"Well?" I asked. "What do you think?"

"Doesn't seem to be evil."

"That was the impression I got. In your reading on the shard, were there any ill effects from wearing it?" I asked Agata.

"No."

"How did this ancestor of yours die?" Kesyn asked.

"He committed suicide, so it was said."

"That's not good."

"No, it's not. When he returned from Aquas, he was interrogated by the Khrynsani. Soon after his release, he was found impaled on his own sword, and the king confiscated his house and tore it apart."

"Sounds familiar."

"Yes, it does."

Kesyn handed the ring back to me. "So the disk and ring themselves are probably safe. It's just having the things that can get you killed."

"I think we can safely say both of these have the same capabilities as the motherstone, only on a smaller scale," Agata told us. "Once we've landed, we should be able to use it as a compass of sorts to find Nidaar, and once in the city, to find the motherstone. I'll use the time on the voyage to attune myself to it. If I'm to use it to locate Nidaar, I'll need to wear one of them. I'm thinking the pendant, since the ring was clearly made for a man."

"You might want to try it on here and now," Kesyn told her. "We'll have your back if it gets nasty."

I tensed. I knew how the beacon to the Saghred had attached itself to Raine. She hadn't been able to take it off until she'd found the Saghred itself—that is, if she wanted to continue breathing.

Agata slipped the chain around her neck.

Nothing happened.

"Do you feel different?" I asked.

"No. But for it to be effective, I'll need to wear it next to my skin."

"I had a feeling that would be the case."

Agata pulled back the neck of her tunic. "Here goes hopefully nothing." She dropped the disk down the front of her tunic.

Immediately, the disk's glow became visible through the cloth of her tunic.

"Aggie," Kesyn said in warning.

Agata remained completely calm. "No need for concern. I'm merely injecting a small portion of my gem magic into the disk." She smiled down at the disk, almost fondly, and put her hand over the outside of her tunic, as if she was holding a kitten. “Bonding with it, if you will. It has no intention of harming me. I assure you, it’s quite benign. This has happened before. It just means the disk has accepted me. That’s good. We should work well together.”

“Can you take it off?” I asked. “Or should I say, will it let you take it off?”

Raine hadn’t been able to.

Agata lifted the chain from around her neck along with the disk. The glow dimmed, but not completely. I got the impression it was pouting. Then she put it back on, and the glow brightened.

“You’re still breathing,” I noted with no small measure of relief.

“Very well, in fact.” She put the chain back over her head, dropping the disk back down the front of her tunic.

I glanced down at the ring. “It appears to be my size, or close to it. And since I’m not a gem mage, there should be no danger of the thing biting me. I don’t see any reason not to try it on, do you?” I asked Kesyn.

“I don’t like it, but can’t think of any.”

I quickly slipped the ring on my finger.

Nothing.

That was good, disappointing, and not unexpected.

Good that nothing happened, though disappointing, but expected since I wasn’t a gem mage and there was no Heart of Nidaar nearby for it to track.

I took the ring off.

Still nothing.

That was definitely good.

I put it back on with the intention of keeping it there.

Kesyn stared intently at me for a few moments. "Feeling evil?"

"No." I would have added "of course not," but I was rather surprised—and relieved—myself.

"Well, if you start feeling evil and find you can't remove it…" Kesyn grinned and pulled a small knife out of his robes. "I'll just cut your finger off."

I looked at him.

"What? Which would you rather lose, boy? Your mind or a finger?"

"Neither, if I can help it."

"You're going to start wearing it?" Kesyn asked.

"Let's just say I don't want it going anywhere without me."

After replacing the shattered lightglobes and helping Barrett clean up the mess we'd made, we put everything back in the chests and secured them in the armory vault in my bedroom. Seeing my armor and weapons reminded me of a few more things I needed to pack.

It also made me very much aware that with her house burned to the ground, Agata Azul had nothing to pack—as in nothing to wear.

"This isn't a proper thing for a man to ask a woman—especially when they've just met—but necessity is more important than propriety right now."

"The only clothes I have are the clothes on my back." She paused. "That's what you were getting at, wasn't it?"

"Um, yes, it was. I don't know whether the assassins at your home were after you or me—or after you because of me; that is, me asking you to go to Aquas to find the Heart of Nidaar. Regardless, I feel I am indirectly to blame for your loss, and wish to remedy the situation. When we return, I want to have your house rebuilt and refurnished. At the moment, we have the rather pressing need to get you some clothes."

"We leave the day after tomorrow. Even the best palace clothiers can't work that kind of miracle."

"They can't, but if you will make a list, and make it complete, Barrett will take care of everything in our absence and have your wardrobe replaced by the time we return."

Agata smiled, enjoying my discomfort. "And in the meantime…?"

"All of us will be traveling light—"

The smile didn't fade. If anything, it broadened. "Naked is a bit too light in my opinion."

"What I'm getting to is that you and my mother appear to be the same size. I know she wouldn't mind if you took enough from her wardrobe to see you through the expedition. And being a mortekal, she has ample clothing suitable for where we are going and what we'll be doing once we get there." I started down the hall. "I'll show you to her room and then to your guest room for the night."

Talon arrived an hour later via mirror from my parents' estate. We'd both had a long day. I told him he needed to do two things now: a bath and then to bed. The only bath he would get between here and Aquas would be if it rained on him, and on board the *Wraith,* his bed would be a hammock.

I fully intended to go straight to sleep myself, but stayed

up longer than I should have. When I finally made my way to my bed, I overheard voices from Talon's room.

"It's my last night in Regor. I should be out with my friends. Instead I'm—"

"In the finest mansion in the city," Barrett said, "bathing in a tub that once graced the imperial baths of Kaleh, sipping hundred-year-old brandy from two-hundred-year-old crystal, and eating what took hours to prepare all because your father said you might enjoy it before being subjected to ship's fare. But why would you want this when you could be surrounded by young men and women who are not your friends vomiting ale into a disease-infested gutter?"

Silence.

I had to bite my bottom lip to keep from laughing.

"I'm an ungrateful brat from the Lower Hells, aren't I?" Talon said.

"Yes, young sir, you are. But we have hopes for you. Will you be needing anything else, sir?"

"Aside from good manners, I'd like a few more of those cherry tarts. They're very good. In fact, I've never tasted better."

"Yes, sir. I'll relay your compliments to the cook."

I continued to my own room, grinning broadly. I was really going to miss Barrett.

17

"Good morning, Your Grace."

Barrett's voice filtered down to me through the remains of a nightmare that included the mage who had attacked us last night, but instead of a demonic zombie horde were multiple copies of Sarad Nukpana and Rudra Muralin. Agata wasn't the only one trapped with me. Talon was there as well.

Needless to say, I was relieved to wake up.

Waking up to what I knew was a bright, sunny morning provided neither relief nor comfort.

Nocturnal instincts died hard.

"There is something good about it?" I muttered.

"I was being optimistic, sir," Barrett said. "The morning sky *is* unreasonably bright."

"You didn't open the curtains."

"No, sir. That would have been cruel to both of us."

I sat up and pushed my hair out of my face. "When I leave, the house can get back to normal."

"While we look forward to once more sleeping during the day, I speak for the entire household staff in saying that we would rather you didn't have to go."

"That makes all of us, Barrett." I swung my legs over the side of the bed and stood, Barrett holding my robe open for me. "Someone has to do the dirty work."

"For which you are eminently qualified, sir," he said with a straight face.

I gave him a quick grin.

"It was the highest of compliments, Your Grace."

"I'm sure it was. Is Talon awake?"

Barrett gave me a look. "Is that a question you truly need to ask?"

I chuckled. "Of course not. What time did he get to sleep?"

"When the cook arrived two hours ago, she found him foraging for a snack. Lord Talon has adapted very well to nocturnal life."

I scowled. "He's about to get a rude awakening. Literally. I told him he needed to be up this morning."

"Director Kalis and Magus Azul are downstairs to accompany you to investigate the remains of her home. After that, Captain Phaelan Benares arrives from the Isle of Mid." Barrett gave me a meaningful look. "You will be gone. We will be here. For the sake and sanity of the staff, Your Grace, let Lord Talon sleep."

Agata Azul's house had been completely consumed, reduced to ash, even the stone foundation.

Whoever had fired the canisters didn't need to be a firemage; the canisters' contents had been crafted by one—a master of his or her art.

Or a master of demons.

The stench of freshly harvested brimstone was strong in the air. There were two types of fresh brimstone: molten and quick-dried into powder. The canisters would have been packed with the latter.

Fresh meant the firemage had recently made a trip to the Lower Hells. Very recently.

I gazed around at the destruction. This had been meticulously planned, which lessened my guilt somewhat about being the cause, but did nothing to affect how I planned to deal with it.

Find the perpetrator and take it out of his—or her—hide.

I wasn't eager to go up against the dark mage again, but since she hadn't gotten what she wanted last night, I was certain that we would be encountering her again.

Encountering her again made me think of another who might be crossing my path again soon.

Sarad Nukpana.

Fresh brimstone of this type came from the Lower Hells, which was where Sarad Nukpana was now—or at least where he was supposed to be. Before the destruction of the Saghred, Sarad had been after Agata Azul. He had needed her then just as much as I did now and for the same reason. The dark mage had said that Sarad had warned her about my strength. Did this mean that she was working for Sarad? Was she his representative on this plane since he was presently unable to leave Hell? Or was he already here and had more important things to do—for now?

Agata had walked over to where a burnt limb from a nearby tree had fallen onto her small "lawn" of crystals, now blackened. The crystals had disintegrated into a cloud of ash. Agata bent and touched one of the larger crystals surrounding her property. It collapsed, the flakes carried away on the breeze.

The heat produced by those incendiary grenades had burned so hot that indestructible sentry crystals had been reduced to ash.

"This was no firemage work," Imala said. "A pyromancer did this. I know Tam has some high-powered enemies, but do you?" she asked Agata.

"A Khrynsani agent has been insisting on a meeting," Agata said. "I refused him. I believe this is the result."

"This wasn't a spur-of-the-moment attack," Imala said. "This was planned."

"She's right," I said. "When did the Khrynsani agent first contact you?"

"Last week."

"Those canisters would have taken longer than that to make. A pyromancer can't just throw some ingredients together and stockpile them. They also had to have been highly customized to destroy your sentry crystals. If this was Khrynsani work, it was planned before they contacted you."

"They knew you'd refuse," Imala said. "This was their backup plan. When Tam showed up on your doorstep, they knew he needed you for the same purpose and they couldn't wait any longer." She paused. "You know as well as I do how the Khrynsani react to refusal."

Agata nodded. "Retaliation and revenge."

"And they don't stop until they get it. They're known for making an example of those who defy them."

"I know. They do not tolerate refusal." Agata's dark eyes narrowed dangerously. "I have news for them, I do not tolerate being threatened."

18

Phaelan Benares arrived around noon.

Most of the mirrors capable of trans-kingdom travel were located in the palace. Most, but not all. I knew the absolute last place Phaelan would want to step out of a mirror into was the Mal'Salin palace. To tell you the truth, it wouldn't have been my favorite destination, either. You couldn't listen at a mirror as you would a door before stepping through. You had no way to know what was waiting on the other side. I'd never found that to be a particularly comfortable sensation.

Within two days of returning to Regor, I'd had a mirror installed in my study that could easily handle trans-kingdom travel, and had a talented—and trustworthy—mirror mage on retainer.

When Phaelan stepped through my mirror, it appeared to

be under his own power, without Raine's boot applied to his backside. His weapons weren't drawn, but he had hands on the grips of two swords.

The elf pirate instantly went into a fighting stance.

"Welcome, Phaelan." I raised my hands, having already stationed myself out of blade reach. I'd also made sure that other than my mirror mage, we were alone.

I'd had the lights turned up. When a highly nervous, mirror-hating, heavily armed elf came for a visit, you wanted him to know there was no danger lurking in the shadows. It was a little bright for my or any other goblin's comfort, but assuring Raine's cousin that he hadn't walked into a nest of goblin assassins was more important.

"Your house?" Phaelan glanced around, his shoulders relaxing.

"My home. Be welcome and at ease. You are safe here. You have my word."

The elf lowered his hands from his weapons. Reluctantly, but he did it. I'd already alerted the staff against making any sudden movements, and to announce their presence when entering a room. Goblins made no sound when they walked, especially indoors. I didn't want any accidents.

I stepped forward to shake his hand.

Funny thing, hand shaking was supposed to indicate that you were unarmed. Phaelan was bristling, and I was only less so, and only because I was in my own home.

"Are Gwyn and Gavyn here yet?" Phaelan asked.

"Not yet. They're due on the tide within the next two hours. I've had a mirror installed in a warehouse next to the harbor for your crew to come through."

Phaelan nodded in approval. "I couldn't just have them sit around and wait for the *Fortune* to be repaired. It's a waste of good talent. They'll come through when they have a ship to board, and Gwyn and Gavyn to keep an eye on them. I thought that would be best."

"I think everyone would agree with that."

Nearly a hundred heavily armed elven pirates suddenly appearing on the capital's waterfront could cause a situation none of us wanted to deal with. I'd kept the expedition as secret as I could. Ships were provisioned in Regor's harbor all the time. The *Wraith* was a sleek merchant ship that ran between Dragalon and Nabé in Nebia, and the Caesolian port cities in between. At least that was her cover. The merchant who owned the *Wraith* on paper was an actual merchant. If she was stopped, her hold would contain what was listed on the trading manifest. She was fast, sturdy, and exactly what we needed.

Imala, as the director of goblin intelligence, was the true owner.

The *Wraith,* and the goblin intelligence agents who sailed her, was one of the best sources of information on the west coast. Imala wouldn't be going on the expedition, but she would know what happened every minute that we were gone. The *Wraith* was discreetly gunned to protect herself from pirates. How ironic that on this voyage, pirates would be protecting her. Barrett appeared at the door. "Your Grace, may I offer your guest refreshments?"

I turned to Phaelan. "Do you require refreshing?"

The elf pirate glanced around uneasily, hands twitching to be on his weapons. "Yeah. Salt air and water as soon as possible."

Regor's warehouses, shipping offices, inns, and taverns resembled any other large city waterfront in the Seven Kingdoms. What was different was that it was nearly deserted.

Goblins were nocturnal, as were our businesses' operating hours, and it was late morning on a bright, sunny day. I had been readjusting myself to a daytime existence for the expedition. It had taken only a few days for me to revert to being awake at night and sleeping during the day. Most of those going with us were elves or humans—day dwellers. The crew of the *Wraith* was used to being among humans, so it wouldn't be much of an adjustment. I'd had enhanced protective spectacles made for the expedition's goblins, though they were more like goggles. Our sensitive eyes weren't made for a desert environment. Fortunately, we would be doing most of our travel at night when goblin eyes were at their best. For that, I'd had goggles made with clear lenses as well to protect our eyes from blowing sand.

After what had happened last night with Agata, I had four guards accompanying us, courtesy of Imala. Also with us was my best friend, Count Jash Masloc. He was a battle mage and tactician without peer, and would be going on the expedition as my second-in-command. The guards were staying out of sight, and I'd glamoured myself and Phaelan in dress and appearance as minor merchants. Jash did the same for himself.

To keep Phaelan's mind off of goblin assassins jumping out at him—even though to anyone who might see him, he was a goblin—I filled him in on what Raine might not have told him, since I'd only informed Mychael of it yesterday.

The Heart of Nidaar.

Phaelan stopped in the middle of the street. “The rock has a name?”

“Yes.”

“You give them a name; they give you trouble. Especially with a name like the Heart of Nidaar. That’s worse than a name. Now the damned thing thinks it’s important.”

“It’s just a rock,” Jash said.

Phaelan jerked a thumb at him. “This guy didn’t get up close and cozy with the Saghred, did he?”

“Fortunately for him, no,” I said.

The elf turned to Jash. “Anything with a name like that is never ‘just a rock.’ The only stones I want anywhere near me are the two I was born with—or the shiny kind I can sell. This Heart of Nidaar doesn’t eat souls, does it?”

“No,” I told him.

“Good.”

“The legend says it powered a city in ancient times,” I said.

“And now the Khrynsani want it to power Gates.”

“That’s what we believe, yes.” I felt the weight of the ring on my finger. I sighed. Best to tell him now and get it over with. I tilted my hand slightly so he could see the ring. “This is a piece of the Heart of Nidaar.”

Phaelan jumped back a solid five feet. “You’re *wearing* it?”

“We believe the Khrynsani tore apart my house looking for it. So yes, to keep it safe, I’m wearing it.”

“I would ask if you’re crazy, but you just answered my question.”

“Feeling evil?” Jash asked me.

"Of course not."

"Can you take it off?" Phaelan asked.

In response, I did.

"And you're still breathing," he noted with something that vaguely resembled approval. "That's a start."

"Not all jewelry is evil," I told them both. "If this is part of the Heart of Nidaar, then this may well help take us there. Our expedition gem mage is wearing a pendant with a slice of the Heart."

Phaelan went pale. "Another pendant? We're doomed."

Phaelan, Jash, and I had been waiting inside the warehouse's office. From the way he'd been pacing for the past hour, I wouldn't have been surprised if Phaelan had jumped into the harbor and swam to meet his father's ships.

He wanted that badly to be off of a goblin dock and back on a Benares deck.

I didn't blame him. I was equally impatient to get underway. Sandrina Ghalfari had a head start. We'd been playing catch-up. Until we got to Aquas, we would have no way of knowing whether we were too late.

Sandrina and the invaders might already have the Heart of Nidaar. If they did, our mission would go from being merely dangerous to probably suicidal.

We would do what we had to do.

The *Wraith* was docked near the warehouse. Supplies for the expedition were being loaded in the unmarked, well-used crates used by merchant ships all up and down the coast. Even our clothing was chosen to blend in with the crew of the

Wraith. Their typical garb included shirts and trousers with sturdy boots. For going ashore or dealing with bad weather, a long or medium-length coat was added. The canvas and leather was treated to be waterproof and warded to be blade resistant. The length also allowed concealment for the bladed weapons that no goblin would ever go into a strange port without. Stylish, yet eminently practical.

The reason I'd given at court for my upcoming absence was another trip to the Isle of Mid. With the possibility of an impending invasion, no one would think anything of me going to Mid and holing up in the Guardians' citadel for secret tactical meetings. Gearing up for a war took place behind closed doors, and that's where those in the palace thought I was going to be. The only people who knew otherwise were A'Zahra, Imala, Barrett, Chigaru, and Mirabai. Those going on the expedition, other than the ship's crew, would be using a glamoured disguise.

I hoped there hadn't been a leak, but this was Regor, the goblin capital, filled with goblin courtiers who loved secrets more than life itself. What had happened last night with Agata Azul had been an attempt to kidnap her and force her to work for the unidentified mage. At no time did the mage who had used demon zombies to attack us mention anything about what she wanted Agata to do for her, nor did she mention the Heart of Nidaar.

"Gwyn and Gavyn are twins," Phaelan was telling Jash. "There's not much magic in our family—at least not on Dad's side—but what Gwyn and Gavyn have goes beyond the bond that some twins have." The elf grinned. "They're telepathic, which can come in handy when working the high seas together."

"And of unquestioned value when crossing that sea," Jash noted.

"I haven't seen either one of them in almost three years, but Dad said they're the best choice for what you need—after me, of course."

"Of course."

"And naturally," I said, "the legend of a city filled with treasure had nothing to do with your desire to accompany us."

Phaelan clutched his hand over his heart. "You wound me. Raine trusts me to protect the fleet on the way to Aquas."

"And to look to your own interests once we arrive."

Phaelan raised a finger. "Extracurricular activities that coincide with your own."

"We may have to destroy the Heart of Nidaar, which may destroy the city—and its treasure—as well."

"And I may try to talk you out of that, at least until I can fill a few bags."

I gave him a grin filled with challenge. "You're welcome to try."

19

Phaelan and his spyglass were scanning the northwest horizon for signs of his siblings. The scowl told me he couldn't see them. Yet.

We were waiting inside the warehouse where the mirror had been installed.

I knew how Phaelan felt about mirrors. However, other things were waiting inside the warehouse to be loaded onto the ships that the elven pirate captain would like even less.

A dozen firedrakes and four sentry dragons.

Each ship would be carrying three firedrakes and one sentry dragon—including Phaelan's new ship, the *Kraken*.

Jash jerked his head toward Phaelan. "Did you tell him?"

"Not yet."

"Oh good, I get to be here to watch."

"You don't have to sound so happy about it."

"Sure I do. Besides, it's fun."

I walked over to where Phaelan stood gazing out the window. He inhaled and his nose twitched. He smelled something here in the warehouse and his nose didn't like it. The rest of Phaelan would soon share that opinion.

The east coast of Aquas was four weeks' sail from Regor. A sentry dragon's range was three days. They were essentially overgrown hunting hawks—that is, if a hunting hawk was the size of a warhorse. Unfortunately, they often behaved like warhorses, too. The vast majority of sentry dragons in service were females. They were larger and stronger, and while they weren't any more intelligent than the males, they had infinitely better focus. The males were easily distracted. Not a good quality for an animal in military service. When it came to firedrakes, the males and females were equal in intelligence and focus. We would be bringing both with us. As to telling Phaelan that we'd be bringing some ladies on board—and not the species he preferred—once again, I knew it was best to simply get it over with.

"Phaelan."

He turned and I gestured him over.

The closer he got, the worse the smell, and the elf's face screwed up.

"What the hell is that stench?"

"Passengers."

Phaelan stopped and his eyebrows went up.

I went to the other side of the warehouse and partially slid back the section of wall that separated us from the smaller of Phaelan's new passengers. One shock at a time. The elf's eyes went wide, and while he didn't reach for a blade, it was obvious that he wanted to.

It was equally obvious that Jash wanted to laugh at Phaelan's reaction. I shot him a warning look.

There were a dozen cages on tables, each containing a hawk-sized firedrake. They were a range of colors, but when in flight they took on the color of the sky, and when on the ground they were either a shade of brown or green, or both. They were rather like chameleons in that respect, except these chameleons could put hunting hawks to shame with their speed and maneuverability—and they breathed fire.

It would be that last trait that Phaelan would have the most difficulty getting past, though the smell would run a close second. When a creature breathed fire, it usually smelled like brimstone, or rotten eggs to those not familiar with dragons. On the closed quarters of a ship, it wouldn't be pleasant, but neither would being ambushed by the Khrynsani or their allies. With a twenty-mile range and an uncanny homing instinct, firedrakes would prove invaluable where we were going.

"These are firedrakes," I told Phaelan. "We'll be using them as scouts and lookouts. They'll be fitted with harnesses equipped with spy gems to get a real-time look at anything we need to see that we either can't or don't want to get close to ourselves. I've used firedrakes before, and they're invaluable as scouts. As an added bonus, they're more than qualified to protect themselves, their fire being every bit as hot as that of a sentry dragon. Plus, they're faster and even more nimble than any hunting hawk."

"You're not thinking about putting any of those firebreathers on my ship, are you?"

"I'll need each ship to transport three firedrakes, plus one sentry dragon and its pilot. The pilot will care for the firedrakes as well as the sentry dragon."

Phaelan blanched. "Sentry dragon? I am *not* carrying one of those crazy things on my ship."

I sighed and slid the section of wall back the rest of the way. Four sentry dragons stood in absolute silence in their stalls, their yellow eyes locked on Phaelan. Sentries were highly intelligent. They knew when they weren't liked. I looked from Phaelan's glare to the ladies' eyes glittering like raptors from the shadows, offended and insulted raptors.

"Do Gwyn and Gavyn know about this?" Phaelan asked, backing up a step as smoke started curling up from the sentry dragons' armored nostrils.

"They do. They didn't see it as a problem."

"They knew I would, and they didn't tell me."

"Maybe they wanted to see the look on your face," Jash piped up.

I shot him another look. I thought about telling Phaelan that at least Jash wouldn't be on his ship, but decided to keep that to myself.

"You've carried horses on board before, haven't you?" I asked.

"Yes, but—"

"They're the size of horses," Jash said cheerfully. "Just think of them as horses with wings."

"That *breathe fire*."

"An added bonus. Plus, they'll hunt for themselves—and us—while at sea, so we don't need to carry food for them. Which would be problematic anyway, considering that they like their food alive and kicking. They're very sporting creatures."

"Jash," I said in warning.

My friend spread his hands. "Simply pointing out the benefits of traveling with sentry dragons. No fishing necessary on our part. Heck, they can even cook what they catch if you don't mind having the outside extra crispy."

The elf pirate stood his ground. "There is no way that—"

I quickly interceded. "Phaelan, I take it Raine showed you the recording of the battle dragon on the other side of that portal on Timurus."

"Yes." He didn't know where I was going, but he'd already decided not to like it. "It was one of the biggest things I've ever seen."

"Sentry dragons are the largest *we* have on our world. If the invader has already brought even one of those beasts with them—"

"We're toast," Jash finished.

Phaelan and I both glared at him.

"I'll wait over here with the dragons," he said. "The ladies have a better sense of humor."

"We need all the advantage we can get," I told Phaelan. "Four sentry dragons isn't what I would call an advantage, but these are the best and most highly trained that we have. Our best pilots will be going with us. If there's a battle dragon waiting for us, we probably *are* toast, but I'm going to give us every chance I can at survival. I know you don't have a problem with survival."

"Never have, never will." Phaelan glanced uneasily over at the sentry dragons. "The pilots will be staying with those things?"

“Those ‘things’ are highly intelligent, and instinctively know when they’re not liked; but yes, the pilots do stay with their mounts.”

Phaelan shot a sidelong glance at the closest sentry dragon, who I could swear was smiling at the elf pirate in anticipation. Of what, I could only guess. I made a mental note that that one wouldn’t be on the *Kraken* with Phaelan.

The elf sighed. “If we have to…”

“We do. If I didn’t think it was necessary, I wouldn’t bring them.”

“So, are any of these things housebroken?”

20

The harbormaster had been told of the arrival of the three Benares ships—a harbormaster who also reported to Imala.

The *Raven, Sea Wolf,* and *Kraken* wouldn't be flying Benares family flags, at least not until we cleared the Rheskilian coast. Phaelan had assured me that his brothers and sisters were experts in passing undetected in nearly any harbor in the Seven Kingdoms. He may not have liked magic, but the rest of his family had no such reservations. Glamours could be used even under sail, and the Benares family had mages on board every ship for communication, wind manipulation, and disguise. Admittedly, those disguises were most often used to get within striking distance of ships with cargos they wanted to take, but they also served the purpose of not attracting cannon fire from a nervous harbor artillery battery.

However, a Benares ship had never dropped anchor in the harbor of the goblin capital when said capital had recently undergone the overthrow of not one but two kings—if you counted Sarad Nukpana's brief reign of a few hours (I didn't)—and the establishment of a new monarch, a monarchy that was now preparing for the possibility of war against not only the Khrynsani, but an off-world army as well.

Three unfamiliar ships entering the harbor wouldn't simply arouse curiosity. The harbormaster would report them as Caesolian vessels, which in all likelihood they were—before they'd been pressed into Benares service. But to preserve the peace and avoid any unfortunate incidents, the three ships would anchor in the harbor and not approach the docks. That should prevent any violence that we had neither the time nor inclination to deal with.

The harbormaster, with two of his pilots, would be rowed out to the lead vessel to review the paperwork for the small fleet. Thus cleared, the ships would remain for the evening and leave on the pre-dawn tide. The *Wraith* would follow soon after.

I was on the harbormaster's vessel along with Jash and Phaelan. Jash and I were glamoured as two of his pilots. Phaelan would be glamoured so as not to be noticed at all. Under usual circumstances, Phaelan would remain to take command of the *Kraken,* and Jash and I would return with the harbormaster. Our situation wasn't normal. Phaelan's crew who would be manning the *Kraken* were still in Mid, though they'd be coming through the mirror set up in the warehouse within the hour. To avoid any unnecessary tensions, Phaelan would return to shore to be there when his men arrived.

"Once we're on board," Phaelan was saying as we were rowed out to the three ships, "there will be a veil between each ship and the harbor. Kind of like a haze. We'll still be visible from shore, but no one spying on us will be able to see any details, like faces."

"We can drop the glamours," Jash said. "Good. The damned thing makes me itch."

I just looked at him. "Itch?"

Jash shrugged. "Magic can itch."

"Mine doesn't."

Phaelan's eyes glittered. "Maybe you're doing it wrong," he told Jash.

I groaned inwardly. And the payback for the firedrakes and sentry dragons began.

We would be meeting Phaelan's siblings on the *Raven,* Gwyn Benares's ship. Gavyn had come over from the *Sea Wolf,* and both were waiting for us on deck when we boarded.

Phaelan's boots had barely touched the deck when a beautiful and statuesque brunette lifted him off his feet in a crushing hug which he enthusiastically returned. No sooner had she set him down than a handsome dark-haired elf of equal height to his sister but larger muscles hoisted Phaelan in his arms for more of the same.

After his not-so-little brother put him down, it took Phaelan a few seconds to regain enough air to speak. "Gwyn, Gavyn, this is King Chigaru's chancellor, Duke Tamnais Nathrach; and this is Tam's second-in-command on this trip, Count Jash Masloc. Tam, Jash, this is my sister Gwyn and brother Gavyn, captains of the *Raven* and *Sea Wolf.*"

Hands were shaken, and pleasantries exchanged.

"Let's adjourn to my cabin," Gwyn said. "We can speak in private there."

While Jash and Imala's harbormaster agent remained on deck to receive the doctored documents confirming the three formerly Caesolian ships were perfectly harmless merchant vessels, I went below with the three Benares captains.

There were no signs that Gwyn Benares's cabin was her personal quarters. There was a rectangular table with six chairs around it and a map spread on top, a few more chairs positioned out of the way against the walls, and a small sideboard built into the hull of the ship itself.

"Would anyone care for a drink?" she asked.

"None for me, thank you," I said.

"You have to ask?" Phaelan muttered. "This morning I was on the Isle of Mid. Now I'm on the other side of the Seven Kingdoms." He tossed a meaningful glance at his siblings. "Then I was told I'll have four, flying, fire-breathing lizards on my ship—three little ones and a monster that doesn't like me. For some reason, I was not told any of this by my own brother and sister."

Gavyn grinned and poured himself, his sister, and Phaelan a whisky. "Because we knew it was a good idea and didn't think it worth mentioning."

"I can see where it's not a bad idea, but I sure as hell think it was worth mentioning."

As we sat around the table, Gavyn and Gwyn sipped their whiskey like connoisseurs. Phaelan tossed his back in a single shot.

Gavyn and Gwyn may have been the youngest of the Benares children, but they reminded me of the eldest—Mago

Benares. Mago was a banker and a cunning financial genius. In the face of recent events, Mago had resigned from his position and had taken one with elven intelligence. Mago was tall, outwardly reserved, commendably cautious, and possessed a keen and quick mind. Perhaps a Benares escort would be better and more beneficial than I'd originally thought.

We confirmed the route we were taking, the stop we would make in the Lastani Islands approximately halfway between here and Aquas, and the harbor where we would moor once we arrived at the continent. It was farther north than where the previous Khrynsani expeditions had landed, but the one we'd chosen would be safer for us and the ships, and just as close to where the city of Nidaar was rumored to be.

Each ship would carry enough provisions for ten weeks—sufficient to get us there, two weeks to search, and the four weeks it will take to return. Fish would be plentiful in the north Kenyon this time of year, but we'd take only what fish we could at the speed we had to travel. As Jash had said, the sentry dragons were proficient hunters. They could feed themselves and the crews. Being at sea and having to be quartered in the ships' holds, the dragons would prefer to be out hunting. We would eat very well on the voyage over and back, and each ship was carrying sufficient salt to dry provisions for once we arrived in Aquas. Previous expeditions had reported little to no game on the coast, at least not in size and quantity to sustain the crews of four ships.

"What about the west coast of Aquas?" Phaelan asked. "Is the access any closer?"

"According to the Mylorans, there's an unclimbable escarpment running the length of the coast," I told him. "Or at least as far as they cared to explore. As far as they're concerned, no enemy came from Aquas and no fun prey showed itself, so they left it alone."

"The winds will be with us," Gwyn said. "Four weeks at the most to reach Aquas's east coast. Probably less."

"Then there's reported to be four days of desert between the coast and the mountains where Nidaar is," I told them.

Gavyn leaned back in his chair and away from the map. "Once we get there, what are your plans? Raine and Mychael weren't able to give us much by way of details."

"Wait'll you hear this," Phaelan muttered.

I told them about the Heart of Nidaar, what it was capable of, and what Sandrina in all likelihood would use it for should she secure it before we could.

To their credit, Gavyn and Gwyn Benares accepted the information without reaction, at least not outwardly.

"And you have the means to find this city of Nidaar and the stone?" Gwyn asked.

"I do. We'll have one of the best gem mages in the Seven Kingdoms with us, and we have two shards from the Heart of Nidaar itself. Magus Azul will use them to guide my team to the city. The plan is to render the Heart inoperable or, if necessary, destroy it."

"You have no plans to bring it back?" Gwyn asked, sounding more than a little surprised—and relieved.

"We've learned from our experience with the Saghred," Tam said. "Just because the Heart of Nidaar is said to be self-sufficient—"

"Not a soul-eater," Phaelan clarified.

"—doesn't mean we can risk it falling into the wrong hands,"

I finished. "We don't know anything about its capabilities, other than it was said to have powered the entire city of Nidaar. If it could do that, it can do more. Guarding and hiding the Saghred cost far too many lives through the centuries. We're not doing that again."

"And the city is abandoned?" Gavyn asked.

"Unknown. We assume so, since there were no reports of civilization from the most recent expeditions. However, the last recorded expedition was over three hundred years ago."

"Sandrina Ghalfari has the same knowledge about Nidaar as you do?"

"Yes. I've read every book and document the Khrynsani had concerning Aquas and Nidaar. Yesterday, I came into possession of a book discovered in a secret compartment behind one of the library's shelves." I grinned slightly. "Before it was hidden, the temple's librarians had been most helpful by cataloguing the book and marking it as pertaining to Nidaar. It's magically encrypted, and I haven't had the opportunity to break the encryption to study it. I'll rectify that as soon as we're at sea."

"Is there any chance of this book going boom?" Phaelan asked.

"I'm familiar with the type of encryptions used," I assured him. "Of course, I will take every precaution with shields. Safety will not be an issue."

I didn't mention the author's name or whose personal shelf it'd been found behind. Phaelan wouldn't react well to hearing them, and to tell the truth, I didn't want to say them. Words had power. Names of mages even more so, rather like summoning an evil genie from a bottle. Just because Rudra

Muralin was dead and Sarad Nukpana was still (hopefully) a prisoner in the Lower Hells, didn't mean either one couldn't cause trouble. Sarad Nukpana had eaten Rudra's soul, and Sarad was apparently very much alive. If Sarad was alive, Rudra's soul was still inside Sarad, along with the souls of six of history's most evil mages.

No, I wouldn't be casually tossing any of those names around.

I didn't see the need to share any of this with the Benares siblings. There was nothing they could do about it, and they would sleep better not knowing.

I would be losing enough sleep for all of us.

breathing dragons. I didn't know which one had scared them more: the mode of travel, the destination, or the welcoming committee. I was suddenly feeling exposed. Yes, I could handle the pirates who had already come through, but I'd have to use some nasty magic to do it, which would make an already bad situation critical.

The elves knew who I was and what I could do. They were heavily armed and so was I, but Jash and I would be woefully outnumbered. We could even or better those odds with magic, and they knew it.

This was Phaelan's move to make.

Phaelan's eyes were on mine, and mine were on his.

We had a standoff.

Our mirror mage broke the tense silence. "Sir, I'm trying to contact the Guardian mage on the other end to find out what happened."

I nodded once, my eyes still on Phaelan's.

"Allan?" Phaelan said, not moving.

"Aye, Captain?"

"Contact that Guardian telepath, what's his name..."

"Ben."

"Contact him and find out what the hell is going on."

"Aye, sir."

The elf, who I assumed was Phaelan's ship telepath, braced his feet, closed his eyes, and bowed his head. Seconds and then minutes passed, and the only sound was the shifting of the sentry dragons in their stalls.

Allan guffawed and raised his head. "Captain, Bart Vane was skittish about stepping through a mirror. Some of the boys got their hands on him, but he broke away, tripped, and..."

"Let me guess," Phaelan said, "he broke the mirror."

"Aye, Captain."

Colorful cursing arose from Phaelan's men, though it was aimed at Bart Vane and not at me. I started to breathe normally. Phaelan trusted me only to a point. I didn't know what that point was, but I suspected we'd all come entirely too close to finding out.

Our mirror mage cleared his throat. "How many more men do you have to come through, Captain Benares?"

Phaelan took a glance back at his crew. "This is only half."

The mirror mage winced and glanced at me. "Sir, it'll take the Guardians' mages at *least* twelve hours to set up another mirror to transport that many men."

Phaelan and I locked eyes again.

"We don't have that kind of time," Phaelan said before I could.

I shook my head. "No, we don't."

An explosion shook the building.

Screams and shouts erupted from outside, dragon roars from inside.

A second explosion rocked the floor beneath our feet, toppling the mirror, shattering it to bits.

I ran for the door, Phaelan at my heels.

A black cloud from the explosion roiled into the air, and fire engulfed the dock where the *Wraith* had been.

The *Wraith* was gone. Only bits and pieces of wood and flaming debris remained.

Very often survival depends upon immediate action. To delay, even for an instant, could mean death.

I knew this, and still I stood in that open doorway and

stared for a good three seconds. Someone could have picked me off, but the people who didn't want an expedition going to Aquas had just administered their killing blow, and were probably standing in the crowd that was gathering, to admire their work.

I didn't ask myself how anyone could have discovered that the *Wraith* wasn't being provisioned for a trip down the west coast, how this voyage was any different from any other. A secret could be kept, but when your enemies were masters of black magic, plans could be discovered, secrets uncovered, and your cover literally blown.

"Stay here," I told Phaelan, quickly shielding myself.

"Like hell." He turned and shouted to his men. "Stay put and hold this building." He paused a beat and added, as if he couldn't believe he was actually saying this, "And protect the flying lizards."

22

The remnants of black magic swirled with the oily smoke high into the morning sky.

My skin prickled and the hairs on the back of my arms and neck stood up as if I had been too close to a lightning strike. The sky was clear with no clouds.

I'd seen and personally experienced enough Khrynsani black magic attacks to know it when I saw it. This was Khrynsani work. I had no doubt.

How they had done it was something else entirely. The *Wraith* had been guarded day and night. No one and nothing had been allowed on board unless they and it had been thoroughly examined first.

This entire end of the waterfront was chaos.

I ran toward where the *Wraith* had been. I shielded myself

and extended it to include Phaelan. I didn't use a glamour. I needed these people to obey me without question. To do that, they needed to know who I was.

The buildings closest to the *Wraith* had been flattened by the concussion from the blast, and others were pocked with smoking, blackened holes where the debris had hit as if shot from a cannon. They were mostly wood. If one of those buildings caught fire, the entire waterfront could go up. If that happened, the city could be next. Perhaps that was what the arsonists had planned. Their primary target was the *Wraith;* Regor going up in flames would be a welcome bonus.

It was the middle of the day, so the waterfront was mostly deserted. The curious onlookers might have been awakened from their beds, but we quickly put them to work operating manual pumps to get water from the harbor, using hoses to spray down any structure that may have caught fire, or have been hit by debris. Phaelan had been seen by my side, and only a few had tossed a questioning glance at me before they started taking orders from him as well. I imagine Phaelan had had plenty of experience putting out fires caused by flying ship debris.

None of the crew who had been on the *Wraith* at the time of the blast needed a healer.

There had been no survivors.

"Vaporized." Imala was shaking with rage. "Instantly vaporized. Every man and woman on board. They were my people, my agents."

She had arrived on the scene within minutes. I wasn't the only one not getting much sleep.

She was covered in soot from head to toe. She looked as if

she had personally searched the wreckage for each and every one of her missing agents. They were dead, blown up with the *Wraith,* but that hadn't stopped Imala from searching.

Slightly less than half of the crew had been sleeping onboard, including the captain. It'd been a last-minute decision. We didn't know how long we'd be gone, so the captain had ordered those with families to spend their last night in Regor with them.

For those on the ship, it had been their last night alive.

"They destroyed the *Wraith* to keep you from going to Aquas," Imala was saying. "I hope they enjoyed waking up this morning to set those charges, because I will do everything in my power and the power of my office to ensure they never live to see another sunrise."

I wanted to put my arm around her shoulders and pull her close, but I couldn't. Imala was here as the director of goblin intelligence and the secret service. In the aftermath of terrorist violence, she couldn't be seen as anything other than completely in command and control.

Anyone who had been in the immediate vicinity of the *Wraith* had been injured by flying debris from the blast. A few were in serious condition, none critical. It was nothing short of a miracle that there hadn't been more deaths.

"This wasn't a bomb," I told Imala. "It couldn't have been."

"The crew checks anything brought on board, and anyone, but you know as well as I that devices can slip through."

"I know that. That wasn't what I meant. The *Wraith* was targeted—from outside." As I worked through this in my mind, it sounded more and more likely. Telemetric conjuring wasn't necessarily black magic, but when it was used to strike and destroy a ship and everyone on her it wasn't only black magic, it was murder.

Phaelan appeared at my side. "What are you talking about?"

"Telemetric conjuring. In magic, it's performing a spell in one location to affect a result in another."

"So whoever did this wasn't here when it happened."

"I seriously doubt it. They would need a quiet place where they could focus, but that doesn't mean they didn't have anyone here to ensure it worked as it was supposed to."

"The harbormaster closed off the harbor immediately after the blast," Imala said. "They're questioning everyone and getting names before releasing them."

I didn't need to say that some would get through, and more than likely those would include any Khrynsani mages or observers. Imala knew that well enough.

"I don't like it either," she said, "but it's the best we can do. If this was telemetric conjuring, how was it done?"

"They would have needed a piece cut from a larger part of the *Wraith*. For example, a beam, mast, or yard. Though it would have been more reliable if it came from a part near or below the waterline. The spell would evoke a reconnection between the piece in the mage's possession and the part of the ship it was taken from. The mage would then destroy the piece they had, triggering the same in the ship."

Phaelan was incredulous. "That's possible?"

"I've heard of it being done. I've never witnessed it myself—until today."

It would take an incredible amount of power and focus.

Just like the amount of power Agata and I had experienced last night from that mage. And while her ultimate plan could encompass more than Agata, I didn't think she was responsible for what had happened here. Telemetric conjuring on this scale would have taken days of preparation. She had the power, but I didn't believe she had the motivation. This was Khrynsani work. The who, how, and why could wait. What couldn't wait was finding another ship.

"A Khrynsani dark mage could have done it?" Imala was asking.

I nodded. "There were about half a dozen who were strong enough."

"I take it not all of those six have been accounted for."

"Only three."

"Dammit."

"Agreed."

There were still Khrynsani, their agents, and their sympathizers in the city and throughout Rheskilia. Just when we thought we'd found them all, someone would turn over a rock, and more would scurry out.

I wasn't surprised that there might be both Khrynsani and their sympathizers still in the capital. What surprised me was the boldness of the attack. They knew what the penalty was should they be discovered and captured: interrogation to ferret out any accomplices, and then death. With the black magic talents of many of our prisoners, allowing them to live meant a constant threat hanging over the new king and queen, and the government we were building. Failure was not an option for us; therefore, mercy wasn't an option for them.

They knew they would be killed if they were caught, but

with the Khrynsani temple taken and its leadership either dead or on the run for the first time in their history, they had no other choice. Kill or be killed. They had lost everything except their lives, and without power, those lives were worthless to them. They had nothing left to lose, and everything to regain.

As I had said on more than one occasion when Sathrik and Sarad were still in power—it's not treason if you win.

Destroying the *Wraith* didn't necessarily take a Khrynsani mage, just Khrynsani gold.

"What's to stop them from doing the same thing to your new king and queen?" Phaelan asked.

I nodded toward Imala. "Her."

"So she's supposed to check all their furniture, so the thrones don't explode under them?"

"Done at least three times a day," Imala said, her sharp eyes continuing to scan the crowd.

"The same can be done with hair, nails, or blood," I told him. "Precautions are being taken against that as well. When I leave, I'll take this trouble with me, or at least the target that's on my back. My parents and Nath will be back later today, Imala. Ask for their help. They'll be more than glad to do anything they can."

She almost smiled. "Between the three of them, they ran the entire goblin Resistance. They can do quite a bit. We'll find those responsible and they will pay."

Unfortunately, I wouldn't be here to do the finding, but I had no doubt that Imala would locate those responsible and extract the appropriate retribution—after she extracted the name of who had hired them and supplied them with a piece of the *Wraith*. By "name" I didn't mean Sandrina Ghalfari.

Her involvement was a given. I wanted any Khrynsani who had eluded our local purge, as well as any Khrynsani-sympathizing civilians.

"You'd better come back," Imala said.

I smiled. "You'll miss me?"

"You're leaving me here to hold back chaos by myself. What do you think?"

23

I didn't have a ship, or provisions, or a full crew. Sandrina was far enough ahead of us. We couldn't afford any delay.

We were in the warehouse, regrouping, and taking stock of our situation, which didn't take that long considering we were an expedition without transportation. The *Wraith* and her crew were to have been more than my transportation and guards on the way to Aquas. They were to have played the critical role of mission backup, security, and support for me and my team in Nidaar. In addition to being seasoned sailors, they were some of the best agents that goblin intelligence had. Being chosen for duty aboard the *Wraith* was considered to be a great honor.

Now half of those men and women were dead.

Phaelan was as soot-covered as the rest of us. He took a seat. "How many men are you taking with you?"

"An incursion team of myself and five others. Jash is one of the five. There will also be Agata Azul, a gem mage."

"So seven."

"Yes."

"Thanks to two broken mirrors, I have only half a crew. Thanks to the Khrynsani, you have only half a crew, and no ship or provisions. The *Kraken* is waiting out there with no crew and fully provisioned."

"You're proposing an alliance?"

"I don't see as we have much choice. Not going is not an option, right?"

"Right."

My smile had grown with each reply. Raine had said that when it came down to it, Phaelan would be all business, and that he had hauled her out of trouble more than once. Trusting him had never been an issue. I realized something and chuckled.

"What?" Phaelan asked.

I told him what I'd said to Raine about my misgivings concerning him. To his credit, Phaelan sat sprawled in his chair, not in the least bit offended. In fact, he seemed to find it amusing.

"If I had a kugarat for every time someone underestimated me, I'd be even richer than I am now."

"I didn't exactly *under*estimate you," I said.

"I didn't even enter into your estimation at all. No offense taken. I'm a pirate, a very good pirate. What most people don't realize is that you have to be very proficient at many things to be a successful pirate. How to avoid being trapped on land after your ship has been blown to smithereens is one of them."

"This has happened to you before?"

Phaelan narrowed his eyes in thought. "Four...no, five times." He grinned and spread his hands. "I'm here and whole, meaning I escaped every time." The grin vanished. "I made sure my best men came through that mirror first, just in case something went wrong. The Guardians' mirror is broken and now so is the one here. I don't even want to think about how much bad luck we had dumped on us when that happened. The crew I've got is what I have, but they're not enough to sail the *Kraken* across the Sea of Kenyon. Also thanks to the Khrynsani, you have no ship, and half of your crew is dead. From what Raine told me, you and your people put a big dint in the Khrynsani population, nearly wiping them out."

"Not nearly close enough." I thought of Sandrina, her inner circle, and the Khrynsani mage who had vaporized the *Wraith* and nearly fifty men and women.

Phaelan stood and slung his sword belt into position. "Then what do you say we cross that oversized pond together so you and yours can finish the job?"

We weren't waiting until tomorrow to leave. High tide was in three hours, and we would be sailing with it.

Once again my survival depended on getting out of Regor as quickly as possible.

The *Kraken* stayed right where she was—moored near the entrance to the harbor along with the *Raven* and the *Sea Wolf*. We weren't about to risk bringing her any closer to shore. She could be destroyed by any number of means, but those were all mundane. Storms or cannon were all I wanted to worry about, and those were normal concerns for any ship going to sea. No one had carved a chunk out of the *Kraken*'s hull, and no one would get the chance.

Since we now had only three ships, one sentry dragon and its pilot would return to their squadron. I left that choice to the senior officer, Calik Bakari. The other two dragons' pilots had saddled and prepped their mounts. Calik would follow on his dragon, Sapphira. They would fly them out to the ships and land them in the holds. The dozen firedrakes would be rowed out separately, four per ship.

My team had arrived. They were cloaked, hooded, and masked. If they were seen, they would be marked. Their identities couldn't be known to the public. Not yet, possibly not ever. I'd been forced out of Regor. They had been forced into hiding. We had the same impetus—a reason from our pasts to bring down and destroy the Khrynsani. Plus, they all had military backgrounds.

Each carried their weapons and a duffle containing clothing fit for where we'd be going, plus additional gear. Phaelan had assured me that all three ships carried more than enough weaponry to outfit double the number of people on board the ships. Weapons got broken and if they couldn't be repaired, they needed to be replaced. But like soldiers the world over, my team preferred their own.

They were given a wide berth as they loaded their gear in the next boat to go out to the *Kraken.* Mundanes felt the urge to get out of their way; lesser mages experienced the same compulsion, but they knew the reason for it. Dark power rolled in waves off of these three men and one woman.

Needless to say, I was no longer concerned with stealth.

The Khrynsani knew what we were up to, and had blown the *Wraith* out of the water to keep us from doing it. I didn't know why they hadn't waited until we were in the middle of the harbor or out to sea and beyond hope of rescue. That was what I would have done. For whatever reason, they decided to do it when they did.

Imala and I had spoken with the remaining crew of the *Wraith.*

Then we introduced Phaelan as their captain for the voyage.

It went much better than I thought it would.

The crew of the *Wraith* were basically seagoing spies who gathered information in the ports they visited to benefit goblin intelligence and the secret service. Phaelan's crews did much the same thing, but to benefit the Benares family coffers and business interests. The remaining crew of the *Wraith* had no doubt gathered extensive information on the Benares family and Phaelan in particular. So it was almost as if they already knew him. They knew what kind of man he was, probably more so than I did.

They actually liked him—and he them.

I leaned down and whispered in Imala's right ear. "I think this is a good thing, but I'm not entirely sure."

"A combined crew of elves and goblins," Imala mused. "Most definitely a first. And from a tactical standpoint, a good idea. Goblins can take the night watch and elves the day."

Minutes later, Kesyn, Talon, and Agata arrived under full guard, courtesy of Imala. I had them take the boat out to the *Kraken.*

Everyone and everything being shuttled to the *Kraken*

was being searched for magic-activated trackers or explosive devices. That included me. Though unlikely, someone could have gotten close enough to slip a tracking stone on us. If we blew up in the middle of the Sea of Kenyon, I wanted to die knowing I'd done everything possible, probable, or merely likely to have prevented it.

I'd assigned two of my team members to each of the other Benares ships. Bane Ahiga and Elsu Lenmana would be on the *Raven* and Dasant Kele and Malik Chiali would go to the *Sea Wolf*. Kesyn, Jash, and I could take care of the *Kraken*. The sentry dragon on each ship would be prepared to defend it. What had happened to the *Wraith* meant that we needed to be on guard against black magic attacks at any time throughout the voyage. If that happened, we needed to fight fire with fire, and I wasn't referring to cannons. We could signal quickly enough between ships, but I wanted help to be onboard in case of an attack. When dealing with black magic, a second could mean the difference between an unsuccessful attack and complete destruction.

24

All three ships had put on every yard of sail throughout the night to take advantage of the good winds that we'd encountered soon after leaving Regor's harbor. All hands had been needed. The crew remaining from the *Wraith* were assimilating well into Phaelan's half crew. Considering that the ship's operation and our very survival depended on a crew working seamlessly together, they'd had little choice. For the most part, the goblins would take the night watches, with the elves on duty during the day.

The goblins had pushed what had happened to the side as they did their jobs. Agents in goblin intelligence and the secret service took their lives into their hands on a daily basis. Living until retirement age as a field agent was virtually unheard of. They knew the dangers and took the risks. Still, to have nearly fifty men and women who you served with and worked beside every day be vaporized in an instant went beyond horrifying.

They had died in their sleep, or where they had been standing guard, with no chance to fight an enemy to defend themselves. The enemy had already been there, taken a piece of the *Wraith,* and left. The mage who had brought death to those men and women didn't look them in the eyes as he killed them. He or she had been in a closed room, risking nothing.

A coward.

A coward who would pay.

Imala had said she would keep me posted on the investigation via ship's telepath. I didn't expect that she would find any evidence or clues that would lead her to the mage who had worked that spell. They would have had to have been within five miles to have been guaranteed success. Regor was the capital city of the kingdom. There were thousands of people within five miles of the waterfront. But just because they wouldn't be found immediately didn't mean any of us would stop looking. We would never forget. Someone would talk; they always did.

The guilty would be found.

The crew of the *Wraith* would be avenged.

Having a ship vaporized within hours of leaving on an expedition made you forget a few things—like ensuring that your son who had only set foot on a ship once in his life took precautions against seasickness.

Though he was old enough to take responsibility for himself.

Or so I would've thought.

With full-blooded goblins, it was difficult to tell by looking at them if they were about to feed the fishes.

Talon was half-elf. His skin was a paler gray than a full-blooded goblin's. Right now he was obviously green. It wasn't a good color on him.

Luckily we had two ship's doctors—one goblin and one elf. Phaelan had said he'd had his most important crew sent through the mirror first. I was grateful he'd considered his doctor indispensable—though he had come through the mirror after the gunners. Between the two doctors, they determined the best treatment for a seasick goblin/elf. They had recommended that Talon come up on deck and get some fresh air while they mixed a tonic for him.

While at our family's country estate, Talon had fallen in love with our hunting firedrakes, and they with him. He had spent as much time as he could out with them. He'd already spoken to Calik about helping to take care of them on the voyage. Calik had agreed. It would help him to have more time for his sentry dragon, Sapphira, and it would give Talon something productive to keep him occupied and hopefully out of trouble.

One of the drakes had already adopted Talon as his own. Indigo was a deep blue, almost purple firedrake with black stripes. Since the drakes considered the ship their nest, there was no danger in them flying off. Indigo had taken to staying with Talon. He was presently perched on the ship's railing that Talon was leaning over.

Talon had just managed to raise his head from where he'd been hanging it over the side. I had a firm grip on his belt.

Even with the tonic, Talon wouldn't be guaranteed of keeping food on his stomach. The doctors had a draught for that problem, too—nutrient-rich and quickly digested. I hoped Talon would adjust and wouldn't need it, but I wasn't holding my breath. The sea was shallow here, just west of Rheskilia's northernmost islands, and today the sea was smooth as glass. As we neared the Lastani Islands, we'd likely run into rough seas. That'd be the true test of the tonic—and Talon's stomach.

I had a spell that would help, but it also had the unfortunate side effect of grogginess. If Sandrina knew we were coming—and I was now sure that she did—I wanted Talon to have all of his wits about him.

The *Wraith* being destroyed was proof that someone didn't want us reaching Aquas. Sandrina and any allies she might have in Regor had access to telepaths the same as we did. If so, she knew the *Wraith* had been destroyed, but that the expedition had set sail ahead of schedule.

She would try again. Whether using magic means, mundane, or both, Sandrina wasn't about to give up. When she did, I wanted Talon able to not only defend himself, but help protect the ship and crew as well.

Kesyn had said Talon was strong. I'd seen enough firsthand evidence to know that for myself. I also had no doubt about his control, his ability to hold on to a spell once he launched it. Controlling his impulses was where he needed work—a lot of work. Becoming a mage was equal parts knowing when and when not to use magic than having the necessary strength for more advanced work. And as I knew from my own experience, such knowledge didn't necessarily come with age. I'd had to hit rock bottom only a few years ago before realizing that I was in trouble.

My parents weren't mages, so there was only so much they could do to rein in a magically precocious son.

I was determined that things would be different with Talon.

Whether he liked it or not.

I knew that pushing too hard could be just as bad as not stepping in at all. It was a fine line I would be walking, but it was a journey I was determined to get right.

Starting with this voyage.

Our first morning at sea had dawned unnecessarily and ferociously bright. All of the goblins and many of the elves were wearing heavily tinted glasses. Talon had narrowly avoided having his fall off when he'd had to quickly lean over the side.

Agata Azul strolled toward us, dressed in one of my mother's sets of leathers. Agata must have been slightly larger in a few places. I knew this because I was a keen observer of my surroundings, and my powers of observation couldn't help but notice the laces were being pulled in some rather intriguing directions.

Talon shakily stood up and leaned on the ship's rail. He'd noticed, too. In fact, his noticing put some much-needed color back in his cheeks.

Kesyn had introduced his present student to his former student on the dock before they'd gotten into the boat to be rowed out to the *Kraken*. Agata had been her usual cool and collected self.

Talon? Not so much. He actually stumbled over a word or

two. He recovered quickly, but not quickly enough. I'd heard it, Kesyn had heard it, and most importantly to Talon, Agata had heard it.

He'd tried to be smooth after that, even helping Agata into the boat—though completely lacking in sea legs, he'd needed it more than she did. Once on board, he tried to affect indifference, but failed miserably. Surprisingly, Agata had sought him out twice now, whether from pity at him being violently ill or actual interest, I couldn't tell.

"Dammit," Talon managed.

"Dammit, what?"

"I'm sick."

"I think everyone knows that." I paused and smiled in realization. "Ah, Agata's strolling over, and it's hard to be suave while hanging over the side of a ship."

As Agata walked toward us now, Talon groaned dramatically and sank to a crate near the rail. He risked a quick glance at her out of the corner of his eyes.

I rolled mine. If you can't be suave, evoke pity.

I leaned down to Talon's ear. "Just don't throw up on her."

Talon went pale, no acting needed. "I didn't think of that."

"Be sure to get your face over the rail before it happens. And get a good grip on the rail, not her. Dragging her overboard with you won't earn you any points."

"Noted."

I looked up and saw the goblin doctor arrive with a cup. Saved by the tonic.

I patted Talon on the shoulder. "Help has arrived. Behave yourself, I'm going below."

25

Those who could were below for some much-needed rest after having been up since noon yesterday, getting crew, passengers, dragons, and supplies loaded on the *Kraken* and then setting sail. We'd need all hands soon enough; the crew needed to sleep while they could.

The *Kraken* didn't have much room for passengers. In fact, there was only one passenger cabin, and that went to Agata Azul. I would be sharing the captain's cabin with Phaelan, Talon, Jash, and Kesyn—that is, if the old man had found a way to keep his snoring under control. If not, Jash and I told him we'd string a hammock for him on deck. That way, those of us below could get some sleep, and the crew topside would have no choice but to stay awake.

Sharing the captain's quarters had been Phaelan's idea.

He'd insisted, especially when it became obvious that Talon didn't have sea legs. As he put it, "The kid will need fresh air."

Phaelan Benares rose even further in my estimation.

I pulled up a chair to a small table. Normally, I'd have read in bed, or in this case my hammock, but I wasn't about to lie down with a book written by Rudra Muralin. I wanted to be able to get away from it quickly, not get tangled in a canvas sack.

I'd brought a set of my usual court clothes with me in case I needed to look presentable. After trudging across miles of rocky wasteland, I seriously doubted my wardrobe choices would be anywhere near the top of my needs, but I was Chigaru and Mirabai's representative. If we encountered civilization, I needed to have the means to present myself properly.

But on the *Kraken,* I wore shirt, trousers, and boots topped by a light canvas coat that offered highly desirable inner pockets for an assortment of weapons both magical and mundane that I wasn't going anywhere without.

I'd hidden the book in a warded inner pocket. I'd wanted to put off examining Rudra's little book of evil until after I'd had sufficient sleep, but what had been done to the *Wraith* had changed my plans. I didn't know for certain that it was evil, but it had been written by Rudra and hidden by Sarad, so I felt safe in assuming it wasn't a collection of nursery rhymes.

Sometimes books fought back, especially volumes of black magic. Khrynsani black magic books always fought back. It wasn't an exaggeration to say that you were literally taking your life into your hands when you opened a book written by a Khrynsani dark mage.

I knew I'd be multiplying my risk by ten opening a book written by Rudra Muralin.

It would be bad.

If you wanted to delve into the mysteries of black magic, breaking the code on books was a talent you either developed or paid for. Men and women who had the gift could name their price for their services. I would have done the same if I had been in their line of business. They risked their lives and even their immortal souls every time they opened an encrypted book. They deserved to be paid accordingly. But some volumes they wouldn't touch for any price.

Rudra's book would have been one of them, or any other book found in the Khrynsani temple library.

Even if I hadn't been at sea, I would have had to have done it myself.

I wasn't Khrynsani. Never had been, never would be. However, I had been possessed briefly by Sarad Nukpana, their leader. I had seen his thoughts, his memories, his knowledge, and had been unable to rid myself of any of it.

I wanted to forget all of it, but more than once, my knowledge of Sarad's mind—he had revealed his intentions to me while he'd held my soul and body prisoner—had saved us all.

Now was merely another one of those times.

I felt like a thief about to break into a heavily warded and defended vault. I had the key, but didn't know whether I'd be attacked for using it.

The door opened, and Phaelan stepped into the cabin. He stopped just inside the door and stood perfectly still, his eyes narrowing and meticulously scanning the entire space. "That book isn't in here, is it?"

I sighed. “It is.”

It wasn’t as if I could lie about it. I’d said I’d be reading the book, and I would be staying in the captain’s quarters.

I patted the right side of my coat. “Wherever I am, it is.”

“And you’re going to be doing a lot of night watch, right?”

“That is correct.”

“So when I’m sleeping, the devil’s diary won’t be under my pillow or anything.”

“You have my word.”

Phaelan exhaled. “Good.” He came the rest of the way into the cabin, giving me and the book a wide berth. I couldn’t really blame him.

Kesyn and Jash came in.

I felt an eye roll coming on again. “I take it the two of you are here to watch me read.”

Kesyn pulled a chair out and sat opposite me. “If you’re reading it, we’re watching. It’s bad enough that A’Zahra isn’t here as well, but we’ll make do.”

Jash remained standing. “Gee, thank you for the vote of confidence, sir.” He turned to me. “Let’s see…a book from Sarad Nukpana’s secret stash written by Rudra Muralin. If any book could eat your face off, it’d be that one.”

Phaelan took an obvious sniff in Kesyn’s direction. “You’re not hauling around any of that nasty cheese Raine told me about, are you?”

I snorted. The night the Saghred had been destroyed, Kesyn had broken the concentration of the Khrynsani mages maintaining a ward around the stone, enabling Raine to destroy the Saghred and save the Seven Kingdoms. He’d been arming himself, so to speak, by eating a particular odoriferous type of cheese. The mages' concentration broke when Kesyn broke wind.

One fart had saved us all.

Kesyn was all innocence, which was an impressive achievement coming from him. "Would I do that?"

"In a *stinking* heartbeat," Phaelan said.

"That's not the end you should be worried about," I muttered, removing the book from my coat's shielded inner pocket.

I immediately had the attention of everyone in the room.

Phaelan headed for the door. "I'm outta here. My crew needs me."

Jash pulled out a chair, straddled it, and crossed his arms over the back. "And Tam needs us—whether he wants to admit it or not."

I put the book on the table. I would readily admit that even to touch it set off my alarms. "Need? Hopefully not. Want? I can't say I don't appreciate the company."

"What are you going to use?" Kesyn asked solemnly.

"Shield myself and set up a ward around me, the book, and the table. If anything happens, it'll be contained and won't damage the ship."

Kesyn nodded in approval. "How about you shield you, and we ward your immediate vicinity."

"That way you've got more juice left to protect yourself," Jash said.

I swallowed against a sudden lump in my throat. "Thank you, both. I would appreciate that."

"You still think it's only spell-locked?" Kesyn asked. "Think, Tam. This is Rudra Muralin's work you're dealing with."

I raised my hands a few inches above the book, focusing my will. “I won’t know until I get it open.”

“That’s what I’m afraid of.”

26

Unlocking Rudra Muralin's book on Nidaar wasn't the problem. That had been simple. Too simple. Now I knew why. Reading what was inside would be the difficult—and dangerous—part.

The book itself had been spell-locked.

The words inside were blood-locked.

That meant I would need to write my name in my blood on the first page to unlock the rest of the book.

I had encountered books like this before in my darkest days of practicing black magic. Some of them still haunted my nightmares.

Merely writing my name wouldn't give me access to the entire book. At any given point, the words could vanish, requiring more blood from the reader, this time a fingerprint.

If you wanted to read, you had to pay, with your own blood. And once you unlocked the book and began to read, you had to keep your hands in contact with it. Break the contact, lock the book.

A mage's name was powerful. Our blood was even more powerful. Using both was asking for every kind of trouble. The vilest of curses could be worked with the blood signature of a rival mage. I'd heard of a mage using a blood-locked book to kill his rivals—all of whom had read it by signing their names in their blood.

It was risky as hell.

I had to take that risk.

"Wait," Kesyn told me. He went to his duffle and dug around until he found a small leather-bound book, two pens, and ink. "I brought blank books with me. You read, I'll write, Jash will listen and stand by to step in if necessary." His face darkened with a rage I'd never seen from him. "You're only doing this once."

I took out a small knife. Without a word, Kesyn passed me one of his pens. I knew he would either clean it thoroughly afterward to rid it of any trace of my blood, or destroy it outright.

I carefully pricked the tip of my middle finger over my open and cupped palm, squeezing it with the finger on either side until the blood began to flow. When I had enough in my palm to sign my name, I dipped the pen's nib into the blood, took a deep breath, and wrote my name in the first page of Rudra Muralin's book.

The blood didn't sink into the fibers of the paper and dry. It remained bright and fresh. Then the page suddenly rose from beneath, as if the book was taking a deep and satisfied breath. As the book exhaled, my name and blood was absorbed into it, vanishing completely.

When the page again lay flat, I could see words appearing on the next page.

I pressed a cloth into my palm to absorb the blood there, and steeling myself, turned the page.

On the inside cover, Rudra Muralin had written a brief summary of what was inside.

Rudra had called it an "interrogation record." I called it a written account of psychic rape. Rudra Muralin had performed a ritual called a memory drain on Kansbar Nathrach. Rudra had forced his way into Kansbar's mind, pushed his soul aside while he ransacked his memories. And when he found the ones he wanted, he took them, only then releasing his victim.

Rudra could have been careful, but I know he hadn't been.

The official story had been that Kansbar had committed suicide shortly after being released from Khrynsani custody. After Rudra Muralin had finished with him, Kansbar's mind would have been in shambles, all but destroyed. Kansbar hadn't been a mage; he'd had no way to protect himself. He'd been completely helpless against Rudra's assault.

I now believed my ancestor had taken his own life.

Kesyn and Jash couldn't see the pages. Only I could.

I didn't want to, but I had to.

Sarad Nukpana was still alive. And somewhere inside of Sarad was Rudra Muralin. As long as Sarad lived, so would Rudra. Sarad had taken Rudra in much the same way as Rudra had taken my ancestor.

It had been divine, ironic justice.

But it hadn't been nearly enough justice.

One day Sarad would show himself, and on that day both Sarad Nukpana and Rudra Muralin would pay.

How do you read a detailed account of your ancestor's mind being raped?

It didn't matter that Rudra Muralin had done this to Kansbar Nathrach nearly nine hundred years ago.

It felt as if it were happening to me as I read.

What Sarad Nukpana had done to me in that bunker under the Isle of Mid had been appallingly similar.

I had met Rudra Muralin only a few months ago. He had somehow discovered that Talon was my son. He then proceeded to use Talon's safety against me. If I failed to turn Raine over to him, he would have had Talon kidnapped and sold in the Nebian slave markets. Rudra didn't need to tell me what kind of slavery awaited a half elf/half goblin as beautiful as Talon. He didn't need to tell me, but he had. The Khrynsani had a long reach, so I knew I couldn't send Talon away to keep him safe. The closer he stayed to me, the better. If I had tried to warn Raine, Rudra would have had Talon killed outright.

So as I had many times in my life, I walked a tightrope, feigning cooperation while plotting retribution.

I denied Rudra his chance at controlling the Saghred by having Raine as his captive, and I—along with some of the dark mages on the list I'd given A'Zahra and the four I'd brought with me on this voyage—had kept Talon from being sacrificed to the Saghred, and Raine from having Talon's murdered soul pulled into the Saghred through her.

It had been a good and satisfying night's work.

However, Rudra had escaped, and I had no doubt that I was at the top of his "kill slowly in revenge" list.

Sarad Nukpana had gotten to him first, consuming his soul and his life force, and leaving nothing but a dried husk. Imala had decapitated him and had his body burnt and scattered to the winds.

But if Sarad still lived, so did Rudra—in a way.

Rudra had written this book. Sarad had read it.

Both would love to watch me read it.

I was surprised that Rudra hadn't told me what he had done to Kansbar. Perhaps he'd been waiting for a time when it would have inflicted more pain.

I glanced up. Kesyn and Jash were patiently waiting, not judging. Understanding.

"Sorry," I told them both.

"Whenever you're ready," Kesyn said almost gently.

I began to read.

Rudra had absorbed Kansbar Nathrach's memories, incorporating them into his own. He recorded what he had learned for the benefit of a Khrynsani reader, spending more time on sections that would have been of interest to them. What was of interest to Kansbar did not matter. Rudra had ripped out every memory Kansbar had of the voyage and expedition, so he could shift through the knowledge later at his leisure.

Inexplicably, Rudra had written down Kansbar's background. I couldn't imagine what interest that could have had for the Khrynsani, but he had included it.

Kansbar was a young nobleman and a member of the Nathrach family. He was the youngest of five brothers, and as such, under the inheritance traditions of that time, would not have inherited a sufficient portion of the family estate to support himself to the level in which he had grown up. Once his schooling was complete, Kansbar had taken to the sea for adventure and to seek his fortune, as did the younger sons of many goblin families, noble or common.

The king at that time, Omari Mal'Salin, had ordered an expedition to Aquas to find the legendary city of Nidaar, the city of the golden-skinned goblins who were said to have been our distant cousins, separated from us thousands of years before when the continents had split. Omari sent an ambassador to speak in his name and establish diplomatic relations with any civilization, if found.

Kansbar was a goblin historian and scholar of ancient goblin languages. If our distant cousins did exist, the language they spoke would likely not be our own. Kansbar was asked to become the expedition's official translator. He immediately accepted the position, eager to possibly be the first to discover proof of the existence of this legendary race.

What Kansbar had not known, but Rudra had recorded, was that the ambassador and his staff were all Khrynsani, and that their assignment was to secure the Heart of Nidaar. At this point, Rudra Muralin and his Khrynsani still had the Saghred. Not satisfied to possess and wield one stone of unimaginable power, Rudra wanted any he could get his hands on. Others on the expedition had equally dark intentions. There were treasure hunters and slavers. If these golden-skinned goblins existed, they would bring a high price, as would the gold their city was said to contain.

Two ships left Regor for Aquas. The voyage to the continent was uneventful as far as Rudra had been concerned. He had written only a few sentences. As for Kansbar's thoughts of his first trip across the Sea of Kenyon, apparently Rudra didn't think them worthy of recording.

Halfway through the journey, the ships stopped in the Lastani Islands for fresh water, and to make some minor repairs to one of the ships.

The bay on the east coast of Aquas where the two ships had moored two weeks later was approximately fifty miles south of where we would be making landfall. The bay was large and protected, the same location that every expedition coming to the continent had used. Kansbar's expedition hadn't been expecting an ambush. We, on the other hand, had to be on guard for anything.

Once they reached the coast, a smooth beach awaited them. Beyond the beach was a lush landscape of forests, valleys, and fields, filled with plants and animals that had never been seen before. There was ample fresh water in lakes, rivers, and streams. To the goblins weary of over a month at sea, it was nothing short of a paradise.

This was the first account I'd seen of the interior of Aquas being anything other than barren rock and desert. Subsequent expeditions to the exact same location told of a nearly unclimbable escarpment that extended as far north and south as the eye could see. Beyond that lay dried-up lakes and riverbeds and a parched and rocky landscape. The map we had had told us as much. I had hoped whoever had drawn that map had been exaggerating.

Aquas had apparently been named for what it had been, not what it was now.

Later expeditions had found no sign of the city of Nidaar or its golden-skinned goblin inhabitants. One expedition had remained a year in the area where Nidaar was said to have been, without success, leading to Nidaar's reputation as a city of legend rather than one that had actually existed.

Kansbar's expedition arrived at the foot of the mountains after nine days of travel and camped in a cave they discovered, after posting their usual guards outside.

The four guards were found dead the next morning. Not just dead, but shriveled as if they had been drained and dried from the inside out.

I suddenly felt magic slide against my shields, oily, nauseating. It wasn't black magic, at least not as I'd ever known or experienced it. It wasn't merely different. It was alien.

I glanced up sharply at Kesyn. He had stopped writing. He felt it, too.

Jash leapt to his feet and flung open a window. There was shouting from the deck and above.

"Ships off the starboard bow!"

I closed the book.

27

The three of us rushed up on deck. I continued up to the quarterdeck with Phaelan.

"What have we got?" I asked him.

"They're Nebian, Captain. Frigates, I think," came the call from aloft.

"That's what we've got," Phaelan shot back. "Hot on our tail and gaining."

I couldn't believe it. Then again, I could. "The bastard didn't want an alliance because he already had one."

Phaelan had a spyglass up, looking in the direction of the ships. "This bastard have a name?"

"Aeron Corantine, the Nebian ambassador. Said the rest of us were committing suicide by forming an alliance against any invaders."

"So you're saying he couldn't sign on with you because he was already in bed with this Sandrina Ghalfari."

"Figuratively, I've long suspected. I haven't considered a literal interpretation. I certainly wouldn't put it past her or him. Though none of that changes what's closing on us."

"No, it doesn't." Phaelan lowered the glass and passed it to me. "They look fuzzy to me, and I haven't had a drop to drink all week. Are they wearing wards?"

I raised the spyglass to my eye and focused it. Or attempted to. It was a veil, a good one, and large enough to cover multiple ships. No wonder the lookout couldn't make a positive identification. I summoned just enough discernment magic to let me make out two separate forms. If they didn't know we'd spotted them, I didn't want to be the one who gave us away.

"They are frigates, and they've got veils," I told him. "Good ones."

Phaelan snorted. "Two Nebian frigates coming after three Benares warships? Now that's suicidal."

"I don't want to be the bearer of bad news, but they've got dark mages on board. That's why I came up from below. I sensed them. So did Kesyn and Jash."

"And we have three ships, and you and your four buddies. I'm still taking bets on our side."

"I wouldn't know how to act if someone wasn't trying to kill me." I looked through the glass again. "They're flying every scrap of canvas they've got, and they're gaining on us."

"If they want to die before sundown, who are we to deny them?"

I hissed out a breath. "I don't want to say this, but I have to. They're flying the pasha's flag. We can't touch them."

Phaelan turned on me.

"Unless they fire the first shot," I told him. "We can't attack two royal Nebian ships."

Suddenly, we had the attention of every crewman—goblin and elf—who wasn't occupied with sailing the *Kraken*. The others were listening, too. They just couldn't give us their full attention.

Half the crew were goblin, the other half elf. The captain was an elf, I was a goblin and head of the expedition. The goblins were also agents of the crown and sworn to aid, serve, and protect the royal house of Mal'Salin. My last name was Nathrach, but I was the king's chancellor, temporary heir, and his voice on board this ship.

We had many more weeks at sea together. I knew the Nebians didn't have friendly intentions, but as the representative of the goblin king, I could hardly go around blowing another ruler's ships out of the water.

"I know as well as you that's why they're flying that flag," I kept my voice down and my expression neutral. "So we don't blow them out of the water on sight."

"The deck you're standing on doesn't belong to a goblin ship," Phaelan said quietly. "We're flying Benares flags. They know who we are, and they're still coming after us."

"You're a wanted man and we're in interkingdom waters," I countered. "They could claim they're apprehending wanted felons."

"Shit." Phaelan clearly hadn't thought of that.

"Yeah." I had thought of that. "I've got the Mal'Salin royal standard *and* a Guardian flag on board, and I sent a set over to Gwyn and Gavyn with my team before we set sail. To attack a Benares ship is enforcing the law, however suicidal. To attack a Mal'Salin or Guardian vessel is a declaration of war." I grinned. "Aeron Corantine and I had several disagreements while on the Isle of Mid. I recommend flying the Guardian flags. You and Raine are more like brother and sister than cousins. That makes Mychael Eiliesor your almost brother-in-law."

Phaelan smiled. "He wouldn't mind at all."

"Not in the least," I agreed.

"And family lets family borrow things."

"That they do. And I don't think the Nebians are *that* suicidal."

"They'll keep following us. We'll keep watching our backs." Phaelan flashed a grin full of white teeth against his swarthy face. "I wouldn't know how to behave if someone wasn't trying to kill me, either."

"Sirs?" Calik stood on the stairs to the quarterdeck in full flight leathers, helmet tucked under one arm, smiling up at us. "If we really want to encourage the Nebians to go home, may I suggest letting the ladies out for a little exercise? Besides, the girls won't like being cooped up that close to the gun deck should you start firing those cannons. I think a little fly-about would be in everyone's best interests." He chuckled. "Well, except the Nebians'."

Phaelan and I exchanged a glance. He raised his hands. "I'm the captain of the ship. You're commanding the expedition. The lizards are all yours."

"I would never dream of denying a lady a good time." I grinned broadly. "Release the dragons."

The Nebian ships had been closing distance.

As soon as the three sentry dragons cleared the masts, our pursuers had second thoughts about their course of action. They had third and fourth thoughts when the ladies roared and exhaled columns of fire half as thick as a mast.

The frigates slowed their pursuit, but they didn't retreat.

"They're determined to be a problem," I said.

"The ships or the mages?" Jash asked.

"Yes."

The ships were a known equation. The dark mages were unknown. We'd only sensed them for a moment, but we knew they were there, and they were powerful. Now they were quiet. Not just quiet, completely silent, as if they were no longer there.

We knew better.

I'd been in contact with my four team members on the *Raven* and *Sea Wolf*. They'd sensed the same thing that we had. It was the stirrings of magic that felt like nothing we had ever sensed before.

I'd heard similar words said—about the invaders who had wiped out civilization on the world of Timurus.

Talon had come up from below. "Why would the Nebians have alien invader mages on board? Aside from the fact that they can probably kick ass better than Nebian mages."

"It's the Nebians' nature as traders to hold out until they get the best offer," Jash said.

"Or their natures as traitors," I told them both. "It's not only the pronunciation that's similar. Nebian leaders have a favored tactic in times of war—wait for the winner to emerge. Their history of neutrality isn't due to politics or distain for conflict, but a desire to emerge on the winning side."

Talon blinked. "They'd side with the Khrynsani, or someone not even from our world?"

"Whoever wins. The Nebians prize self-preservation above all. Loyalty really doesn't enter into their thinking."

"So the weasels would betray us."

"If they believed it was in their best interests, then yes, they would act without hesitation."

If the Nebians had allied themselves with the Khrynsani, it was but a small step to have the alien invaders involved as well. The Khrynsani wouldn't be the only ones with a vested interest in keeping us from reaching Aquas.

I didn't tell Phaelan my theory. If I was right, there wasn't anything he could do about it. This would be a battle fought by only a few of us; and even then, our opponents might be too much for us. We wouldn't know until they attacked. And attack they would.

After standing watch for nearly two hours, I'd decided that an attack wasn't imminent. So I went back to our cabin and tried to unlock the book again, but it was unresponsive.

From past experience, I knew that it could be hours or it could be days before it allowed me to read further.

Kansbar Nathrach had obviously survived whatever had attacked the landing party. I was only a third of the way through the book when I'd had to break my connection to it. We had only been at sea for a few days. We had at least four weeks before we reached Nidaar. While I needed to know what we could be facing once we reached Aquas, we still had time.

What I needed now was sleep. I wanted to take tonight's watch, but it was a little over five hours until full dark. When our followers decided to act, I wanted to be well rested.

I checked to ensure that Rudra's book was securely bound in the interior pocket of my coat. I removed the coat, draped it over myself as a blanket, and within minutes was asleep.

28

I looked out over a scorched and blighted landscape. Nothing grew as far as the eye could see. The sky was that clear, crisp blue found over land in which there was no water. Even though the sun shone brightly, the light didn't hurt my eyes.

It was a welcome change.

"Beautiful, isn't it?" said a familiar voice from behind me. "You see a wasteland, I see sunlight, fresh air, and wonders."

I drew blades and shielded.

At least I tried to.

I had no weapons and no magic.

With Sarad Nukpana now standing next to me.

He smiled and spread his hands. "I am without weapons as well." Sarad gazed out over the barren landscape. "You realize that you take so many things for granted, when you no longer have access to them. That's what several months languishing in Hell will do to you."

The last time I'd seen Sarad he'd been attired for his coronation and wedding in black and purple silk and velvet with a scarlet sash. Over that he wore black chest armor intricately embossed with a silver scorpion, the Nukpana family crest. And who could forget the crown? A silvery ring of scorpions with their tails intertwining.

Now he was wearing tunic, trousers, and boots of a dark indeterminate color. While by no means an inferior fabric, it wasn't what Sarad would've worn by choice.

"You're not the worse for wear," I noted.

Sarad shrugged elaborately. "I much preferred my royal raiment. How is the youngest Mal'Salin? Happily married and securely enthroned?"

"Yes to both."

Sarad shook his finger. "You're lying about the latter. No goblin king is ever securely enthroned, unless a plague has taken out every courtier and noble and left the king unscathed. Any who thinks so is a fool and a liar, or merely delusional. You're not any of those, Tamnais." His eyes narrowed shrewdly. "So who have you left to babysit the young upstart while you're off playing the bold adventurer?"

"Why don't you ask your new lady friend? We weren't properly introduced, and the lady didn't tell me her name, but she would have been remiss if she did nothing except try to abduct Agata Azul while she was in Regor."

"Ah, Bricarda."

"Bricarda."

"It's the name she's using now. I imagine when you've

lived as long as she has, you become bored keeping the same name." Sarad smiled fondly. "Older, but ageless, women are a rare treat. So much knowledge and experience, so glad to teach. You should try it."

"I'll pass. I prefer a lady who's non-murderous, wears a scent other than brimstone, and doesn't travel with a zombie demon entourage."

Sarad leaned forward and peered over the side of the outcropping where we stood. "My, that's quite a fall." His dark eyes glittered. "Do you think you would survive it? They say if you take such a fall in your dreams and don't wake up before impact, you will die. Do you believe that?"

"It's possible," I said. "What I can't believe is that in all my choices of who to dream about, my subconscious chose you. When I wake up I shall have to have a long talk with it. Or perhaps you standing here is the result of something disagreeable that I ate."

"You weren't my first choice, either," Sarad told me. "But alas, the dreamscape of the fair Raine has been denied me."

That was a relief. She and Mychael—and probably Justinius Valerian as well—had successfully warded her against psychic attack. Mychael not only had taken my warning seriously, he'd taken action.

I should have taken my own advice and done the same.

If I had, I wouldn't be standing on the edge of a cliff with Sarad Nukpana.

"Her loss is your gain, Tamnais. Though in a way it is your loss as well, isn't it? The gallant paladin won her hand—and the rest of her, leaving you alone and bereft. Or have you sought comfort and consolation in the arms of the lovely

Imala? Or perhaps you've visited the cabin of your delectable gem mage, young though she is. However, I can tell you from personal experience that instructing and corrupting the nubile and innocent is intensely satisfying." He sighed dramatically. "Satisfaction I have not had in far too long, thanks in large part to you. Did Agata tell you that I courted her myself?"

"She mentioned that you had attempted to persuade her to help you find the Saghred."

"That's all? How disappointing. I expended some of my best seduction techniques on that young lady, promising her riches and sensual delights beyond her imagination."

"It sounded to me like she didn't want to imagine it—or you."

"The young have no appreciation for the finer things in life." Sarad brightened. "And how is the young scion of the noble Nathrach family?"

"He is well."

"Too bad. I understand Talon was responsible for killing several of my generals and destroying the entrance to the Khrynsani temple."

"It was a team effort. We all did our part that night."

"And all of you have yet to pay for what you've done."

"I take it you're here to gloat that our time is up and our doom imminent."

"No."

"No?"

"You don't need me to tell you that," Sarad said. "You already know. The terror's in the details, details you will begin experiencing soon. I wouldn't want to ruin the surprise. I understand you've been reading Rudra Muralin's little travel guide."

"You mean the record of my ancestor's torture."

"If he had cooperated, Rudra wouldn't have resorted to such drastic and distasteful measures. He would have accepted the information, killed him cleanly, and been done with it. Your ancestor, Kansbar, was it? He brought his madness on himself. I do hope you've learned from his obvious mistakes."

"I have yet to find that Kansbar made any mistakes."

"Really? You must not have read very far."

"I had to temporarily stop reading about a third of the way through. I took my hands off of the book and the words vanished."

"Ah yes, Rudra's tiresome games. When you unlock the book, take care not to overfeed it. You won't like what will happen if you do. Though I don't believe you will like it now. I read the book as well, and wrote my name in my blood on the same page as you. The book absorbs the blood—blending your name with those of us who had read before." His lips spread in a slow smile. "You had to ask yourself what would be the consequences of your actions, consigning your name in your blood on the exact sheet of paper as so many others before you." The smile stretched into a grin as Sarad Nukpana spread his arms. "Ta-da. And here we are sharing a dream. Cozy, is it not?"

I choked on my next breath.

"Yes, it was quite the surprise to me, too." Sarad said. Though unlike me, he probably wasn't experiencing the sudden urge to be sick.

I had unwittingly bonded with Sarad Nukpana—and every mage who had read Rudra Muralin's book.

Including Rudra Muralin.

These weren't men and women I wanted to be anywhere near, let alone able to share my headspace.

"By the way," Sarad said brightly, "Rudra says hello. He's not in any condition to make a more personal greeting, but he's hopeful that will change soon. He's cute when he's optimistic. Rudra keyed the book to shut down when it caused the most discomfort for its reader. You're certainly experiencing discomfort now, aren't you? I managed to read it nearly all the way through the first time. The torture didn't bother me. It was getting to a part that I really wanted to know. The book sensed it and the words vanished. It refused to cooperate for another two weeks. Rudra was a sadistic bastard, and those are strong words coming from me." Sarad smiled slowly. "Though I fixed it so he won't toy with anyone ever again."

I had to know. I tilted my head toward him. "So Rudra is in there."

"Oh yes. And just for fun, I've kept his soul intact. Rudra wants out again very badly, especially now that the game is about to become so enjoyable and entertaining. I may let him out again, though I would never release him into just any body. If I'm going to go to all the trouble of releasing him, it would be into a vessel that would provide me with maximum amusement. I've always wanted a pet weasel."

"I take it your mother has read Rudra's book?"

"She was the one who gave it to me. It was one of the few things she wanted me to know. You didn't have to expend all that effort conjuring your bull demon to carry me away. My mother was plotting my assassination. She wouldn't have succeeded, of course. I, in turn, would have been left with no recourse but to have her executed. If you'd only had a little patience, you wouldn't be dealing with her antics now."

"I would probably be dead, along with all of my family and friends, with the entire goblin kingdom at your mercy. No, wait, I take that back. The kingdom wouldn't be at your mercy because you don't have any."

Sarad smiled and tapped the tip of his nose. "Right on the mark. We could have been friends, you know."

"No, we couldn't. I summoned that demon because I judged you not only the greater of two evils, but of all evil."

"Why Tamnais, that's the nicest thing anyone's said to me in months."

I shrugged. "It cost me nothing to say."

His smile turned calculating. "What do you want in return?"

"The location of the Heart of Nidaar."

"It's in Rudra's book. Hidden, but there. I've committed many despicable acts in my life—and if I enjoyed them enough, I would do them again—but I would never dream of spoiling the ending to a book."

29

The Nebian ships continued to follow us, not closely, but they kept us within sight.

We didn't feel the alien magic again, but the sense of it was there, oppressive and dark.

We remained alert and ready.

I also watched my back for Sarad Nukpana—and any other readers of Rudra Muralin's book who might attempt to contact me.

Including Sandrina Ghalfari.

Good sense would dictate that I ward my sleep as Raine had done. However, good sense and I had parted ways the moment I decided to go to Aquas after the Heart of Nidaar. Many went. Few returned.

That was what kept me from protecting my sleep.

I needed information, some kind of advantage over Sandrina Ghalfari. If Sandrina herself wanted to come to me in my sleep, it was an opportunity I couldn't pass up.

Sarad had to know what his mother's plans were; he had read Rudra's book, and his body now held Rudra's soul prisoner. So if there was a motherlode of knowledge, Sarad Nukpana was it. And since he had now gained access to my dreaming subconscious, I knew he wouldn't be able to resist another visit, or two, or three.

I needed an advantage over Sandrina, but I already had one over Sarad.

He was lonely.

And he had been right about one thing—we could have been friends. That is, if Sarad hadn't been a manipulative, utterly insane, megalomaniacal sadist.

In addition to being lonely, and perhaps more important to him, Sarad Nukpana was bored.

Visiting me in my dreams assuaged both feelings.

He was using me; I would use him.

Sarad would know perfectly well what I was doing. We had crossed actual swords often enough in training and more than a few times with deadly intent. We knew each other's moves. However, we'd never limited our dueling to steel, or even magic. This would be a duel of minds, attempting to outmaneuver each other, trick the other into revealing information. At this point I couldn't think of anything Sarad wanted to know from me. Though that didn't mean there wasn't anything. I would be on my guard as I always had been with Sarad Nukpana.

It was night, and I was on watch, as was my team on the other two ships.

Bane Ahiga was taking the night watch on the *Raven,* and Elsu Lenmana the day. Dasant Kele was on night duty on the *Sea Wolf,* with Malik Chiali braving the daytime sun.

If the Nebians, the alien mages on board, or an enemy who had yet to show themselves made a move against us, I wanted one of my dark mage team alert and able to take decisive action.

"Do you think it was real?" Kesyn asked.

My teacher was on deck with me. I was watching the Nebians.

Kesyn was watching me.

I didn't blame him. If I had a student who was getting dream visitations from someone like Sarad Nukpana—with the possibility of those even more evil, if that was possible—I'd be standing watch over him, too.

I nodded. "He was real."

"And no dreams with Sarad before now?"

"No."

"Not even after the possession?"

"No. Nothing."

"So it was the book."

"I don't see Sarad lying about something like that. I knew there would be consequences to signing the book, and now I know what they are."

"Okay, say this was Sarad paying you a visit from Hell," Kesyn said. "Since Sandrina also signed and read the book, it also means Sarad could be visiting her as well."

"Lovely. Just lovely."

"Though Sarad barely tolerated Sandrina. But if you were going to kill her, he might want to be around to watch. That I could see."

I smiled slowly. "And apparently, Sandrina barely tolerated Sarad. In fact, she had been close to doing our work for us. Sarad discovered that she had been plotting his assassination. If he had managed to remain king for a few more days, she would have killed him—at least she would have tried. Then he would have had her executed. Though since he's not the wasteful type, he probably would have sacrificed her to the Saghred. Of course, that wouldn't have done us any good. After that night in the temple, let alone a few days, neither one of us would have been alive to be having this conversation. Our families and friends would be dead as well—or wishing they were dead."

"And I would've been the first one in line," Kesyn said.

Kesyn knew what I had done in an attempt to ensure that Sarad didn't live through that night. I'd used black magic to call a demon to take Sarad Nukpana to the deepest pit in the Lower Hells. I'd used black magic, and to rid the world or a monster like Sarad Nukpana, I'd do it again.

Kesyn was aware of this, too.

Soon we would likely be crossing paths with Sandrina, and possibly Sarad himself.

I wouldn't hesitate to use anything in my arsenal to destroy either one of them.

I could tell he was worried.

He knew I was determined.

We stared at each other.

It was a familiar standoff for both of us.

"Speaking of killing Sandrina, my mother wants her head."

Kesyn blinked. "Really?"

"She wants me to bring it home to her as a souvenir. Preserved, of course. Mother says she's not entirely a barbarian."

"Come to think of it, I could see that, too. She did take it personally that she didn't catch Sandrina, didn't she?"

"Oh yes."

"Remind me not to piss off your mother."

"I don't think either one of us needs to be reminded of that."

We stood in silence for a few moments. The wind was coming from the north, and had a cold bite to it. The closer we got to the Lastani Islands, the colder the wind and the water would get.

"You told me that Sarad's soul possessed you for nearly five hours," Kesyn said. "That's more than enough time to establish a soul bonding."

I felt a chill that had nothing to do with the wind. "Don't you think I know that?"

"Sarad is patient. He could have left you alone until he needed to exploit the bond."

"If I had a soul bond with Sarad Nukpana, I would know it."

"You might know it, but would you admit it?"

"Not only would I admit it, I would do everything in my power, yours, A'Zahra's, Mychael's, and Justinius Valerian's to rid myself of it. I do have pride, occasionally too much, but I am no longer too proud to ask for help when I need it."

Kesyn didn't respond. I glanced over at him.

My teacher was smiling. "Again, I knew that. I was just checking."

"I wish you would stop doing that."

"Maybe one day I will." His eyes searched my face. "You'll

have to bear with me, son. I only recently got you back. I'm just assuring myself we're not going to lose you again."

"We?"

"Me, your family, A'Zahra." He paused. "Imala."

"Are those the members of the Tam intervention team?"

"Those are the people who care about you and don't want to see you fall again."

I clenched my jaw against a swell of emotion. I didn't have time for that now. "Thank you, sir. If that's the case, then I suppose I can give you permission to continue being annoying."

Kesyn grinned. "That's good, because I wasn't going to ask your permission. Why should I start now?" His grin vanished. "Think back over the dream, Tam. Are you sure it was on Aquas?"

I thought back over the dream.

"I was on an outcropping, almost a cliff," I said. "I'd never seen it or anything around me ever before."

"A cliff? Not a good choice for a dream that includes Sarad Nukpana."

"He pointed that out. I didn't pick the location or recognize it, but I have a feeling it was Aquas, or what my subconscious thinks Aquas will look like." I described it to him.

Kesyn nodded slowly. "Sounds about right."

"He said he was in my dream because Raine's dreamscape had been locked against him."

"Perhaps we should think about doing the same to yours."

"No, I want him there." I explained why—Sarad was lonely, bored, and had information that we needed. "If I can keep him talking, I'm counting on getting some of that information. He did tell me that the location of the Heart of Nidaar is in Rudra's book. Sarad said it's hidden, but it's there. So as little as I like going to sleep knowing that Sarad is lurking in my subconscious, I need to keep myself unwarded."

"I'm sure he threw that in just to keep you on the hook."

"I'm certain of it, but I'm equally certain that he's not lying. The next time he visits, I've thought of something I'd like to try."

"Such as?"

I told him.

Kesyn chuckled. "Got room for a third in that dream of yours? I'd like to watch that."

"If it works, I'll tell you all about it." I paused, remembering something. "Is the name Bricarda familiar to you?"

"No. Should it be?"

"That's the name of the mage you took on in the street the night before we left."

"The demon zombie queen."

"That's her. Sarad said that's the name she's using now. He said when you've lived as long as she has, you become bored using the same name. If you haven't heard of her, I thought I'd contact Mychael about it. Perhaps Sora Niabi, the chairman of the college's demonology department, might be able to enlighten us about her."

"Good idea."

"And if he is to be believed, Sarad did more than ask Agata to help him find the Saghred. He claimed he courted her, and in his words, 'expended some of my best seduction techniques on that young lady, promising her riches and sensual delights beyond her imagination.' Did you know anything about this?"

Kesyn's eyes hardened. "Not one word. Aggie always considered her personal life her own business. She kept her nose buried in her books, so I never worried about her that much. I believe that time has now passed. If Sarad is bored and looking to disrupt this expedition, Aggie as our gem mage would make an irresistible target. Raine didn't read the book and Sarad made an attempt to contact her. He could very well try the same with Aggie. The bastard could be infesting her sleep as we speak."

"I wouldn't put it past him. He found me, and he knows Agata is here." I hesitated. "Since you know her better, you go first and I'll back you up. Be careful of the rocks. She has a pile beside her bed."

Kesyn grinned, fully showing his fangs. "Who do you think chipped this fang?"

30

Once below, we were met with the sight of Talon picking the lock on Agata Azul's cabin door.

"Talon!" I shout-whispered.

He yelped and jumped straight up.

Kesyn caught him by the scruff of the neck before he landed in a heap on the floor. "What the hell are you doing?"

"She's having a nightmare," Talon said. "A bad one."

I swore and gripped the latch, intending to unlock it by magic, and if that didn't work…

The latch turned.

"It's not locked," I said.

Talon flashed a grin in the darkness, holding up a picklock. "I'd just finished picking it."

From inside the cabin, came the sounds of a struggle. Agata called out.

I flung the door open and ran inside.

The next thing I knew I was picked up and thrown out the door, across the passageway, and slammed into the far wall.

I dimly heard Kesyn say, "What happened to you letting me go first?" At least I think that was what he was saying. I had ringing ears to go with the spots in front of my eyes.

"Aggie, it's me!" he shouted.

The next instant, a glowing crystal the size of my fist hit the wall where my head had just been.

"Sir, I don't think she cares that it's you," Talon noted.

Agata Azul was sitting up on her cot, mostly fully dressed, covers on the floor, hair in disarray to put it mildly, clutching a blazingly bright crystal in each fist.

She was furious.

"Son of a bitch!" she shrieked.

Kesyn nodded. "Yep, that's Sarad, all right."

When Sarad didn't find me asleep, he went looking elsewhere for company.

I don't think he got what he expected.

Agata Azul's dream had taken her to the same place I had been.

A barren, desolate landscape.

With rocks.

Lots and lots of rocks that Agata made good use of.

Sarad Nukpana had not had a nice time.

I really would have liked to have been there.

"You think you brought enough crystals?" Kesyn was asking her. "It's a damned miracle you haven't sunk the ship."

The small cabin was filled with angrily pulsing crystals. They were on the floor, arranged around her cot, and filling what few shelves the cabin had.

Agata glared at him. In fact, that's about the only expression she had right now. Her crystals seemed to share their mistress's mood. Agata was sitting crosslegged on her cot, covers pulled up around her waist, seemingly as angry with us as she had been with Sarad.

Beneath that anger I detected fear.

"What did he say?" I asked quietly.

"He was most interested in the pendant," Agata said. The slice of the Heart of Nidaar was now hanging on its chain outside of her shirt, its sharp flickers indicating it liked seeing Sarad about as much as Agata had. I was glad I'd quickly turned my ring away from his view when we'd met in my dream.

Agata went on. "When I refused to give it to him, he attempted to take it." Her mouth curled in a smug and gratified little smile. "He paid for that—immediately and dearly."

A low growl came from the corner of the cabin.

Talon.

"That was when the three of you barged in," she said.

"That was it?" I asked.

Her color heightened slightly. "Yes, other than I think it's been a while since he's seen a woman. However, I could be mistaken, since that was usually how he behaved around me."

Talon growled again.

Kesyn rolled his eyes. "Boy, do you have something caught in your throat?"

Talon ignored him. "Isn't there anything we can do to stop him from coming after her again?"

"Yes," I told him. "And we will." I glanced around at the crystals. "Can any of these be used for reinforcing wards?"

"What do you think I was using them for?" Agata shot back.

"Were you warding your sleep?"

"And my body. He got through both. Why do you think I'm so pissed off?"

"We can fix that so it doesn't happen again."

"Would those be the same wards you used for yourself? I hear I wasn't the only one Sarad visited."

"I didn't ward my sleep," I told her. "And I don't plan to for the foreseeable future."

Talon was incredulous. "You want him in your head?"

"No, but I need information. Information that Sarad has."

"Well, if he gets grabby," Agata said, "don't be shy about using rocks. It worked for me. I hit him right in the eye." Her dark eyes shone with a wicked glint. "And other places."

Agata's wasn't the only sleep we would be warding. I didn't want Sarad Nukpana in Talon's head, either.

"Are you sure you haven't had any dream with Sarad Nukpana in it?" I asked him.

"I think that would qualify as a nightmare," Talon retorted, "and yes, I'm sure. I think I would have remembered that."

We were back in the captain's cabin while Kesyn helped Agata give her crystals an extra surprise for the next time Sarad came knocking. I knew he would; it was simply a matter of when.

"Then have you had any nightmares?" I asked.

"No."

"You're not dreaming at all? That means you're not sleeping well. You're going to need all the rest you can get before we get to—"

"I didn't say I wasn't dreaming," Talon snapped, color rising in his face. "I just that none of my dreams have had Sarad Nukpana in them."

"You don't have to get—"

Talon took a deep breath and blew it out. "I'm sorry. It's just that…"

I waited—and while I waited, I realized.

I'd already known that Talon liked Agata. That much had been obvious from the moment they'd met. Less than half an hour ago, he'd growled whenever she'd mentioned Sarad trying to lay hands on her. I might not be correct in my assessment, but then again, I thought the chances were pretty high that I was. So I did what I thought a father should do, and—pressing my lips together against a smile—waited some more, until it became painfully obvious that Talon was experiencing something else besides love for the first time.

A loss for words.

If one of us didn't speak up soon, we were going to be here all night.

It appeared that if any speaking was to be done, it would have to be by me. "You like Agata, don't you?"

"Yes…I think so."

"For someone who only thinks so, you've been rather obvious."

Talon groaned and dropped his face into his hands. "Am I making an idiot out of myself?"

"No."

"Are you sure?"

"Quite sure."

"But not absolutely."

"Talon."

He dropped his hands to his sides and slouched in the chair, head thrown back, eyes to the ceiling.

Oh, the drama.

"Do you think I stand a chance with her?" he asked, eyes still on the ceiling. "She's not that much older than I am, but she seems that way."

Honesty would be best here, at least I thought so. Talon had probably had as much experience falling in love as I had being a father. We were both treading deep, unfamiliar waters here.

"I met Agata less than two weeks ago," I told him. "Kesyn used to be her teacher, so he's known her for at least a few years. He might be able to give you a better answer than I could. Or maybe not. He just told me that she was the one who chipped his left fang."

Talon sat up and looked at me. "With one of those crystals of hers?"

I shrugged. "Or a rock that was close to hand. At the very least, he might be able to tell you what would make her throw a rock at you. If so, you should avoid doing that."

"Do you know anything about crystal magic?"

"Next to nothing."

Talon slouched again. "Damn."

"Sorry."

We grew some silence between us.

"I do know one thing," I said.

"Which is?"

"Stop trying to impress her and just be yourself—or at least a non-arrogant and less-impetuous version of yourself."

"In other words, it's past time for me to grow the hell up."

I glanced over to see my son grinning. I joined him.

"I don't even believe I'm grown up yet," I told him. "I think your grandmother is still awaiting that blessed event—for me and your uncle Nath. If you grow up before we do, your grandmother won't be able to withstand the shock—and neither will I."

31

The Lastani Islands were rocky and barren, and the only source of food was the seabird population, extremely large turtles, and the eggs they both laid. That being said, the birds' cliff-side nesting locations, and the turtles' poisonous spit and bile, ensured their continued survival. Few were desperate enough to expend that much strength on so meager a return, or take that much risk on a creature whose meat, depending on your poison tolerance, might or might not cause you to die in agony.

As a result, the seabirds and turtles thrived.

But the main island had two things that made it popular with vessels that ventured this far west—a harbor offering protection from storms and an easily accessible fresh water supply from natural cisterns that dotted the main island's interior. We planned to take full advantage of both for the next twenty-four hours.

Two ships would be on guard at the harbor mouth at all times while the third replenished its water supply and the crews had a little time on shore. The Nebians had fallen farther behind, but they were still there. We weren't about to let our guard down.

Talon squinted at the cloudless blue sky through his sunglasses. "Is there a chance we're going to get rained on anytime soon?"

"Maybe, but most likely not," I said.

"Damn."

"We've got enough water."

"Yeah, for drinking."

"I warned you that bath would probably be your last."

"You said probably, not definitely."

"Your nose is too sensitive, boy," Kesyn said, lowering himself to sit on one of the island's many flat rocks. "Soon enough we'll all stink so bad your nose will stop smelling it."

"From traumatic overload."

Kesyn shrugged. "Works just as well either way."

Talon stood and swayed on his feet. "What the hell? Okay, I'm on dry land. Why can't I walk straight?"

"It's called sea legs," Kesyn told him. "You finally have some. So now you're having trouble walking on something that's *not* moving."

"You're kidding, right?"

"Would I do that?"

"All the time." Talon looked to me.

"He's telling the truth," I said. "At least this time. In fact, you might want to get back on the ship as soon as you can. If you get too used to being on land, you might get sick again once we're back at sea."

Talon swore, creatively and extensively.

"Your choice, boy," Kesyn pointed to where Agata Azul was disembarking from a ship's launch. She had an empty sack over one shoulder. "Though if you want to stay off the ship for a while longer, Aggie said she was going to add to her rock collection. Why don't you go play pack mule for her?"

I don't think Talon heard the "pack mule" part of the sentence. He was off and running at "why don't you go play."

"Are you sure that was a good idea?" I asked him.

Kesyn lay back on the rock with a contented sigh. "Sure. He's a good kid. Basically. And Aggie has one hell of a throwing arm—and a right cross. At least she'll be fine. Whether he'll be fine is up to him." He sighed again. "You know, the sun isn't all that bad. In fact, I kind of like it."

I glanced up and squinted. Even with the darkest lenses in my glasses, the sun was still uncomfortably bright for me. If Aquas's wasteland was anything like my dream, I was going to be only slightly less than miserable. Those who would be going on to Nidaar with me had goggles for the trek across the desert to the mountains to keep both light and sand out of our eyes.

Our twelve firedrakes swooped and played near the cliffs, having been released to feed. Unlike the sentry dragons, firedrakes preferred a more diverse diet. Goblin sentry dragons—at least those native to the coastal regions—ate mostly seafood. The expedition's three sentry dragons were enjoying time out of the ships' holds and were presently basking on the rocks much like Kesyn was doing. Meanwhile, their stalls were being cleaned. The crews had drawn lots for that duty. Those who had drawn the short straws would be paid a substantial bonus.

The sentry dragons were sunbathing.

Not the firedrakes.

They were happily hunting.

They'd earned it.

At the beginning of each watch since we'd left Regor, a firedrake had been released every hour to check the surrounding seas for pursuit or intercepting ships—in addition to checking the position of the two Nebian vessels. Each drake wore a harness equipped with a spy crystal that would send real-time images back to the ship it had been released from. With four firedrakes per ship and a dozen total, each drake would be released twice a day, perfect for exercise and their feeding schedule. We had food for them on board, but if a drake spotted prey, they would take it. If something under the water spotted them and determined them to be prey, the drakes were more than capable of convincing them otherwise. They'd also quickly cleaned the ships of rats.

While we couldn't reach the thousands of seabird nests, our firedrakes had no such problem. They probably liked fish well enough, but the eggs and the birds were a welcome treat. Thankfully there were plenty of seabirds, and drakes had enough sense not to gorge themselves. In the wild, a drake that couldn't outmaneuver drakes from a rival flock when fighting for mates or territory didn't live very long. When they were full, they stopped eating.

Unfortunately, a few of them had discovered the turtle nests.

I quickly went to where Calik was filing Sapphira's claws while she dozed. I was careful to stay out of the sentry dragon's torching range. I took a seat on the rocky beach near Calik and pointed out the adventuresome diners.

"Not a problem," Calik told me. "Drakes and dragons can eat most anything. If you breathe fire and belch sulfur-scented gas, a little turtle toxin is just seasoning. They'll be fine."

Phaelan was sidling over to where we were, trying to give Sapphira a wide berth. The deep blue dragon opened one reptilian-pupiled eye into a slit and watched him. Phaelan saw and sidled faster.

"Don't worry, Captain Benares. She won't fry you," Calik said. "I've told her not to. She always does as told." He winked at me. "Most of the time."

Phaelan saw the wink and chose to ignore it. "The two drakes that went out to have a look at the Nebian ships just came back."

I sat up. "And?"

"They're still there, about five miles out."

Both Phaelan and Calik were looking at me.

Kesyn had wandered over. "That's getting to be annoying."

"As much as I'd like to, we can't simply blow two ships out of the water just for following us," I told them.

"Why not?" Phaelan asked. "And don't give me that 'I'm the king's representative' crap. They're not tailing us because they want to make friends. They're waiting for an opportunity—or a signal from someone."

"We're sitting on a beach and our dragons are asleep." Calik lifted one of Sapphira's newly manicured claws, released it, and it fell limply to the sand. That was a seriously relaxed dragon.

I nodded. "I know. I've been giving it a lot of thought. They know we're going to Aquas, and we can't risk them following us the rest of the way there. I'll be taking my battle mages with me when we go inland, which will leave our ships magically defenseless. The mages on the Nebian ships aren't Khrynsani. They're worse, which until now I didn't believe was possible."

"What are the chances they're not from around here?" Calik asked.

Meaning they were part of the off-world invaders. We had all been thinking it, but no one really wanted to say it.

"Their magic is unlike anything I have ever sensed," I said. "Kesyn?"

"Slimiest magic I've ever felt. Even the blackest Khrynsani magic seems cleaner."

"What do Gwyn and Gavyn have to say?" I asked Phaelan.

"They're all in favor of clearing our wake. We've got enough trouble ahead of us; we don't need it creeping up behind us, too. There are smaller islands on our way once we leave here."

"You're suggesting an ambush."

"Strongly suggesting."

"We'd need to completely conceal the ships," I said. "Douse all signs of life and magic, but even that won't be enough. We'll need to conjure a realistic projection."

"Fake ships?" Phaelan asked.

I nodded. "Just to give them something to chase, or at the very least distract them. It'll be close. I'm sure they're expecting something."

Unless they had a surprise for us first.

32

Imala needed to know what we were about to do, as did Mychael Eiliesor. Destroying two Nebian ships who had yet to fire on us was essentially a declaration of war. It didn't matter how many alien dark mages there were on board.

Once again, I was about to be at the center of an inter-kingdom incident. Though this time, I'd be taking it one step further.

I'd be starting a war.

It was a decision I had to make on my own—and right now.

The *Raven* and *Sea Wolf* had each gone to shore and restocked their water supplies.

I had tried to contact Regor and the Isle of Mid to obtain official sanction for what I was about to do.

My attempts had been solidly blocked.

Not just blocked, slammed down—by the mages on the Nebian ships.

All three of our ships were flying Conclave Guardian flags. Diplomatically speaking, we were untouchable. I didn't need to ask what Justinius Valerian would do. He was the supreme head of the Conclave of Sorcerers, the commander in chief of the Conclave Guardians, and the most powerful—and vicious, if pushed—mage in the Seven Kingdoms.

We'd just been on the receiving end of a sucker punch.

Justinius Valerian wasn't one to turn the other cheek.

"So you feel better now about blowing them out of the water?" Phaelan asked cheerfully.

"I'm positively enthusiastic about it," I said. "We're too close to Aquas to let them follow us any longer. In magespeak, what they just did by preventing us from contacting the mainland was firing a cannonball across our deck."

Phaelan's grinned fiercely. "Now that's something I know how to respond to. And while I like a straight-up fight as much as the next pirate, I value my fleet over fun. Let's set us up an ambush."

If there were multiple angles to a plan—and multiple scenarios that could go wrong—I wanted them covered. Decisive action had its place and was all well and good, but judicious caution had kept me standing on top of the ground, rather than lying in a crypt beneath it. And I had no plans to go underground—or underwater—any time soon.

The Nebian ships had held their position on our southeastern horizon until our three ships emerged from the harbor close to sundown. The setting sun was in our eyes, but it was also in theirs. A good wind took us quickly to the last cluster of small, mountainous islands before we would again be in the open sea. We sailed just past the last one and turned sharply north, letting the island's mountains act as a natural windbreak to slow us down. Phaelan expertly timed our arrival as the Nebians had begun gaining on us. When the Nebian ships cleared the last island, we would be waiting for them.

They never arrived.

"They should be here by now," I murmured to myself.

"Don't you think I know that?" Phaelan snapped from beside me.

I didn't take Phaelan personally. We were all tense.

I ran down the stairs to the main deck and over to the open hold doors. All three ships had left their holds open. The ladies had a big part to play in tonight's performance.

"Calik?" I called down, loud enough to be heard, but not loud enough to carry across the water.

"Sir?" Calik said from below.

"Get a drake aloft. We need to see what's keeping our guests."

We had turned to the north after passing the last island. The two Nebian ships had turned to the south and were holding their positions as well as they could. They were out of our cannon range, going no farther south, but coming no closer to where we were concealed.

They knew we were here, and they were waiting.

"What the hell are they doing?" Talon asked for all of us.

I allowed myself a moment of anger and then focused on what I felt, had been feeling, but had dismissed in favor of the threat I could see.

The Nebian ships had no intention of attacking us, at least not directly. An attack was imminent, but it wasn't coming from any direction on the compass.

It was coming from below.

I ran to the rail and leaned over, staring down into the depths.

And saw a ship.

It wasn't a reflection of the *Kraken* cast by her lanterns. It was the masts of a ship beneath the surface, sailing directly under us on the currents, getting clear of the *Kraken*.

Once it was clear…

I took the stairs to the quarterdeck in two strides. "We've got demons." I kept my voice down for Phaelan's ears only.

Fortunately, the elf was facing toward the Nebian ships as they drifted into view just past the last island, but still out of cannon range. Our crew was rushing to battle stations, focused on their duty. That was good, because the color drained from their captain's face.

"Demons? On my ship?"

"Not yet, but they're coming—from below."

"The hold?"

"The water. Under the water."

"Sea monsters?"

The shouts came simultaneously, from fore and aft. Moments later, shouts rang out from the *Raven* and *Sea Wolf*.

Masts and sails erupted from beneath the waves, as a ship rose from the depths.

A red glow appeared beneath the surface off the starboard

side, as a second mast broke the surface, followed by rotten sails, both black in the last rays of the setting sun. Twilight, the edge of darkness, when things that didn't belong here could break through into the realm of the living.

"Ghost ships!" came the scream from aloft. And it was a scream, born of disbelief and terror.

The crews of all three ships went deathly silent as two ships, black of sail and wood, the decks and yardarms glittering with points of blood red light, surged to the surface, water sloughing off the decks as they settled on the waves. It took a few seconds for me to realize that what I was seeing weren't lights.

They were eyes.

The eyes of countless demons of every size, gleaming in eager anticipation as they scurried across the deck and up the masts. Still others were launching themselves with bat-like wings onto the yardarms. All with one purpose—to board and take our ships. There would be no prisoners taken, no mercy shown.

We wouldn't be captives.

We would be food.

The demons were aloft, but what stood silently on the decks were worse than demons. They were what any man or woman who went to sea feared above all else.

A ship of the dead.

A ship of the damned.

Given life, animated, in this place and at this time by dark demonic purpose.

The Nebian ships never had any intention of fighting us. The alien mages had conjured demons and the dead to do their fighting for them. These weren't translucent phantoms. They may not have had blood, but they had flesh. Flesh that had been long dead. We couldn't kill what was already dead. But I knew these dead could kill us.

Some of the demons looked all too familiar.

Demonic zombies, courtesy of Bricarda, brimstone-scented mage, and lady friend and fiend of Sarad Nukpana.

The demonic vessels had risen between us and the *Raven* and *Sea Wolf*—their intended victims.

Our slice of hell didn't arise out of the depths, it sailed out of a sudden manifestation of mist between us and the island.

The *Wraith.*

No.

A growl started to build low in my chest and I let it. My lips peeled back from my fangs and the growl became a snarl and then a full-throated, enraged roar.

I wasn't the only one.

Whoever had committed this blasphemy had made a very bad mistake.

Shock, fear, and raw agony showed on the faces of the goblins with me on the deck of the *Kraken*. The blackest magic was at work here. The appearances of the dead on the ghost ship's deck were those of the men and women they had served with. To be attacked by their closest friends went beyond desecration. I swore by all I held dear that whoever was responsible would pay with their lives and souls. There would be nothing left.

"They're not real," I called out, using a touch of power to amplify my voice to carry throughout the *Kraken* and across the water to the *Raven* and *Sea Wolf.* The elven crews didn't count the phantoms as friends, but they would have been afraid of a ghost ship of dead goblins regardless.

Jash tightly gripped his crossbow. "They could be constructs."

"I know."

"What the hell is a construct?" Phaelan's voice was tight, but that was the only indication that what he was seeing was probably scaring him to death. I was impressed. This was a man who'd been ready to jump out of a second-story window rather than risk being in the same room with just one reanimated corpse.

"A construct is a conjured re-creation of a living being," I told him. "Given enough power behind them, they can function just as they did while alive."

"Meaning those things could kill us."

"Yes."

"But we can kill them, right?"

"If the mages who created that are strong enough, you could kill the constructs, but they would come right back."

"That is not what I wanted to hear."

"That wasn't the answer I wanted to give you."

If they were solid enough, we would have to kill them. To the goblins on the *Kraken,* it would be like losing their friends twice: once by explosion, again by their own hands. If they were recurring constructs, the goblins on the *Kraken* would have to kill their friends again and again. This was premeditated. Those who had done this had also been responsible for the destruction of the *Wraith.* They would have known who had been on board. Someone had been watching and recording before the explosion, gathering the images of those who had been about to die. They had a backup plan in place in case the expedition could continue without the *Wraith* and half her crew.

The Khrynsani had been involved.

In my dream, Sarad had said: "The terror's in the details, details you will begin experiencing soon. I wouldn't want to ruin the surprise."

Somehow, Sarad Nukpana had been involved. If he valued what was left of his life, he would stay in the Lower Hells. I wouldn't use black magic or a bull demon to extinguish his miserable life.

I would use my bare hands.

The mages on the Nebian frigates were controlling all of this. Those ships wouldn't be coming any closer. They didn't need to. They only needed to be within sight of the construct they had created. I'd never heard of a Khrynsani mage who could manage constructs on this scale, enabling each creation to act independently. The work and craft involved was staggering.

The magic couldn't possibly be of this world.

One of the goblin phantoms was manning a deck cannon aimed at our mainmast.

Phaelan stood straight. "Mr. Lucan?" he called.

"Sir!"

"Ready a broadside. On my order."

"Aye, Captain."

I couldn't kill one of my countrymen in cold blood, but these weren't my countrymen. They were images, re-creations of the living, nothing more.

"Give me the bow," I told Jash.

"But—"

"You can't do this. It should be me."

Jash understood and handed me the crossbow. I was the leader of this expedition. If we had to fight the constructs of the *Wraith*'s dead crew, the responsibility or blame for that first kill to determine exactly how solid they were needed to fall squarely on my shoulders.

Phaelan stood still, waiting. A quick glance at me said he was holding the command to fire only for the sake of his new goblin crew members.

The phantom gunner lowered a glowing slow match to the cannon's touch hole.

I snapped the bow to my shoulder and fired.

The bolt took him squarely in the chest.

An eldritch scream echoed across the distance between the ships. The gunner's image flickered and vanished. The relief from the goblins around me was palpable. They were constructs. They might have looked like their dead friends, but they weren't them.

We waited.

We didn't have to wait long.

With another flicker, the gunner reappeared and smiled…

…and fired the cannon.

"Fire!" Phaelan screamed.

A broadside from the *Kraken* tore into the side of the *Wraith*.

The cannonball from the *Wraith* took a chunk out of the foredeck railing.

They didn't want to destroy our ship.

They wanted to board us.

How can you fight opponents who can regenerate as soon as you kill them?

You kill the mages maintaining and regenerating the construct.

We had to get to those Nebian ships.

Phaelan had drawn a wicked, curved sabre, prepared to join his crew in repelling boarders. "Can you stop this?" he shouted.

"Yes." I ran toward midship—and the hold.

33

Calik Bakari had Sapphira saddled and ready to join the fight.

"I need her," I said quickly. "They're constructs. Kill them and they come back. The mages controlling those things are—"

Calik flashed a fierce grin in realization. "On those Nebian frigates. Say no more, I'm on it. A couple of grenades and they'll lose control of everything, including their own—"

"You're good, Calik. The best. But those mages are protected. The Nebians won't leave any survivors. They can't risk it."

Calik stood back with a flourish, revealing a double saddle strapped to Sapphira's back. "While you work your magic from the backseat, me and Saffie will keep you out of harm's way. She'll toast 'em." He grinned broadly and tossed a grenade in his hand. "And I'll roast 'em."

I vaulted into the saddle. "Let's do it."

I'd planned to signal Bane and Dasant as soon as we were airborne, but it wasn't necessary.

As Sapphira rose farther above the *Kraken* with each beat of her powerful wings, Bane flying with Amaranth and her pilot had already cleared the *Raven*'s mainmast. Dasant with Mithryn and her pilot were emerging from the *Sea Wolf*'s hold.

All three dragons had been shielded against attack, magical and mundane.

Phaelan and the crew of the *Kraken* were successfully keeping the *Wraith* from closing to grappling hook and boarding distance. Kesyn and Talon were working together to spread a ward net to keep the constructs from swinging over from the *Wraith* into our rigging. Agata had armed herself with crystals glowing even a brighter red than the demons' eyes. I didn't know what those crystals could do, but I suspected the constructs weren't going to like it.

Until we could take out those mages, the crew of the *Kraken* was on their own against the *Wraith* and her goblin phantoms. The *Raven* and *Sea Wolf* were fully occupied with the two ships full of the dead and demons.

If there were any mages left on the two Nebian ships who weren't directly involved in maintaining and controlling the three ghost ships, they weren't making themselves known. We'd reached the halfway point between our ships and theirs, and I sensed no attack preparations. Though I'd believe that when nothing or no one tried to blast us from the sky.

Regardless of what was waiting for us, our ships didn't have time for us to feel out their defenses.

We attacked.

"Hold on to your crystal balls," Calik shouted before he sent Sapphira into a dive.

The dragon roared in sheer joy—right before she raked the upper sails with a column of blue fire. Calik timed his grenade drop for when we were directly over the Nebian's midship.

Seconds later, a gratifying amount of the ship's deck exploded upward.

So much for the ship being shielded.

Calik whooped and sent Sapphira sharply to the side, avoiding the resulting shrapnel.

I readied a fireball and hurled it down toward the ship's stern and the bank of windows that indicated the captain's quarters. I couldn't imagine a cabal of Khrynsani mages huddling in a dank hold to conduct their dark work. As glass and timber exploded outward, I glanced back at the *Kraken* and *Wraith*.

The *Wraith* and the ghost ships were still there.

Dammit.

Bane saw what had not happened and readied a fireball in each hand, his dragon's pilot going into a dive on the second ship.

The Nebians in the second ship were ready for them.

Black-hooded mages appeared in a circle around the Nebian ship's mainmast, the mast forming the nexus of spell maintaining the constructs and controlling the demons.

Amaranth must have sensed the incoming strike and banked sharply to the left, but the blinding column of red light took the dragon in the right side and her pilot and Bane in the right legs. Screams rent the air as the dragon went into a spin, leveling out at the last moment before crashing into the sea. Amaranth and her pilot's reflexes were all that had saved them from being roasted alive.

Through Bane's best shields.

It was as if they hadn't even existed.

They were hurt, badly.

And out of the fight.

Discharging that spell had given me a moment's glimpse of the top of the Nebian ship's mast, glowing with the same red light as the *Wraith.*

They were using the mast as a signaling device, linking the mages to the construct they'd created.

Break the mast, break the spell, destroy the ship.

I fully intended to do all three—especially the last one. The Nebians weren't the only ones who didn't want word of what was happening here to get back to the Seven Kingdoms, and to the Conclave and the Guardians in particular.

I didn't want the Nebians and the Khrynsani to know that they'd failed.

And fail they would.

I saw precisely how I could make it happen.

"Get close to Dasant," I said to Calik, nearly having to yell over the wind.

Calik turned Sapphira to intercept Dasant's dragon. When Dasant had us in his direct line of sight, I communicated my plan in the hand signals we knew all too well. Even at that distance, I saw Dasant's eyes widen as I gestured.

That made two of us. I couldn't believe what I was about to do, either.

I knew Bane would give us what support he could, but I wasn't going to count on it.

Dragons attacked from the air, usually from above.

The mast was protected and so were the mages and the ship, from the top of the mast to the waterline.

We were at sea, with wind and waves.

As the ship moved, so did the waterline.

The mages' shield didn't. It couldn't. Manifesting and controlling the constructs that were the *Wraith* and its dead crew took all of their power and concentration.

As a result, the shield was like a glass dome over the ship, rigid, inflexible.

Sentry dragons were very flexible.

We would strike in that instant when the ship rolled with the waves, exposing a sliver of the ship's hull.

Dasant would execute his attack run from port near the bow. I would strike from starboard near the stern. We would bank sharply toward open water, staying below the ship's guns to get clear.

I quickly told Calik the plan.

I had never seen such an evil grin. He liked it. He liked it a lot.

"So, how low can she go?" I asked.

"Your legs strapped in?"

"Yeah."

"Good. Those fancy boots of yours might get wet."

Calik and the other pilot sent the dragons into a broad swoop, then a dive from farther out than would be needed for a conventional attack run, but vital for gathering speed.

Sapphira leveled out mere inches above the waves, her

wings tightly tucked, her body like a fire-breathing arrow aimed directly at the Nebians' waterline. We had to be far enough away to maintain speed, close enough to be targets for the Nebians' guns. Only I could see the gap between water and the shield where the hull was exposed. Sapphira would fire on my signal. Then Calik would rein her sharply up and to the stern, toward open water. Mithryn's pilot would bank her toward the bow. The goal was to avoid the mages' shield and the destruction caused by each other.

At least that was the plan.

It sounded great in theory, brazen, suicidal even.

Brazen if we lived. Suicidal—and stupid—if we didn't.

I summoned fireballs to supplement Sapphira's flame. She was aiming at the waterline. I would target just below the surface. Water extinguished fire, even a dragon's. Mine wasn't normal fire; it was formed and propelled by magic. Dasant and I could go under the mages' shield and right through the hull of the Nebian vessel. The pilots would make any minute adjustments to our mounts to keep us on target and out of the water. However, Calik couldn't do anything about the spray sent up by the force of Sapphira's bulk and speed flying over the water.

One bobble, one wingtip in the water, could send us into a deadly, neck-breaking tumble, where we'd be easy prey for the Nebians' guns.

Calik was nearly horizontal in the saddle, lying flat against Sapphira's neck. I did the same as much as possible, but instead of Sapphira's neck, my cheek rested against the saddle bow, giving me an angled view around Calik without affecting our wind resistance.

I knew I might die in the next few seconds, but I'd never felt more alive.

I held my hands down and out of sight, relying on my harness to stay in the saddle, keeping the fireballs out of the sight of the shouting and screaming Nebians on the deck until the last instant. I felt Sapphira's sides expand against my legs, inhaling in preparation to breathe fire. I raised my arms slightly, my fists holding the concentrated red fire ready to launch.

If I miscalculated, Sapphira's fire would hit the shield and the backblast would consume us all.

My field of vision narrowed, focusing on the section of the hull most likely to clear the water for the best exposure, but before Sapphira had to peel away or crash into the side of the ship.

"Fahrat!" I screamed. *Fire.*

Sapphira fired, I launched, Calik veered us all away.

Explosions punched holes in the waterline of the Nebian ship.

The plan had been for Sapphira to half extend her wings to get enough leverage and wind to stay below the ship's railing. A similar maneuver had been part of her training.

Sapphira had other ideas.

I didn't know if it was that she'd seen her sister struck by the mages' spell, or whether it was the heat of battle, pure stubbornness, or all of the above.

Sapphira fought the bridle, ignored Calik's commands, and went for the mast that was no longer protected by a shield. Having a ship blown out from beneath you would break the most focused mage's concentration.

The power channeled through that mast had hurt her sister. Sapphira was determined to hurt that mast.

As she soared up its length, Sapphira snapped her massive tail like a whip, breaking the mainmast in half as the ship exploded.

"Must have hit the powder room," Calik shouted as Sapphira allowed herself to be brought back under control.

Just before the ship exploded, I got a good look at the faces of the alien mages. Taller than the human Nebian sailors by at least a foot, they had dark green faces, *scaled* dark green faces.

One face wasn't green or scaled. It was pale gray and beautiful. A goblin. I recognized the cloak and hood.

Bricarda.

Her hood fell back as she smiled up at me and waved, then she vanished just as she had in the street two blocks from my home—a spilt second before the Nebian ship exploded.

"When the second ship blew, the *Wraith* and the two demon ships disappeared," Phaelan was saying. "Even a cannonball that was headed straight for our mainmast vanished into thin air."

Talon was having his arm wrapped by the ship's doctor. It was a relatively minor injury, so he had waited until others with worse injuries had been treated. One of those had been Agata. Talon had insisted that she go before him. She refused because Talon's injury was worse. He re-insisted. Agata refused his re-insistence. Then they argued until Kesyn stepped in, took charge, and got them both patched up.

"He did a fine job," Phaelan was saying. "You would have been proud." He paused and thought. "Or maybe pissed. Proud and pissed."

I smiled. "I often experience that with him. What did he do?"

"Put himself and his blades in front of four of my wounded crew. Most of the goblins have some fighting magic to go with their blade work. My elves don't. Maybe I need to think about recruiting some battle mages."

"Present and possible future situations considered, I think that would be a good idea. Markus Sevelien is Imala's equivalent in elven intelligence. I'm sure he'd be able to make some recommendations and introductions."

Phaelan glanced back at Talon. "He's a brave young man. Refused to back down. I didn't want to leave him on his own, but I didn't have a choice. We were overrun."

"Casualties?"

Phaelan scowled. "Ten. Which is ten too many considering we were fighting magic replicas of dead men."

"You said ten," I said quietly, seeing the bodies covered by tarps. Six had pale skin. The other four had gray. "Not six elves and four goblins."

"I did, didn't I?" he said, looking out over the main deck at the crew clearing the debris and making repairs. "They're not elves or goblins now; they're my crew, and they will be for as long as this voyage lasts."

From his tone, Phaelan Benares sounded as if he wouldn't mind making the arrangement permanent.

"Your teacher deflected a yardarm blasted over from the *Wraith* that would've killed at least half a dozen more,"

Phaelan continued. "Magic killed ten of my crew, but it saved far more."

"So you're saying magic isn't the bane of your existence any longer?"

"Let's just say that I'm reserving judgment."

34

Once the two Nebian ships were destroyed, communication was restored, and I contacted Regor and the Isle of Mid with a report of what had happened.

Not surprisingly, the Nebians had not lodged a complaint or filed charges against us with the Conclave. Either they knew of their ships' destruction and chose to remain silent, since they had been the aggressor, or we had taken out the ships before they could send a distress signal.

Hopefully, this meant the only danger would come from ahead of us in Aquas, but we would keep an eye out for pursuers—by sea, air, or from beneath the water.

The last option was what was keeping all of us on edge.

We were slightly past the halfway point of the voyage.

If the weather held, another two weeks would put us on the shores of Aquas.

I debated attempting to unlock Rudra Muralin's book again, but instead I chose what I hoped would be a more enjoyable and satisfying option—a nap. After what I'd done, my body could use the rest, but that wouldn't be the enjoyable or satisfying part.

That part would come when Sarad Nukpana put in another appearance in my dreams and I could get my hands around his neck.

I've always been a patient man, but there was nothing like the sensation of immediate gratification.

My dream's location was the same as last time. Once again, Sarad Nukpana was waiting for me.

And I was ready for him.

This was my dream and I took charge of it.

The next instant had me slamming Sarad onto the rocky ground with my hands around his throat.

No demons battling in our stead, no magic, just us.

Now this was more like it.

If I needed any more proof that somehow, some form of Sarad Nukpana was wreaking havoc in the dreamscape, I had it now. Sarad Nukpana had a black eye, courtesy of Agata Azul and her rocks.

Though right now Sarad wasn't choking.

He was laughing.

I wanted to tighten my grip, snap his neck, and permanently

wipe that smirk off his face, but curiosity as to why he was laughing won out.

I could always resume choking him later.

"I had nothing to do with that attack," he managed. "But that doesn't mean I can't admire the artistry."

My fists twitched with the need to add substantially to the Agata-inflicted black eye. "Artistry?" I snarled. "Men and women died."

"As we will all do eventually. They gave their lives in defense of their ship and comrades in arms. Isn't that the very definition of a good death? You can't tell me you actually want to die in your sleep of old age."

I shoved him away from me and bared my teeth in a ferocious smile. "No, but I'd love for *you* to die in my sleep."

Sarad pulled himself up against a rock and leaned back. "I've discovered through experience that it's impossible to die in a dream—or to kill another. Otherwise, I assure you, my dear Tamnais, I would have made the attempt. I lost nothing in letting you have a go at me. Do you feel better now? Or do you still have additional barbarism to get out of your system?"

"If you didn't personally oversee those mages, that doesn't mean you didn't know about it—or your lady friend, Bricarda."

"I would hardly describe Bricarda as a friend, more like a shapely jailer." He smiled, slow and lascivious. "With certain benefits. I can honestly say that Hell hasn't been all that hellish."

"If I had known that, I would have arranged to have had you taken somewhere else."

"And miss out on getting a chance to choke me? Not to

mention the satisfaction of again having an adversary worthy of your intellect and skill. I have made your life infinitely more exciting. Admit it, you've been bored since I've been gone. I can't imagine how tedious your workday in the palace must be. Attempting to discover who the traitors are, and when you find them, agonizing over their fates."

"Actually, not only have I not agonized over their fates, I haven't even lost sleep over it. They signed their death warrants when they allied themselves with you."

"Death warrants?" Sarad gasped in mock horror. "You don't mean to tell me that you and Imala have been executing people?"

"Imprisonment merely gives them the opportunity to escape. The risk is too great. There is no redemption for these people. Once we're convinced of their guilt, yes, there have been executions. Unfortunately, there will be many more."

"Why Tamnais, I have misjudged you. Perhaps there is hope for you yet."

"Yes, there is hope for me. Unlike you, I derive no pleasure from my actions. They are merely unavoidable. It's the price that must be paid to ensure peace and the survival of the goblin people."

"It will be interesting to see how long your peace lasts. You will find that your beloved goblin people bore easily. There is no challenge in peace, no us versus them, no hunting your enemies in the dark of night. Quite frankly, you've taken away our collective reason to live."

"If you don't wish to go on living, I would be the last person to attempt or even want to stop you."

"I'm sorry, but that decision is not in your hands." He flashed a smile. "At least not here and not now."

"I can wait. I'm certain that you'll con or bribe your way out of Hell eventually." I gave him a smile of my own. "And when that happens, I'll be waiting for you." I leaned back against what appeared to be a petrified tree and crossed my arms over my chest.

My ring glinted in the light, just as I hoped it would.

In my first dream, when Sarad put in an appearance, I'd quickly turned the stone and its dragon setting around and kept my fingers wrapped around it. This time, I make sure the ring was clearly visible.

Sarad's dark eyes glittered in raw avarice when he saw it. "A piece of the Heart of Nidaar. Agata refused to let me examine hers."

I gestured toward his black eye. "So I heard. When a lady says 'no' that is precisely what she means. Get used to disappointment."

"So where were they? I tore your house apart searching for them."

"They were kept safe. And the damage to my home is merely another in the long list of payments that you owe me. Payments I fully intend to collect."

"Get in line, Tamnais."

"If there is a line, I'll be the first one in it."

Sarad's lips curled in a sly smile. "I still say there is hope for you. I was not surprised that Bricarda failed in her attempt to secure Agata's services. I warned her about you. Once again you arrived in time to protect a fair maiden. My mother knows about the ring and pendant, and I would imagine she is aware of Agata as well. Your work there may have just begun. Fun times ahead for all of us."

"Speaking of your mother, you said Sandrina intended to assassinate you."

Sarad hesitated before answering, not sure of my intent. "Yes."

I furrowed my brow. "Then her stealing your body truly doesn't make any sense."

"She stole my what?"

"Your body. The one you regenerated and then abandoned in order to possess me. It was preserved in a crystal coffin and locked in a tower in the Guardians' citadel. Sathrik threatened to go to war to get it back, but I assume by that time you were content to remain in the newly dead body of your Uncle Janos."

I was certain Sarad heard me talking; however, my words were merely background noise to his racing thoughts.

"If your mother wants you dead," I mused, "what could she possibly want with your dead and magically preserved body?"

To say that Sarad had had bad luck as far as keeping a body was concerned was a vast understatement.

The body Sarad had been born with had been vaporized when he'd been consumed by the Saghred. When his soul escaped the Saghred, he had no body for his soul to call home. Sarad resorted to the cha'nescu, a ritual in which he fed on the living, absorbing their souls and life forces to regenerate his body. Once he had taken enough, he became corporeal again. Sarad lost that body when he abandoned it to possess mine. Raine shooting me through the heart killed my body and forced Sarad's soul out. He fled into the newly dead body of his uncle, Janos Ghalfari. Later, after he had stolen the

Saghred, his contact with the stone gave him the power to alter Janos's body and features into his own.

"You sent me to Hell," Sarad was saying, "but I still have my body. What could Mother possibly be up to?"

"She left a note for Raine on top of your glass coffin. It said: 'You destroyed my world. I will destroy yours.'"

"I could see where destroying me would destroy my mother's world. Though it would not be because she'd lost her beloved son. Mother's great gift has always been her ability to use men. Now *your* mother has a talent worth having. She is a true artist. She did an exceptional job killing Sathrik Mal'Salin and opening up the way for me to the goblin throne. She even took out Sathrik's annoyingly persistent chief bodyguard in the process. One bolt, two birds. When you next see her please convey my deepest and most sincere gratitude. My mother, on the other hand, was terribly disappointed when she discovered that she could not bend me to her will. She put on a convincing act, but I'm quite sure she was delighted to see that bull demon carrying me off into the Lower Hells."

"I wouldn't know; I was busy staying alive at the time. I do know that Raine and Mychael found tears on the lid of your coffin along with the note."

Sarad laughed. "Are you sure it wasn't spit?"

"I didn't see it myself."

"I can assure you, my dear Tamnais, my mother has no interest in seeing me freed. She cannot control the Khrynsani. Not due to any lack of iron will. Khrynsani law forbids it. We're strictly a boys-only club. Not to mention my inner circle hates Mother nearly as much as I do."

"Hmm, that's interesting considering who your mother went to Timurus with."

Sarad went utterly still. "Timurus?"

"That was where you told your inner circle to go should the temple ever fall, wasn't it?"

"Yes, but Mother was never told that."

"Have you ever found out about plans you weren't included in?" I asked. "Because I have. Many times."

"Point taken."

"Apparently things didn't go exactly as planned while there." I told him about the unsuccessful Rak'kari infestation, and the new friends Sandrina and Sarad's unfaithful inner circle made while on the alien world.

"For some unknown reason, she's allied herself and the remains of your Khrynsani with the alien invader who stripped Timurus of life about seven hundred years ago. That isn't quite what you had in mind for our world, was it? If the invaders devour everyone, who would you have left to rule, subjugate, and oppress?"

Sarad leapt to his feet and began pacing. "The Sythsaurians? She's mad, completely mad. Nothing else explains why she would do this."

And our potential invaders now had a name.

"The note explained it quite well," I said.

Sarad flicked my words away with a negligent wave of his hand. "Yes, yes. Raine destroyed Sandrina's world, now Sandrina will destroy hers. I hardly think I am, was, or ever will be my mother's world."

"It could also have meant we destroyed her chance at power, even if that power would have been behind the throne."

"Perhaps. But why did she steal my body? I don't think I like that. I don't like it at all. I have committed gruesome acts during my life, but I have never stolen a dead body."

"No, you prefer to steal live ones, suck out that life, and use it to regenerate your own body. Or simply leave your body to possess another, like a hermit crab claiming a new shell."

Sarad sighed. "You're not going to let that go, are you?"

"I think I'm more than entitled to hold a grudge, and it sounds as if your mother feels the same way. If she can't have the Seven Kingdoms, then no one will. She'll see them destroyed first." I pushed away from the tree and strolled toward Sarad. "Some of the attackers on those ghost ships looked familiar. They were astonishingly similar to the demons Bricarda sent after me and Agata. In fact, I got a good look at these Sythsaurians. They're tall, dark, and reptilian. Guess who was among them, helping them manifest and power the constructs of those ships and crews? Your lady friend Bricarda. She even smiled and waved at me, and unfortunately vanished right before the deck exploded beneath her feet, but I'm certain I'll get another chance."

Sarad spat an impressive stream of profanity.

"I wonder if Bricarda has met your mother," I continued. "Bricarda was in Regor and knew to go after me and Agata. Now she worked with the Sythsaurian sorcerers to destroy our fleet. I think Sandrina has another ally. You might want to ask Bricarda about it next time you see her."

Sarad's hard eyes glittered dangerously. "My mother seeks to control my Khrynsani by having an imposter possess my body and assume my place, someone she can control."

"Sounds similar to what you did to me. Payback is a bitch, isn't it?" I purred.

Sarad's expression was pure murder. "And that bitch's name is Sandrina Ghalfari. By the way, where you are going…"

"Yes?"

"When Kansbar arrived on Aquas, he discovered a green paradise. What is it now?"

"Barren wasteland."

"It makes you wonder, doesn't it? It makes you wonder what my clumsy predecessors did with the Heart of Nidaar to cause it. Because they did cause it. Do you still want to control the Heart, Tamnais? If so, you should really be more careful what you wish for."

35

"My nap was every bit as satisfying as I thought it would be," I told Kesyn.

I then filled him in on what I'd discovered.

Kesyn made a face. "Sythsaurians? Never heard of them."

"Me, either."

"Hell, I can barely say it."

"Tricky pronunciation aside," I said, "there are probably professors in the Conclave's college who have heard of them. I'll contact the Isle of Mid right after I talk to Denita Enric. If Sarad was familiar with these things, the Khrynsani temple library probably has something on them. We need all the information we can get and we needed it yesterday." I gestured overhead. "Any sign of more Nebians—or demons?"

"Not a peep. All quiet on all horizons."

"Good. Even more disturbing than the Sythsaurians is the last thing Sarad told me. Kansbar described the land between the coast and Nidaar as being green and lush with rivers and lakes. Now it's nothing but barren rock and desert."

"Yes?"

"Sarad said the Khrynsani not only found the city of Nidaar, they gained access to the Heart and used it. What happened to the land was the result."

Kesyn whistled. "Like when Rudra used the Saghred and created the Great Rift in northern Rheskilia."

I nodded. "Exactly the parallel I drew."

"Sandrina can't get hold of that. No one can."

"Someone has to," I told him. "And right now, we're it." I reached inside my coat for Rudra's book. "While my sleep was satisfying, it was far from restful. I've always found reading to be enjoyable, but this won't be. I need to finish Rudra's book. Now."

Kesyn stood. "I'll get Jash."

I had a thought. "Kesyn?"

"Yes?"

"Ask Agata Azul to join us. If the Heart of Nidaar is capable of changing the geography of nearly a quarter of a continent, she needs to know. And as a gem and earth mage, she may get more out of the rest of the book than we will."

I had a feeling Rudra Muralin's book would open itself to me again.

The book was on the table in front of me. When Rudra

had written this, he'd had the power of the Saghred at his beck and call. I knew better than to discount any threat powered by that.

The door to the cabin opened. It wasn't Kesyn returning with Jash and Agata.

It was Talon.

His eyes went to the book. He knew I had it, but this was his first time seeing it. It wasn't that I didn't trust Talon being around Rudra's book. I didn't want Rudra's book anywhere near my son.

Talon closed the door and came over to the table and leaned forward to see the book, but didn't come any closer. "Is that the book?" he asked quietly.

More than quiet. Tentative, almost fearful. There was no sign of his usual cockiness.

I could hardly blame him. Thanks to Rudra Muralin, Talon had come within seconds of being sacrificed to the Saghred through Raine Benares. I'd nearly been too late to save either one of them.

"Yes, it is," I said.

"You said Kansbar was about my age, right?"

I nodded.

Talon noted the thickness of the book. "Kansbar didn't tell Rudra any of that willingly, did he?"

"No, he didn't."

"Was he tortured?"

"Yes, but not in the usual sense." I hesitated. I didn't want to tell him, but he was asking. He was also an adult, a man now, and with Sarad still alive with Rudra's soul inside of him, Talon needed to know. He needed to know what Rudra had done to Kansbar Nathrach. He needed to know that the danger hadn't ended with the destruction of the Nebian ships and the ghost ships the Sythsaurian sorcerers had conjured. Chances were that the worst and most dangerous part of the journey still lay ahead. Talon already knew that this wasn't just an adventure, sailing the high seas on a pirate ship.

The Khrynsani had vaporized the *Wraith* and nearly fifty of her crew. The Nebians had brought Sythsaurian sorcerers after us and had summoned ships out of nightmare to destroy us. The invaders we dreaded were already here: at least, some of their mages had been before we'd destroyed those ships. If Sythsaurians had been among those pursuing us, I had no doubt there would be others waiting for us when we landed on Aquas. The Khrynsani and others would continue to try to stop us, and more people would have their lives taken before we reached Nidaar.

I told Talon what Rudra Muralin had done to Kansbar Nathrach.

"That's black magic, isn't it?" he asked once I'd finished.

"Of the very worst kind."

"Do you know how to do that?"

"I know how it's done."

Talon's dark eyes were steady. "But do you know how to do it?"

I hesitated. "I do."

"But you never would."

"You didn't ask that as a question."

There was the barest hint of a smile on his face. "I didn't need to."

The door opened again. It was Kesyn, Jash, and Agata.

"Are we interrupting something?" Kesyn asked.

"No, sir," Talon replied.

Kesyn raised an eyebrow in surprise. "Tam?"

"Come on in. Talon had some questions. Do you have any more?"

Talon shook his head. "I'm good. But if it's okay, I'd like to stay and listen." He glanced almost shyly at Agata. "I'll sit over here and stay out of the way."

"Very well."

When I'd last read, Kansbar Nathrach's expedition had arrived at the foot of the mountains after nine days of travel, camped in a cave, and had posted their usual guards. Guards who had been found dead the next morning, shriveled as if they had been drained and dried from the inside out.

The next night it had happened again.

This time Kansbar had witnessed it all and had nearly become a meal himself.

It was a scene any sane person would do anything they could to forget. Kansbar had tried to forget it, pushing it aside any time a flicker of memory tried to surface. Then Rudra Muralin had dragged it out of Kansbar's subconscious, watched it, and then gleefully watched it again and again, enjoying both the carnage and Kansbar's torment.

The creatures—no, the monsters—had fed, and there had been pleasure in the pain they caused during that feeding.

Rudra had described them as giant insects, like armored centipedes. They would tunnel beneath the ground to where their victims were. Their mandibles opened to reveal a feeding spike that, after being driven into a victim's body, injected a sedative to paralyze it, and then a toxin to quickly soften and then liquefy the internal organs and even bones, enabling the insects to drink their meal.

The second night, the insects had tunneled past the guards and into the clearing where the landing party had camped. Kansbar had been unable to sleep, and even he hadn't heard a thing.

But he had seen it.

Not the insects themselves, at least not at first. He had seen the body of the man next to him simply deflate as his insides were drained, leaving only his skin and clothing beneath his blanket.

Kansbar screamed and the others leapt from their bedrolls, grabbing weapons, frantically searching for still-unseen attackers.

Three did not wake. Their blankets were nearly flat against the ground, their occupants reduced to sacks of empty and dried flesh.

One of the Khrynsani kicked aside one of the dead men's bedrolls—and a living nightmare rose from beneath, rearing up like a cobra, nearly double the height of the goblins around it. The thing uncoiled its body to expose dozens of articulated legs, each ending in a razor-sharp point, ideal for burrowing through the ground and capturing prey.

The goblins froze in terror, wide eyes locked on the creature before them…

…and not the two that shot from the ground behind them, sending dirt flying in all directions.

Rudra supplied the words to describe Kansbar's terrified memories of the moments that followed. With their lives threatened, the diplomats revealed themselves to be Khrynsani dark mages, wielding the blackest of magic, which scared Kansbar nearly as much as the giant insects. But even the mages, with their black magic, had been hard-pressed to destroy these creatures. It had been accomplished only after five more of their group had been killed outright. A sixth, pinned against the belly of one of the insects with its legs puncturing his body, struggled futilely as the creature fled into the forest with its meal. Kansbar remembered that the screams seemed to go on forever.

And go on forever they did, with Rudra forcing Kansbar to replay the entire scene many times.

After this attack, Kansbar was the only non-Khrynsani survivor.

He was alone among men who could kill him with a thought.

Even though this had occurred hundreds of years ago, those giant insects could still exist between us and Nidaar.

"I've never heard of such a creature." I sat back in my chair, but was careful to keep my hands on the book. We couldn't afford another delay in getting to the end.

"Me, either," Kesyn said. "And I hope when this is all over, I can still say that."

"Aquas is said to have plants and animals that are different from those in the Seven Kingdoms," Jash said. "In theory, it's because it's an island surrounded by large seas. If it lives on Aquas, it stays on Aquas."

"And Aquas can keep them," Talon said from his chair.

I glanced back down at the book, and at the next words I saw, a slow smile spread across my face for the first time since opening Rudra's account of my ancestor's torture. Not all of the expedition had been death and horror.

"What is it?" Kesyn asked.

"They're real," I whispered.

"Who's real?"

"The golden goblins."

36

The legendary race of golden-skinned goblins was real.

At least they had been when Kansbar Nathrach had been in Nidaar.

Within minutes of the guard being carried off into the forest, the landing party had been surrounded and taken prisoner by heavily armed and armored goblins, their golden skin matching the color of their armor and weapons. After what they had been through, Kansbar felt that being the prisoner of a legendary sister race of goblins was infinitely better than becoming the next meal of monster insects—or being trapped alone with his traveling companions, whom he now knew to be a cadre of Khrynsani dark mages.

What should have been one of the most exciting moments of Kansbar's life, being in the presence of a legendary people whom he'd only read about, was overshadowed by the realization that he was part of a dangerous deception. Kansbar didn't know why the Khrynsani would come to Aquas posing as diplomats, but he knew it wouldn't end well for the golden goblins or himself.

The language the soldiers used was a version of the goblin language that hadn't been heard or spoken since ancient times.

Kansbar understood them. The Khrynsani mages did not. That would be his advantage, an advantage that could save his life.

The soldiers also didn't understand the Khrynsani, something that could save their lives, as well.

Dethis, the senior Khrynsani who was posing as the ambassador, told Kansbar that if he valued his life and very soul, that he would do the task the king had retained him for and no more. If he let these people suspect that he and his men were anything other than peaceful diplomats who wanted to reach out to their distant cousins, Dethis would kill each and every one of them.

Kansbar hoped the soldiers assumed that the tremor in his voice and his shaky smile were due to being attacked by giant insects, not that he was being threatened by a mage who could kill them all where they stood with a single word.

Kansbar would do his job. For now.

Being a historian of ancient cultures, Kansbar knew there was only one thing the Khrynsani could be after.

The Heart of Nidaar.

He introduced those with him as an ambassador from King Omari Mal'Salin and his diplomatic staff and guards, with himself as the official translator.

Rather than greeting them as long-lost relatives, the soldiers viewed all of them with suspicion and barely veiled hostility. Some among them voiced the opinion that they should have left the newcomers to the insects to devour. Kansbar pretended not to have heard those comments when Dethis asked what the soldiers had said. Part of him was glad the soldiers didn't trust the "diplomats," but if the Khrynsani suspected this, the soldiers' lives could be in danger. While Dethis's plan involved getting himself and his men into Nidaar under the guise of diplomacy, Kansbar knew that were their cover blown, they would simply use more direct and deadly methods.

The Khrynsani continued to play the hapless and helpless diplomats. Why should they not? They were being taken precisely where they wanted to go—the gold-filled city of Nidaar and its all-powerful Heart.

The insects had attacked them at the foot of a mountain range overlooking a great lake. Kansbar theorized that the city of Nidaar was located inside one of those mountains. He was unable to describe the exact entrance, though, because their captors tightly blindfolded them, walking them for hours before their surroundings changed to the cool and damp of caves. They were given a brief break to rest, but were not allowed to remove their blindfolds for many more hours.

They were in a vast cavern with gold covering every surface.

Seated on a gilded and bejeweled throne on a raised dais was their captors' queen.

She seemed to be of a similar age to Kansbar's mother, but her amber eyes belied an ancient knowledge. She was attired entirely in white. The queen's robes were simple, and they gave the impression of being just a setting, with her golden body as a precious jewel. Her intricately arranged hair was pure white, and woven within its coils was a gold circlet set with a single stone that flickered as if flame were trapped within.

The senior officer among the soldiers was speaking to her. He gestured Kansbar forward, and when Dethis moved to come with him, the officer sharply motioned the Khrynsani dark mage back.

Kansbar approached the throne alone and bowed deeply. When he raised his head, he was transfixed by the queen's amber eyes. He experienced a moment of disorientation and sank to his knees. He recovered almost as soon as he had been stricken and regained his feet.

The queen knew everything.

With one look, she had read his thoughts, knew what he knew.

The Khrynsani, the black magic, the deception, and the threat of widespread death if they did not get what they had come to steal.

The look she gave him was one of understanding, sadness—and pity.

Yes, she knew it all.

In return for the gift of his knowledge, she gave him her name. Baeseria. Her people called themselves the Cha'Nidaar in homage to the name of their first queen.

Kansbar forced a polite smile on his face and introduced Dethis and his men as representatives from the goblin court in Regor.

The queen knew the truth. It was to be their secret.

For the first few days they were treated as guests, not prisoners, but they were constantly watched and never left alone. The Cha'Nidaar were a matriarchal society, ruled by a queen and her council, which did include a few men. Their hosts had powerful mages among their numbers, and Dethis knew it would only be a matter of time before the Khrynsani's own power was discovered. They had to act quickly to secure the Heart of Nidaar.

As they had discovered, the Heart was the only thing of known value in the city.

The gold that the Cha'Nidaar wore wasn't gold at all. Or at least not gold as it was known in the Seven Kingdoms. It was the same color and could be polished to nearly the same shine, but while Kingdom gold was relatively soft, the gold of the Cha'Nidaar was as hard as Kingdom steel, making for magnificent armor and weapons. Its monetary value was undetermined. However, the Khrynsani fully intended to take some back with them to Regor to have it tested by the mages in the royal treasury.

Meanwhile, the Khrynsani gem mage had used a questing spell to determine where the Heart of Nidaar was located. It was in the center of the city's mountain, but the ways to it were heavily guarded. The Khrynsani devised a plan to overpower and kill the Heart's guards and lock themselves in the chamber with the stone, confident that once the Heart was under their control, they would be able to apply the knowledge they had of the Saghred to access the Heart's power. Then they would bargain for their escape or force it outright.

The day the Khrynsani intended to carry out their attack

and theft, Kansbar had hidden. The Khrynsani still had need of him to act as a negotiator to clear their way free of the mountain once they removed the Heart of Nidaar from its setting. Kansbar knew that once he had served their purpose, he would be killed. He also knew they couldn't risk wasting time to search for him, and instead would leave him to face the wrath of their hosts. Kansbar fled the wing of the subterranean palace they had been given for their use. He told the captain of the guards that had been assigned to them of the Khrynsani's betrayal.

Kansbar was taken before the queen and told her what the Khrynsani were about to do.

Since his last time in the throne room, he had overheard Dethis talking and determined that the goblin king Omari Mal'Salin not only knew of the Khrynsani's plans, but had orchestrated them himself. He told the queen that any future diplomatic overtures from Omari should not be believed. He had also heard Dethis speak of plundering the city's gold, and of the citizens to be brought back to the goblin kingdom as slaves.

Word came that the Khrynsani had gained entrance to the Heart chamber.

The queen beckoned for Kansbar to approach her throne.

When he and the Khrynsani had been brought to the city, the queen had read his mind with a mere glance. Now she reached out and touched his hand. With that touch, the queen determined that Kansbar was a good and noble man.

She told Kansbar that her people's skin color, the interior of the mountain city, and the metals mined there appeared to be gold due to their prolonged exposure to the Heart of

Nidaar. Its power, leaching into the stones of the city, gave rise to the legend of a city of gold. But, she added, a legend was all that it was: its stones were mere rock, the metal was steel, and the skin of their people was once the same gray as Kansbar's.

She then assured him that the Heart of Nidaar was part of the mountain itself and could not be removed.

That was when Kansbar told her of the Saghred, its powers, and the ability of the Khrynsani's leader, Rudra Muralin, and his inner circle, which included Dethis, to use the stone to cause cataclysmic destruction.

The queen looked concerned, even afraid. She told Kansbar that out of respect for the Heart's connection to the earth, they only used the power the stone gave freely, never awakening it and, through greed and a desire for power, forcing it to give more.

There was another way into the Heart's chamber than the one that the Khrynsani had used. It was an emergency escape route should the guards of the Heart ever need it.

But the royal guards failed to reach the chamber before the Khrynsani activated the Heart. The dark mages paid for their arrogance with their lives and the lives of the five guards of the Heart. The Saghred had fallen from the sky. The Heart of Nidaar was part of the mountain that surrounded it. One consumed souls. The other fed from the earth itself. They could not have been more different, yet the power they could unleash was the same.

The Khrynsani mages lost control of the Heart and laid waste the land on the east coast of the continent, reducing that which was once green with life to rock and dust. The earth opened and drained every lake, river, and stream, leaving behind only cracked beds.

All this, and the Heart had been active for only a few seconds.

The mountain city of Nidaar remained undamaged.

The people of Nidaar mourned the loss of their paradise, their land now barren and desolate.

They knew what they must do.

The queen told Kansbar not to return, that neither he nor any of his people would ever find them again. The Cha'Nidaar would guard the Heart against future misuse by anyone. However, in gratitude for his warning of his companions' treachery, the queen gave him a ring and a pendant, each set with a small stone that had once been part of the Heart of Nidaar. These would protect him against the creatures that roamed between the Nidaar's mountain and the coast, enabling him to pass unnoticed.

They gave him enough food, water, and supplies to reach the coast, where the expedition's ship waited. Kansbar would tell them that the others were killed in the massive earthquake that shook the land and drained the waters. He told them that they had never found Nidaar, and that the rest of the party had perished when the earth had opened, swallowing them all, and only he had managed to cling to the edge of the abyss long enough to pull himself to safety. The ambassador and his staff and their guards had been lost. Kansbar's physical condition once he reached the coast reinforced the tale he told.

The ship had been damaged when it had been hit by an earthquake-spawned giant wave taller than the tallest mast. Additional quakes and aftershocks continued to rock the coast. Within an hour of Kansbar reaching the ship, the beach was swallowed and towering cliffs rose to take its place. So Kansbar's story of the landing party falling into an abyss was believed without much question.

One Khrynsani agent had remained on the ship in the guise of the ship's doctor. Kansbar had fallen into a fever soon after being taken out to the ship. The doctor had given him a sleeping draught and had gone through his packs, finding the ring and pendant. He knew of the mission and the description of the Heart, so he knew that Kansbar had lied when he said the party had never found Nidaar. He put the pieces back in the pack, vowing to reveal what he knew once they'd returned to Regor and leaving an official interrogation up to the Khrynsani experts in that art. The doctor befriended Kansbar and tried to get him to talk more about what had happened, but Kansbar insisted there was nothing more to tell…and that what had happened, he wanted nothing more than to forget.

37

The book's final words faded before my eyes as I read them, any secret information regarding the location of the city of Nidaar once again locked away.

I slowly closed the book, my eyes on the ring given to my ancestor by Queen Baeseria of the Cha'Nidaar herself nearly a thousand years ago—a ring that had sealed his fate with Rudra Muralin.

Agata's hand protectively covered the pendant.

We were all silent.

"So that ring of yours isn't gold," Jash noted, breaking the somber mood.

I turned my hand back and forth, letting the stone catch the lantern light. "That's what it sounds like."

My friend chuckled. "No gold in Nidaar. Phaelan is going

to be so disappointed. Please let me be there when you tell him."

"And all of this happened while Rudra was still head of the Khrynsani order," I said. "That meant he hadn't yet used the Saghred to create the Great Rift." I smiled and shook my head. "Rudra must have told Omari what his Khrynsani had done with the Heart of Nidaar. That was when Omari dared him to attempt something similar with the Saghred. He did it, and it killed him. Justice will have the final say."

Kesyn snorted. "Dumb bastard. Too bad he didn't stay dead."

"Then Sarad did to Rudra essentially what Rudra did to Kansbar," I noted. "Justice served again." I mulled over what Queen Baeseria had told Kansbar about the Heart of Nidaar for a few moments. "Sandrina's read this book, so she knows that the Heart can't be moved, and that attempting to use it like the Saghred will destroy a quarter of a continent and kill you."

"Maybe these Sythsaurians know something we don't," Kesyn suggested.

There was a knock at the cabin door.

I tucked the book back into my coat pocket. "Yes?"

The door opened and the ship's telepath peered around the edge of the door. "Chancellor Nathrach, I've got a call for you from the Isle of Mid—from Archmagus Justinius Valerian himself."

The Conclave college's cryptozoology department had *three* preserved Sythsaurians in their basement.

When I'd contacted Mychael, I'd described what I had

seen on the Nebian ship as well as what Sarad Nukpana had called them.

Justinius's face looked back at me from the cannonball–sized crystal ball mounted inside of a rounded steel cage that had been forged to an exact fit. The cage could be opened and the ball removed, but as we were on a ship, that wasn't recommended. The cage was permanently mounted to a pedestal that had been built into the deck itself.

"They've got one of those ugly bastards on display in a lab," Justinius was saying. "And they found two more in preservation cases in the basement." The old man laughed evilly. "What I wouldn't have given to have seen Waere Josten's face when he wiped the dust off the face of that casket. Rumor has it he crapped himself."

"Who's that?"

"Assistant department chairman," Justinius said. "An insufferable ass. Knows his stuff, and isn't about to let the rest of us forget it. The department chair is overseeing the document search, and he put Waere in charge of looking for the bodies. What we've found indicates we acquired the things around seven hundred years ago, which coincides with the Timurus invasion."

"So they were here then."

Justinius nodded. "Probably scouting out their next conquest. We're lucky they never made it back home, or apparently reported their findings, since we aren't all speaking lizard right now. Now if we can just make the same thing happen to the rest of them."

"Plus any Khrynsani in their company."

"I wouldn't want to leave them out of any death wish.

That'd be rude. We'll crack one of the greenies out of preservation and poke around in his insides to find out where they came from and, most importantly, what's the best way to kill 'em. They're still looking for the records of when they were found. The department chairman during that time wasn't the best for holding his staff to any kind of research standards. Some of the faculty didn't even bother to keep records. The department librarian assures me that if those particular records do exist, they have them, because nothing has ever been thrown away." He snorted. "Or even filed, judging from the mess I saw down in their archives. As soon as we have more for you, I'll be back in touch."

"I'd like to know *where* those Sythsaurian bodies were found," I said. "More than likely, there's a portal in that location—a portal that other Sythsaurians could know about. The Nebians had Sythsaurian sorcerers on one of their ships."

Justinius scowled. "So I heard. Imala wanted to kill their ambassador Aeron Corantine back during the peace talks. I wish now that I'd encouraged that behavior. That little gal's a go-getter."

I smiled. "That she is. I'm most interested in how the Sythsaurians were able to destroy the population of an entire world—and how they intend to do the same to us. Speaking of things that want to kill us…" I told him about the giant centipedes from Kansbar's account of the expedition.

"That's something else that doesn't need to be on this world with the rest of us. I won't mention those to the cryptozoo folks. They'll just pester me to get you to bring back a specimen."

"That's a souvenir that will not be coming back with me."

Justinius's expression grew serious. "How's Talon?"

"Once he got his sea legs, he hasn't had any problems."

"That's not what I meant and you know it."

"He hasn't *been* any problem or gotten into any trouble, if that's what you want to know."

"I'm glad to hear it. You take care of yourself and your son, Tam. Folks here don't want anything bad to happen to either one of you."

"I will, sir, and thank you."

The crystal ball went dark.

I had to have some sleep.

Even though I needed to talk to Sarad now that I'd finished the book, I hoped he wouldn't put in an appearance. Every time I'd had a dream with Sarad in it, I'd awoken more tired than I had been before I'd gone to sleep. Though if Sarad didn't pay me a visit, I'd probably lose sleep anyway wondering what he was up to.

Instead of Sarad, I dreamt of a man-eating monster centipede.

A dream that was probably courtesy of Sarad.

The centipede was almost an improvement.

Until it wasn't.

A centipede had caught me and was pulling my body into its underside where the feeding spikes waited to drug, dissolve, and drink me. A spike was sharp against my stomach, pushing in, puncturing, screaming…

I sat bold upright in bed, panting, my body covered in sweat…

...with the corner of Rudra's book stabbing me in the stomach.

And Sapphira's roars sounding outside.

I grabbed the sides of my hammock to keep from falling out. Apparently I'd been thrashing around, too. I spat a string of curses that even Phaelan might have been impressed by, and started pulling on clothes and boots as fast as I could.

Talon slipped out of his hammock, landing in a tumble on the floor.

A few seconds after another thud, Kesyn was standing over me. "What the hell was that?"

"Sapphira," I muttered, still groggy.

"No, your yelling."

Perhaps I had screamed.

Sapphira roared again, this time with a kick that shook the deck beneath our feet.

Kesyn stumbled. "Bloody lizard's gonna tear the ship apart."

I grabbed my sunglasses and ran for the door.

At the end of the passageway there was a hatch to the hold. I put my hand to the wood. It wasn't hot. Sapphira wasn't using fire yet.

I creaked the hatch open and looked inside to see Sapphira frantically clawing her way out of the hold to the shouts and screams of the crew above.

A pissed-off goblin sentry dragon was on the rampage.

The worst thing about being nocturnal was when you suddenly had to go outside during the day, especially on a day as bright as a thousand suns.

I was forced to close my eyes for a few seconds to allow the glasses to darken enough so as not to blind me.

I opened them to a scene out of an elf's worst nightmare.

To escape the hold, Sapphira had hooked her claws deep into the decking, scoring the wood, her eyes wide with terror, the whites showing.

Something had spooked her. No, terrified her. I didn't know of anything that a sentry dragon was afraid of.

Talon and Kesyn came up the stairs behind me.

"Find Calik," I told them. "Quick."

Four crewmen dove aside just as the dragon's tail crashed through the railing where they had been standing.

Jash was on day duty. He swung down into the hold.

Shouts and curses rang out as men scrambled to get out of the way, especially away from Sapphira's head. Flames were banked in her nostrils, meaning she had fire ready. Royal navy dragons were highly trained. They would release fire only if directed to by their pilot. Sapphira had a fire ready to go. With Calik not here to calm her, it was a miracle she hadn't torched the ship.

Sapphira threw back her head and roared, though it sounded more like a scream. She was frantic to get off this ship.

I remembered another ship. A ship with a Gate torn into it. I didn't sense a Gate.

Sapphira's harness was still connected to a fire-proof rope as thick as my forearm. That was all that was keeping her from launching herself up into the rigging.

"Cut her loose!" Phaelan shouted.

In her panicked state, Sapphira would push off with her powerful back legs and go straight up into the rigging, bringing sails, yardarms and probably even a mast down on our heads and leaving the *Kraken* crippled and dead in the water.

A crossbow appeared in one of the gunner's hands.

"No!" I ran forward, snagging a tarp, waving it to get the dragon's attention.

"Ka sa'ffrit!" It was one of the few dragon commands I knew.

Obey me.

Saphria hissed, pushing sulfuric smoke out from between fangs the length of my fingers. I held the tarp ready if it was needed.

"Quiet!" Phaelan barked from somewhere behind me.

"Ka sa'ffrit, Sapphira." This time I did not shout. I kept my voice low and commanding, but not threatening. I wasn't Calik, but Sapphira knew me. I just prayed she knew me well enough to trust me.

I had awakened panicked from my dream to Sapphira's roars. Did dragons dream? Did she dream of a monster centipede and awake to find herself trapped in the hold of a ship?

I had thought to use the tarp to toss over her head as you would a blanket over a panicked horse's head to calm it.

Instinct told me that wouldn't work. If a dream had somehow terrified her, she wanted to escape, to see any threats coming. To see any reassurance.

I dropped the tarp and stepped forward slowly, speaking soft, reassuring words as you would to a frightened child—a fanged, clawed, fire-breathing child, but still a child and definitely frightened.

Once I was close enough, I reached out and cautiously placed a hand on her neck, my murmurs turning to calming whispers in Goblin, the words for her ears alone, as I stroked her neck, the heat from the fire she held ready warm under my hand.

We calmed each other.

Sapphira inhaled, a giant bellows pulling air in.

The crew instinctively drew back, expecting an exhale of flames.

I kept whispering and reassuring as Sapphira gently exhaled in a cloud of sulfurous smoke.

I released my own breath in relief as Jash and Talon helped Calik up the ladder from the hold, a makeshift bandage wrapped around his head, blood showing through.

Calik calmly walked over to where I was, reached up, hooked his hand through Sapphira's bridle and pulled her huge head down to his face, so they were eye to eye.

She gently sniffed at the bloody bandage as several of the crew winced and looked away, not wanting to see the dragon's prey instinct kick in and Sapphira bite Calik's head off.

"Yes, you did that," Calik told her, pushing her snout away from the wound.

The dragon lowered her head and rumbled, as if ashamed of her behavior.

"You *should* be embarrassed, scaring everybody." Calik reached up and scratched Sapphira under the chin like a cat. She bared her teeth in a draconic smile and the men backed up some more. "Is anyone hurt?" he asked me quietly.

I glanced around. "Just you."

Phaelan appeared beside us.

"Sorry about that, Captain Benares," Calik said. "I don't know what got into her. She's never acted that way before."

"Do dragons dream?" I asked.

"Yes, they do."

"I think Sapphira and I might have been sent the same nightmare."

There was no way to ask Sapphira what had scared her.

"Sentry dragons don't scare easily," Calik told me. His head had been re-bandaged. Only a little blood had leaked through the white linen. "A bug the size of what you described coming after her wouldn't normally make her knock down the walls of her stall, but she's in the hold of a ship. My girl felt vulnerable, and the only way she could stop the feeling would be to get out of her stall so she could fight. I suppose it could be possible. If they couldn't destroy our ships with demons and the dead, scare one of our sentries into doing the job for them."

The sentry dragons on the other two ships hadn't had any reaction, so whatever had made Sapphira try to break out of her stall had been contained to our ship. Sentry dragons were sensitive to magic. Perhaps I'd somehow projected my dream as I was having it, but none of the mages or magic-sensitives on board had felt a thing.

It was odd, and not in any way that could possibly be good.

38

The next week passed uneventfully. The book refused to open again, and Sarad Nukpana had vanished from my dreams.

Sarad had said that Rudra had included the location to the city of Nidaar inside the book, but that it was hidden and that I'd have to magically coax it out. Kansbar Nathrach had been blindfolded when he had been brought into Nidaar and when he had left, but he had known where he and the Khrynsani had camped the first time, and where he'd been released when he was left alone. Kansbar had known, so Rudra had known. Yes, we had pieces of the Heart of Nidaar for Agata to use to lead us to the city and the stone, but knowing which section of mountain to concentrate her efforts on would be a huge help.

So I needed to open the book one last time, but I wasn't going to do it until we were on dry land.

It was the morning of the seventh day since Sapphira had terrorized the crew of the *Kraken*.

"Land ho!" came a shout from the crow's nest.

The morning fog lifted, revealing a massive escarpment towering above a rocky beach.

Anyone that could, crew or passengers, stopped what they were doing and stared.

Talon appeared beside me. "The Heart of Nidaar did *that*?"

As the sky cleared to a cloudless blue, we saw that the escarpment extended as far north and south as the eye could see. The map we had had told us as much. Rudra's book had hinted at it. I had hoped both had been exaggerating. So much for wishful thinking. The map indicated that there was no easy way up.

Calik appeared beside me. "Glad we brought the girls?"

"Oh yeah."

We had already decided that those of us going on to Nidaar would get to the top via sentry dragon, as would our supplies. After that, they would remain with the fleet as both hunters for the crews and defense for the ships. Stealth was called for, and that would be difficult traveling with three enormous dragons. However, we would be taking a few firedrakes inland with us as scouts.

The map and the book indicated that our situation wouldn't improve once we reached the top. The rock of the cliffs would give way to a land of sand and rock with air hot and dry enough to shrivel your lungs in your chest. All of this was surrounded by mountains and canyons of rock where no plant could grow. Just because we didn't have to climb this, didn't mean climbing wasn't in our future. Nidaar was somewhere in the mountains beyond the wasteland. We had come equipped, both with ropes and expert climbers. My team usually relished a challenge.

They wouldn't be relishing this.

Neither was I.

I went to where Agata Azul was standing near the bow, staring intently across the water to those cliffs that seemed to grow taller as we closed in on the shore.

"Are you sensing anything?" I asked her.

Agata continued to stare straight ahead. "That is where we must go." One side of her mouth twitched upward. "This information will not be well received."

"No, it will not."

I went to the quarterdeck, standing to the side and out of Phaelan's way as he sailed us northward along the coast until we spotted an opening between two towering cliffs that marked our safe harbor, or as safe a harbor as we were likely to find. At least it was hidden from the sea; however, all an attacker would have to do would be to wait for us to come out. We'd be bottled in. The grim set to Phaelan's face told me he liked it about as well as I did.

A shout from above signaled shallows on either side of the entrance to the harbor. Our final approach would be through a narrow and treacherous channel.

Phaelan gripped the wheel and began a litany of murmured endearments and entreaties to his ship, and curses directed at the continent of Aquas and every rock on it.

Then we saw it.

Dark clouds poured over the edge of the cliffs and

surrounding escarpment like a waterfall. They quickly leveled and spread toward our ships.

"That's not natural," Phaelan said through gritted teeth.

"No, it's not," I readily agreed.

"That Sandrina woman?"

"Or a pack of Khrynsani weather wizards acting under her orders."

I had another suspect in mind. Perhaps Bricarda had escaped the Nebian ship only to teleport here to try to kill us again.

The clouds picked up speed as if recognizing us as their targets and eager to get here.

Phaelan ordered the sails trimmed, and I could hear the same orders being bellowed from the other ships. I couldn't imagine either Gwyn or Gavyn thinking the oncoming storm was natural, but I made my way quickly to the ship's telepath to spread the word to the *Raven* and *Sea Wolf* that things were going to get worse before they got any better.

If it got any better. If Sandrina was behind this, she had never been one for doing anything halfway—especially vengeance. This storm probably wouldn't stop until every ship was under the water. I was no weather wizard, but I could lend my strength to the one we had.

Calik ran up to me. "Tam, if we're swamped, the dragons won't stand a chance."

"Take Saffie and the drakes and get out of here, above those clouds. Can you signal the other pilots to do the same?"

"Done."

Talon darted below with Calik to help release the firedrakes to safety—or to a safer place than we were about to be.

There were two seats on Sapphira's saddle.

"Take Talon with you!" I yelled to Calik's back.

Releasing the dragons and drakes would not only save them from drowning, they could save us in a recovery effort.

If there were any of us left to save.

We were all about to find out the veracity of the Caesolians' reputations as the finest ship makers in the Seven Kingdoms.

There were rocks in those shallows and cliffs looming beyond that. If we were pushed too far in the direction of the harbor, we'd be ground into kindling. I had no intention of being ground into anything, especially not within sight of our goal—or at least the first one.

Phaelan was shouting commands and encouragement. The crew was the best of his elves, and the finest of goblin intelligence agents. Yes, they were all seasoned and battle-hardened, but what was coming straight at us wasn't anything that could be defeated with muscle, steel, or the iron of cannonballs—or probably even countered with our magic. They knew it. We all did. This was the blackest of magic, Phaelan hated and feared it, but you would never know it to see him now.

Captain Phaelan Benares was a figure of strength and confidence, who by the sheer force of his personality was willing his crew to remain calm, stay at their stations, and do their jobs. The crew, elf and goblin alike, fed off of his words, gaining strength and resolve while bracing themselves for what was to come.

The *Kraken*'s weather wizard had already lashed herself to the mainmast, the crew scrambling around her getting the ship ready for the storm rushing toward us. A bank of black clouds had already blocked out the sun and obscured what minutes before had been a clear, blue sky.

Falitta Rondel had sailed with Phaelan's father, Ryn Benares. Ryn had made sure his son had the best weather wizard available. I'd spoken with Falitta many times during our weeks at sea. She was gifted, powerful, and experienced. Lashing herself to the mainmast told me and everyone on the *Kraken* that what was coming was as bad as it could get.

"Lash yourself to something," Phaelan told me. He jerked his head to the right. "There's a stack of harnesses in that bench. Toss me one and take one for yourself."

Phaelan kept his hands on the wheel as I quickly helped him into his harness, which he latched to a steel ring embedded in the deck at the base of the ship's wheel.

"There's another ring by the bench." Phaelan now had to shout to be heard over the wind. "Use it!"

The doors to the hold were flung open and Sapphira dived over the side of the *Kraken* and with a few wingbeats was above the ship, fighting for altitude to get above the storm. The firedrakes followed in her wake.

The seat behind Calik was empty.

I swore and frantically scanned the deck for any sign of Talon. He must still be below. I'd have to believe that he could fend for himself. There was nothing I could do here with Phaelan, but I might be able to help Falitta. There was another ring in the deck by the mainmast.

I unhooked my line from the ring.

Phaelan saw. "What the hell are you doing?"

"Falitta." I ran down the stairs.

The weather wizard's eyes were fixed on the black bank of

clouds racing toward us, her lips moving in silent incantation. I stopped just inside her peripheral vision. She wasn't in a trance, at least not yet. She could still see me, or at least perceive my presence. If there was any help I could give her, she would tell me.

"This is beyond me," Falitta said calmly, her eyes locked on the clouds that were only a hundred yards off our bow.

She couldn't stop or even divert that storm.

We were screwed—and dead.

Like hell.

"Take my strength," I told her. "I can add my—"

The weather wizard finally looked at me. "Power cannot help us now. This is a form of magic I have never encountered. It is not of this world."

Sythsaurian black magic.

"Can we deflect it?"

Falitta shook her head. "It defies my every attempt, sensing my efforts before I make them. My spells evaporate before it. Unless we can somehow ride this out, Tamnais, we're dead."

Suddenly the *Kraken*'s deck shuddered beneath my feet.

I shot a quick glance back at Phaelan.

His face was utterly white.

It was an earthquake, in the floor of the sea beneath us.

I snarled a curse—at Sandrina, Bricarda, the Sythsaurians, but mostly at my own inability to do anything to save our lives—as a wave rose in the distance at our backs, growing taller and wider, until it was a wall of water racing toward and dwarfing our small fleet.

A wave taller than the tallest mast.

A monster wave spawned by an earthquake.

The stone in my ring blazed to life.

An earthquake sent from the Heart of Nidaar.

39

I dimly heard Phaelan's voice cut through the chaos and howling wind. "Brace yourselves!"

I secured myself as best as I could and braced my feet, knowing that it was a pitiful effort against a monster wave, but it was all I could do.

The water rose behind us, obscuring the very sky.

Falitta was right. There was nothing natural about what rose above us. This was malice made water. This wave had been conjured from the depths with only one purpose—utter obliteration. Sandrina wanted to pound our ships to splinters against the cliffs and our bodies into food for whatever lived in these waters. She knew we would be rendered helpless, and if there was any way that she was watching, she would be reveling in our destruction.

With Phaelan standing solidly at the wheel, the *Kraken* lifted herself into the wave, seemingly trying against all odds to preserve herself, to save her crew.

She nearly succeeded.

The ship crested the wave, impossibly high. We were in the sky, the realm of sentry dragons, not ships of the sea. But as quickly as we had climbed and crested, the sea that had carried us up abandoned us, and our world pitched backward.

Screams rent the air as the wind tore hands and bodies from the ropes and rails that were their sole link to this life. The sea, mercilessly manipulated to be the Khrynsani's instrument of death, turned against those it had gently carried only minutes before. This wasn't fate, it wasn't bad luck. This was murder—premeditated, calculated, pure evil murder. As the wind and water tried to wrench my arms from their sockets, I swore that if I somehow survived, I would not stop until I had those responsible dead at my feet.

The *Kraken* had been left hanging in the air for an impossibly long moment before plunging down the back side, her stern pointed straight down, falling backward into the sea.

This was it. This was how I would die, how we would all die. I'd taken what would be my final breath before the sea would close over us.

The *Kraken*'s stern plunged underwater, immediately followed by the rest of her. I instinctively closed my eyes and held my breath, not knowing how we could possibly make it back to the surface, and an instant later knowing with absolute certainly that we were doomed.

Just as my lungs burned white hot and I couldn't hold my

breath any longer, the deck was again beneath my feet, as the ship shot back to the surface.

I swallowed lungfuls of air, seconds before expecting nothing but water, greedily gulping with ragged breaths. I quickly looked around the deck. Some had been lost. Many had survived. And against all odds, Phaelan was still at the wheel, and gave a whoop of pure joy at being alive.

I hoped Sandrina *was* watching.

These goblins and elves die hard, you bitch.

Then I saw it, a wave even taller than the last. Impossibly tall. The sea was shallow here, the volume of water it took to create that monster had stolen the water from the backside of that wave, so that as we crested, I could see the rocks beneath the surface.

The water was too shallow. We would never survive the impact. The *Kraken* would be dashed to bits and us along with her.

I heard a voice cutting through the wind.

Imperious and commanding, ordering the earth beneath that wave to do her will.

Agata Azul.

At the bow.

Soaked, bleeding, defiant.

And at her side was Talon, with Indigo, the little firedrake that had befriended him clinging to his shoulder.

Agata's hands had a death grip on the railing just behind the *Kraken*'s figurehead. Talon had one arm around her waist, helping her remain upright, his other hand clutching the same section of railing.

It was earth magic—raw, primal, and unbelievably strong, even for a mage of Agata's ability.

It was Talon. He was the source of that additional power. His voice carried to me on the wind, a song of strength and resilience, of an undaunted spirit and will. He was sharing his power with Agata. Together they were attempting to counter the wild magic and calm the earth that had been awakened by the Heart of Nidaar itself.

And they were winning. The power rolling from them rivaled the strength of those trying to destroy us.

Agata Azul and my son were doing the impossible.

So instead of diving bow first and being dashed to pieces on the rocks waiting below, the *Kraken* was dropping, the seas spreading out beneath us.

As the seas calmed, the skies inexplicably began to clear.

And as the water fell, so did Agata and Talon. Her hands lost their grip on the rail. Talon attempted to catch her, but his strength was failing, too. They both fell to their knees and slumped to the deck.

The ship was still tossing, but I let go of the lines and unhooked the harness that had saved my life and ran to the bow, to my son and the gem mage who had saved all of our lives. Backwash from the wave broke across the bow as the ship lurched to one side, partially submerging the bow and taking Agata's unconscious body with it.

I ran as fast as I could across the still-tossing deck, jumping and dodging broken spars and debris to reach her and Talon before he was washed overboard as well. I was almost there when the deck pitched and Agata was swept over the side. Heavy lines were wrapped around one of Talon's legs. He wasn't going anywhere and was safe for now. I threw myself across the tangle of downed lines, trying to grab Agata's boot.

I grabbed and missed.

I kicked clear of the lines that'd tangled around my boot to dive in after her.

Agata popped to the surface, coughing.

I lunged for her, but a wave swept Agata up and away from my outstretched arms.

Talon's drake flew shrieking over the spot where Agata had gone down.

Then Jash was there, tossing me a line. I tied it off to the harness I still wore.

"Anchor me," I yelled over the wind, trusting Jash to hold on.

The ship began to rise with another wave. It wasn't tall enough to swamp a ship, but it was more than enough to drown Agata.

If I didn't get ahold of her this time, she'd be swept away.

The wave began lifting the bow, pulling Agata away.

I swam to reach her and got my arm around her chest, pulling her close to keep her head above water. Another wave came, but instead of pulling us under, it carried us further from the ship. I was a strong swimmer, but between the waves and our soaked clothes, it was all I could do to keep us from going under.

Agata had been underwater for less than a minute, but she was unconscious. Conscious, she would have held her breath. Unconscious, and with the water churning, her lungs could have filled with water.

The backside of the wave pushed us both under, tugging at me, pulling me.

Not under, but toward the ship.

Jash, Talon, and Kesyn were reeling us in.

They hauled us over the side, where we landed in a sodden heap.

I coughed and sputtered.

Agata rolled over and threw up the seawater she'd swallowed.

On Kesyn's boots.

I continued to suck air into my lungs as I managed to raise my head.

Anything that could've broken loose had. Lines, rigging, and sails covered the deck as Phaelan shouted orders and the crew scrambled to comply. Amazingly, the masts were still intact. What sails hadn't been lowered before the magic-spawned storm hit had been torn, many hanging in tatters.

Agata weakly raised her head and tried to speak.

"Breathe now," I told her. "Talk later."

Agata and Talon had successfully counteracted who or whatever had activated the Heart of Nidaar.

We all were definitely going to have a talk about that.

40

"I don't know," Talon said for the third time. "I know I'm not a weather wizard, and I don't know why or how the storm went away at the same time the earthquake stopped. I know I've done some unexplainable things in the past, but this time I was only there for the assist. You'll have to ask sleeping beauty over there when she wakes up."

And I fully intended to. Not that I had any problem with what Agata had done. If it hadn't been for her, with Talon's backup, none of us would be alive right now. It appeared to me that Agata Azul had turned aside the power of the Heart of Nidaar. What I had witnessed wasn't a simple deflection, not that magic of that magnitude could ever be called simple. Agata had recognized precisely what was being done, and had used her skill and power along with Talon's strength to make it stop.

Was the attack on us the Cha'Nidaar defending their land from potential invaders, or was the Heart of Nidaar once again in the hands of Khrynsani dark mages? We didn't know. Yet. We would be going inland, finding the city and the stone, and determining the situation we had on our hands. If Agata Azul could somehow manipulate or counteract the effects of the Heart of Nidaar, I needed to know how she had done it—and could she do it again if our team came under attack.

My head was still throbbing, and that Talon was as much at a loss as I was as to how he and Agata had stopped an earthquake and a deadly storm wasn't making it any better.

I massaged my temples. It hurt, so I stopped.

Miraculously, the *Kraken* hadn't sunk. I wondered if Agata and Talon had had a hand in that as well. I squeezed my eyes shut at another stab of pain. One new unexplained and inexplicable talent at a time.

We'd brought Agata into the captain's cabin. Our cabin had windows, hers did not. She and Talon both needed fresh air. A second cot had been brought in for Talon. Both he and Agata were propped up on pillows and bundled in blankets.

The ship's doctor had checked Talon and Agata out and deemed them alive and very likely to remain that way. There was still the concern of pneumonia from all the seawater Agata had taken into her lungs, but we were doing what we could about that—keep her warm and dry, and watch her closely for the next day or two.

The other two ships had sustained only slightly less damage than the *Kraken*. We were all afloat, but none of us would be leaving Aquas anytime soon. We were moored in the harbor and repairs—to both crew and ships—were underway.

Phaelan had been leading the way into the harbor, and the *Kraken* had borne the brunt of the storm's fury. The *Raven* and *Sea Wolf* had been caught on the periphery, and they had witnessed what had happened to the *Kraken*. They had seen us go under and the waves calm as quickly as they'd arisen.

Kesyn came in and closed the cabin door quietly behind him. "How is she?"

"Same as before," I said.

Kesyn brought a chair next to Agata's cot and sat down. "Don't let that she hasn't woken up yet worry you. Aggie did some heavy lifting; she'll need to sleep it off. And when she does, you'll get the answers to your questions."

"Am I that obvious?"

"You're about to pace a rut in the deck."

A sigh came from beneath Agata's blankets. "And what questions would those be?"

Kesyn smiled. "Hey, Aggie girl. How do you feel?"

"How do I look?" she asked flatly.

"You've looked better."

"Then I feel worse." She struggled to sit up.

"Aggie, you shouldn't—"

She silenced Kesyn with a glare and fluffed her pillows at her back, though it was more of a punch than a fluff.

I held back a smile. The doctor was right. Agata Azul was going to be just fine.

"What's happened since I've been out?" she asked us.

We told her.

When we'd finished, Agata turned to Talon with a crooked grin. "We do good work."

Talon met her grin and raised his mug of hot tea in salute. "We're a fine team."

She turned to me. "Thank you all—and Jash—for saving my life."

I inclined my head. "Thank you—and Talon—for saving all of us. We've determined, more or less, that the storm was Khrynsani or Sythsaurian weather magic. How did you stop it?"

"We didn't," Agata replied.

"It dissipated at the same time as the wave."

"It was no doing of mine."

"Told you so," Talon chimed in.

"Was that earthquake caused by the Heart of Nidaar?" I asked.

"It was," Agata replied.

"Do you know who activated the stone?"

"I didn't sense any malevolent intent behind the power, or intent of any kind," she said.

Kesyn leaned forward, elbows resting on his knees. "I've never heard of a stone of power acting alone."

I frowned. "They don't."

"I didn't say it had," Agata said. "I said I didn't sense anyone at the controls. They could have warded themselves against detection, or the power of the Heart could have blocked their presence." She smiled weakly. "It was a massive amount of power. Knowing who activated it would be like trying to see an ant on the ground behind an avalanche."

"It could be the Cha'Nidaar themselves," I said. "They've had goblins land on their shores before. Perhaps this time they took decisive action before we got any closer. To tell you the truth, knowing what's at stake, I almost don't blame them. When the Khrynsani used the Heart, they laid waste to hundreds of miles of coastline. This time, the Cha'Nidaar's land wasn't affected, only the sea beneath our ships."

"It stands to reason that they'd have better aim with their own stone than the Khrynsani," Talon noted.

Kesyn leaned back in his chair. "Well, whoever it was that had their hands on that rock, they didn't count on the two of you."

"Whoever summoned that storm or activated the Heart knew exactly where we were," I told them all. "We're being tracked."

Agata's hand went to the pendant with its piece of the Heart. "I need this to find Nidaar and the Heart, and to do that it can't be warded."

"I know."

Agata gave me a tired, little smile. "Well, Tam, that leaves us with no alternative but to work with the circumstances we are given."

"You called me Tam."

Agata snuggled down into her blankets. "And now I'm telling you I need some more sleep." Her voice was soft and drowsy. "We've got a long trip ahead of us."

There was a quiet knock at the door. It opened and Phaelan stuck his head around the corner. "I came to check on our dynamic duo," he whispered.

Talon sat up and flashed a grin, likewise keeping his voice down. "I'm alive, Agata's been awake and talking, and unless we get an ocean dumped on us again, we're both likely to stay that way."

The elf pirate gave Talon a double thumbs-up. "Badass work."

Talon flashed a grin. "Thank you. We were just both too pretty to die on this ship."

Phaelan snorted a laugh. "At least that's true for one of you. Convey my regards to the lady."

"You're welcome," Agata mumbled from under her blankets. "You men chatter worse than a flock of magpies. What does a woman have to do to get any sleep around here?"

We had survived.

I had no way of knowing if whoever had unleashed the power of the Heart of Nidaar on us knew this. As long as we remained in one place, they might assume we were dead or beyond any chance of continuing our search. I also didn't know if they would dispatch a search team to ensure that if we were alive, that it wouldn't be for long. For now, we had warded Agata's pendant and my ring. She needed the rest, and we didn't need that rest interrupted. We had been moored in the harbor for a day. The team would leave tonight to go inland.

Speed was critical, especially now that the element of surprise was no longer ours.

We'd be taking the three sentry dragons with us. With the probability of the Heart of Nidaar being in the hands of an enemy, whoever that might be, it was imperative that we reach Nidaar as quickly as possible. Agata was up and walking, but despite her protestations to the contrary, she wasn't up to a four-day trek through desert and rocky terrain.

The crews could protect themselves against mundane threats. If mages like those who had conjured the ghost ships and those waves struck while we were gone…

We had no choice. I had no choice.

The only way any of us would survive would be to get to Nidaar and secure the Heart at any cost. It would cost us; of that I was certain.

The plan had been for Kesyn and Talon to wait with the ships for our return from Nidaar.

The plan also had me checking in with Regor and the Isle of Mid before we left to go inland.

Both plans had been sunk as thoroughly as the *Kraken* nearly had been.

All three of the crystal balls used for communication had been either cracked or shattered outright as a result of the storm and the waves. All three being destroyed could either be incredibly bad luck, or they could have been specific targets taken out while we had all been distracted by trying to stay alive. Regardless, contacting anyone for help was beyond our ability, at least for now. None of the ship's telepaths had ever communicated to the other side of the world, which was exactly where we were. They were working on consolidating their powers to magnify the signal and possibly reach Regor that way.

Agata Azul had counteracted the earthquake and subsequent giant wave caused by the Heart of Nidaar with only her skill and the connection to the Heart through the pendant she wore around her neck.

Talon had summoned a vast amount of strength and had

loaned it to Agata. Together they had battled and subdued a force of nature.

We might need that power again to reach Nidaar alive.

Any of us who weren't actively engaged in ship repair were on the rocky beach and out of the way.

Talon was standing next to me.

"The plan was to leave you here with the ships until we returned," I told him.

"I take it that plan has changed?"

"It has, but I need something from you first."

"My assurance that I'll behave myself and follow orders?"

"That would be it."

He looked around, taking in the destruction, the death caused by the Heart of Nidaar. "I felt what Agata did and what we were up against. All I was able to do was lend her as much power as I could call up. I would have been worthless otherwise."

"I wouldn't say worthless, merely inexperienced in that type of magic."

"I felt so small, so insignificant compared to what was coming at us. The Heart *made* those cliffs we were nearly crushed against. I'm not qualified for this."

I felt myself start to smile. "If you were qualified to go up against the Heart of Nidaar, then you would be the first."

"You're not qualified?"

"None of us are. What we are experienced at is finding the people behind this and stopping them from doing it again."

"Uh…I don't think I'm qualified for that, either."

"I'll teach you. Consider it on-the-job training. All I ask is that you listen and do as I tell you."

"That sounds simple enough."

"But you know it's not."

Talon gave me a sheepish grin. "I kind of have a history of doing my own thing, don't I?"

"There's no 'kind of' about it. That needs to change. Right here and right now. All of our lives depend on each member of this team working together."

"And you think I can do that?"

For the first time since I'd met my son, he wasn't sure of himself. It was a good first step.

I put my hand on his shoulder. "I *know* you can."

"You're sure? Because I'm not."

"I'm sure of you. As to what we'll encounter, no one can be sure of that. We'll face it together and do our best."

"Do you think our best will be good enough?"

"It has to be. If the Khrynsani or the Sythsaurians already control the Heart of Nidaar, our job is to take that control away. The fate of the Seven Kingdoms depends on what we do here in the next few days."

Talon swallowed with an audible gulp. "Okay, I'm about to admit something. I'm scared."

"That makes all of us. We push that fear aside and do what needs to be done."

"Is that called courage?"

I smiled. "Yes, it is. And you have it, of that I'm certain."

Talon was quiet for a few moments. "Was my mother brave?"

I clenched my jaw against an unexpected flood of emotion. "Yes, she was. She was one of the bravest women I've ever known." I hesitated. "Talon, when this is over, I'll tell you all I know about your mother."

He looked out toward the ships now rocking gently at anchor and merely nodded. "I would like that."

No, I don't think you will. But it's time. It's past time.

"I need you with me, Talon. You and Kesyn. I think when we go inland, we'll be taking any trouble with us. But if whoever is using the Heart aims it at our ships again… Nothing will save them this time. The only way we can do that is to take control of the Heart away from whoever has it."

"And you think I can help."

"I do." I gave him a crooked grin. "Plus, I know how hard it'd be to keep you from following after Agata like a lovesick puppy."

Talon waggled his eyebrows. "Woof."

Phaelan caught up with me later.

"I want to go with you."

I blinked. "Excuse me?"

"Your ears are as good as mine. You heard me. I want to go to Nidaar." He hesitated. "Okay, maybe *want* isn't the right word. Let's just say I can do more good there than here."

"You have a ship to repair."

"My first mate would be in charge of that anyway. Everyone likes and respects him. They'll be fine. Gwyn can settle any disputes. They like her, too. There's good fishing here, so food won't be a problem, and our cooks know how to turn salt water into fresh."

I smiled. "One more bit of magic you don't seem to mind."

"Any magic that saves my ass, my crew, and my ship gets a free pass."

I chuckled. "You do know that there's not any gold in Nidaar, don't you?"

Phaelan scowled. "Yeah, I do. Jash really enjoyed telling me that."

"There's no gold and you still want to go?"

"That's what I said."

I crossed my arms. "Very well. As the leader of this expedition, what skills will you bring?"

"I can fight. And I can guarantee I won't slow you down. Mainly, I've played the mundane before."

"The what?"

"The mundane. Whoever is tossing that black magic mojo around can track you due to that ring and pendant, right?"

"Unfortunately, yes."

"But you have to have them with you."

"Also yes."

"And every last one of your team is packing dark magic of every kind."

"Yes, and I'm failing to see where you're going with this."

"Yeah, Raine said you can be impatient when you're not in control."

I began to bristle. "Your point?"

"You can't tell me that it's never come in handy to have someone with you who has absolutely zero magic, who doesn't need to tamp down his magical mojo to go undetected. A special someone who is a master at slipping in and out of a place, hearing what needs to be heard, stealing what needs to be stolen."

"The Heart of Nidaar is attached to a mountain."

"Merely a challenge waiting to be overcome."

"Time is of the essence," I said, "so we'll be taking the dragons to the top of the escarpment and from there, on to the mountains."

"I've ridden a flying lizard once; I can do it again." His expression hardened. "Tam, thirty-two of my people and yours are dead, and that's just on the *Kraken*. Gwyn and Gavyn can oversee the repairs, but unless we get into that city and either steal or destroy that rock, ships to get home in aren't going to do us a damned bit of good. Your dark mage team is one man down, and last time I checked, I was a man."

Bane had broken his leg in the attack on the Nebian ships. He was walking around, but was still using a cane. He would be remaining with the ships as defense.

"You're also one of the bravest I've had the honor to know," I said solemnly.

Phaelan opened his mouth, started to say something, then closed it again.

I smiled. "And the good captain is at a loss for words."

"Can you blame me?"

"I am not easily impressed," I told him. "During this voyage, you have earned my esteem, my admiration, and my respect. I do not give these lightly or often. I give them to you now. In turn, I offer you my friendship and the loyalty that goes with it." I felt one side of my lips curl in a crooked grin. "That being said, I'm in charge of the expedition, and if you go, you will be taking your orders from me."

"Raine admires you and she's told me a lot about you," Phaelan began, "but hearing about someone, regardless of how highly I think of the one doing the telling, doesn't impress me. Seeing it for myself does. During the past four weeks, I've witnessed what Raine's told me firsthand. You've got my admiration and respect." The elf pirate's smile was slow and dangerous. "Plus, I've seen you cut loose on your enemies—and from the back of a diving dragon no less." He made a show of hesitating. "I think I can take orders from such a man."

"We leave at dusk," I told him.

"Not a problem."

I put my hand out and Phaelan shook it. I bared my fangs in a fierce grin. "Welcome to the team, Captain Benares. Let's go finish this."

About the Author

Lisa Shearin is the *New York Times* bestselling author of the Raine Benares novels, a comedic fantasy adventure series, as well as the SPI Files novels, an urban fantasy series best described as *Men in Black* with supernaturals instead of aliens. Lisa is a voracious collector of fountain pens, teapots, and teacups, both vintage and modern. She lives on a small farm in North Carolina with her husband, four spoiled-rotten retired racing greyhounds, and enough deer and woodland creatures to fill a Disney movie.

Visit her online at lisashearin.com, facebook.com/LisaShearinAuthor, and twitter.com/LisaShearin.

CPSIA information can be obtained
at www.ICGtesting.com
Printed in the USA
LVOW04s1926291116
514961LV00022B/578/P